A Slice of Sorcery

Magic & Sorcery Chronicles - Book Two

Marie Andreas

Acknowledgments

I appreciate everyone who has helped get these books out there, bought my books, and told others about them.

To my most awesome team of beta readers/typo hunters who plowed through the entire book and helped tighten it up: Lisa Andreas, Patti Huber, Lynne Mayfield, and Laura and Liesel Schilling. And final clean up proof by Faith Williams of The Atwater Group-thank you! Any remaining errors are mine alone.

My cover artists, Joolz & Jarling (Julie Nicholls and Uwe Jarling), for creating an awesome work of art.

Other books by Marie Andreas

The Lost Ancients
Book One: The Glass Gargoyle
Book Two: The Obsidian Chimera
Book Three: The Emerald Dragon
Book Four: The Sapphire Manticore
Book Five: The Golden Basilisk
Book Six: The Diamond Sphinx
The Lost Ancients: Dragon's Blood
Book One: The Seeker's Chest
Book Two: The Finder's Crown
The Asarlaí Wars Trilogy
Book One: Warrior Wench
Book Two: Victorious Dead
Book Three: Defiant Ruin
The Code of the Keeper
Book One: Traitor's Folly
Book Two: Destroyer's Curse
The Adventures of Smith and Jones
A Curious Invasion
The Mayhem of Mermaids
An Intrigue of Pharaohs
Broken Veil
Book One: The Girl with the Iron Wing
Book Two: An Uncommon Truth of Dying
Book Three: Through a Veil Darkly
Books of the Cuari
Book One: Essence of Chaos
Book Two: Division of Chaos
Book Three: Destruction of Chaos
Magic and Sorcery Chronicles
A Touch of Magic
A Slice of Sorcery
A Dash of Devilry

Chapter One

Nevaine threw her knives into the distant target faster than most people could see. *She* could see them perfectly well. And the wobble that each one gave as it left her hand. And the fact that each knife was off-center. They were hitting the far-off target, but none were where they should be.

"Damn it!" she yelled. "Damn *him*," she added under her breath. The former stable that was her weapons room and practice target range was empty—as it should be—but it wouldn't do to have some nosy palace guard walk by and hear her complaining about *him*.

Nevaine was always the most serious of the three royal sisters. Middle of three, she was the calm, cool, and calculating one. Her older sister, Lizeth, was the emotional one. Piallen, the baby, was always active and running about. Nevaine was studious and stable.

Until she let her guard down and fell for the wrong man. Two years ago, a courtier named Trion had decided she'd make a great bride. She finally got him to understand that wasn't going to happen, and decided she wouldn't worry about finding a suitable husband until after the Challenge.

Until she fell for Sean.

Thanks to a decree change Lizeth made upon completion of her own Challenge, royals no longer had to only wed other people of royal or noble blood. That had been a shock to the kingdom, but one that Nevaine welcomed. So, falling for Sean wasn't out of line.

Having him leave her days before her Challenge with a letter stating thanks for the past couple of months, but he had to go get married in another kingdom, was as shocking as it was unacceptable.

Married. She and he had started as friends, then more than that for five months and fifteen days. Then he takes off to get *married*.

Doesn't even have the courage to tell her to her face. Actually, that was probably a good idea on his part, as she was always armed with something.

She stomped to the target, retrieved her knives, and marched back. Lizeth had taken up sketching when she broke her foot a week ago. Maybe Nevaine could get her to draw Sean, and she could tack it to her target for practice. At least when no one was in her room.

"You're holding the thing all wrong, you know. That wobble won't help your aim either." The soft voice of Clait, her grigeen companion, had just enough snark in it, that Nevaine knew a lecture would soon follow.

Nevaine turned to face the grigeen. They looked like oversized cats with wildly large ears, long fur, prehensile tails, and paws that were almost hand-like in their ability to grab things. In Clait's case, she was mostly a silky-white color with bits of soft gray stripes along her body. Every child in the royal family of Astarious was assigned a grigeen guardian at birth. Most of them returned to their forest behind the palace after the royal offspring they'd been assigned to turned fifteen or so. When her sister Lizeth went on her Challenge two years ago, her grigeen, Scruff, had gone along for the trip. Lizeth was now the heir to the throne and also the official guardian of the grigeens. The latter position was one of honor that had not been awarded in over three hundred years.

Which meant there were far more grigeens roaming the palace—and in particular Scruff, Clait, and Tobias, Piallen's young and very excitable grigeen. How he became an official royal guardian of the young Piallen was something that no one had really explained. But Nevaine did think he was part of the reason that her younger sister spent far more time outdoors than inside the palace.

Nevaine didn't mind the grigeens, and certainly not Clait, whom she adored. But right now, she needed to sort out her feelings for

Sean and destroy them. He was gone and could drop dead for all she cared.

Clait would want her to deeply examine her feelings and most likely had a good clue as to why Nevaine's blades were wobbling. Nevaine hadn't shown anyone the letter when it appeared under her bedroom door, nor told anyone; she needed to figure out how to deal with it first.

"I'll throw how I want. Sean's taken off." Nevaine threw two more slightly off-target knives.

"He's gone?" Instead of a lecture, Clait's voice dropped to sorrow. Far worse.

Nevaine threw three knives so quickly that all three were in the air before the first one hit the target. Or rather, the wooden wall next to the target. She quickly wiped her tears, then sat down and dropped her head in her hands.

"He said he's getting married to some woman he was engaged to in Hilath. 'Thanks for the fun, but gotta run.'"

Clait had been on a hay bale behind her but dropped next to her. "He said that?"

"Not exactly, but the idea was the same. I really thought we had something. And my parents turned me down for going to University in Luzangberg. *Again*."

As a princess, Nevaine, like her sisters, received the best education. Her magic tutor, Hisu, also dabbled in history and made every subject exciting. But it was the atmosphere of a university that Nevaine craved. Granted, she knew many referred to her as the cranky princess, but the idea of being around like-minded people, studying new things, was intoxicating. And a risk that her parents wouldn't let her take.

The University of Luzangberg was in the southern tip of the kingdom of Astarious. There were smaller universities scattered about, but Luzangberg was the one with some of the best scholars in the world. And two hundred years ago, an attack from another kingdom had killed the heir to the Astarious throne and his younger sister, who were both studying there. Since then, all royal education took place in the palace. Even though Astarious was a much safer kingdom now and wasn't at war with any neighbors.

They still wouldn't let her go.

She'd hoped that if she agreed to wait until her Challenge, they'd agree. But even massive promises on her side didn't budge them. Going out among the peaceful countries was fine—being a stationary target at a university for two years to complete an advanced degree in magic theory was not.

Going into her Challenge in two days with that failure and Sean's rejection hanging over her was going to be hard.

All royals of Astarious had to face an unknown Challenge before their twenty-first birthday. And no one who'd gone through it could speak of it to anyone who had not. Her sister Lizeth and her husband Finnian could speak to the king and queen about it—but not to Nevaine or eighteen-year-old Piallen.

Nevaine liked study, for the most part. But her magic was a bit different than either of her sisters or their parents. She did better with focused spells that she had to memorize—more like a sorcerer.

Magic and sorcery were different sides of the same art, and they both required different types of skills. Magic users were more likely to be born as such and demonstrated either non-augmented or augmented magic. All three of the royal sisters had augmented magic in different degrees. Non-augmented magic was mostly lower-level spells and more common.

Sorcerers were less common than even augmented magic users. Some were born with the ability for sorcery; others developed it as they aged. Her brother-in-law Finnian had been born with the gift of sorcery, but had to keep it hidden until a few years ago. He'd been born in the land of their enemies, Laiandra, an empire that had banished all magic and sorcery hundreds of years ago. His parents had kept him and his gifts hidden but were murdered by the empress when they were found out when he was sixteen. He had little in the way of sorcery training and was currently working with Gliandra, a mysterious woman who'd lived in the grigeens' forest behind the palace since before the king was born. She was a sorceress and kept to herself, aside from random trainings with Finnian and regular conversations with the grigeen pack.

Nevaine had asked to train with her also, just out of curiosity, but like so many things, it was pushed back until after she completed her Challenge. The Challenge, and her twenty-first birthday, would allow her to be declared the second heir to the throne. Providing that all three sisters passed their Challenges, they would all be declared heirs and would rule together once their parents passed on.

Since Lizeth had not only passed her Challenge but had gotten married and been declared heir, Nevaine and Piallen were technically spares. No one liked it when she put it that way, except for Piallen. The baby of the family wanted to be a queen even less than Nevaine did.

Lost in thought, Nevaine hadn't even noticed that she'd gotten to her feet and thrown all of her knives at the target. Until she saw them hanging in midair.

"What did you do?" She spun on Clait.

The grigeen's mouth was open and her green eyes were wide. "I was going to ask *you*. I didn't do that." Grigeens had low magic, although they could sense it better than most.

"Finish." Nevaine sent a flow of power to the knives, and they all hit the target in a perfect circle. "Are you sure that you didn't do that?" She ran up to the target—a exact circle starting from the one in the center.

Clait ran alongside her. "I don't even know how you did it."

Nevaine channeled her anger at Sean and mentally asked the knives to drop from the target. She was stunned when they did. "My magic doesn't work like that."

"Are you still angry?" Clait sniffed around the knives. "There's a lot of anger coming from these."

"Anger as a magic form?" She picked up her knives. She'd take Clait's word for it. They felt the same to her. "I am furious. But not ready to kill someone anymore, so I guess that's an improvement."

"Ah, this is where it came from. I thought Finnian might be practicing without me." The voice was old but there was a hidden strength to it. Gliandra came in slowly. She used a cane on those few times she came into the palace, but the one time Nevaine had gone to the cabin, she had been moving around fine without it. She claimed that too many people in the palace exhausted her. "It was you." Her smile was broad. She was short, like Nevaine, but stood tall and wasn't bent with age.

"I didn't use sorcery; I didn't chant any spells and I don't even know many." Her magic was a sort of balancing spells one on top of another, and she could sometimes lift and expose hidden spells.

"Ah, but sorcery is far more than just remembering and reciting spells. Goddess knows it took quite awhile to get that through young Finnian's head. There are different routes for sorcery to come through, ones far different than magic. Even your powerful spell-singing sister couldn't have done what you did with those blades."

"That does explain things," Clait said. "Plus, she was extremely angry." She nodded, as if everything was perfectly clear.

Gliandra nodded back. "Ah. Affairs of the heart can be the strongest of fortifiers. Be wary of the power behind that. It can sour easily. It's not something to be counted on."

"I've been angry before, and I've never had such a thing happen." Nevaine shook her head as she put away her knives. There were too many people in here at a time she needed to be alone.

"I could help train you, you know. Finnian has made great strides this past year in his command of sorcery," Gliandra said.

"I'm not a sorceress. I have augmented magic. Aren't the two sort of mutually exclusive?" Nevaine really hadn't looked into it, but she seemed to recall Hisu mentioning something to that effect years ago. She'd wanted to train with Gliandra mostly out of academic research—she didn't think she could actually become a sorceress.

Gliandra laughed. "Oh, dear no. They are uncommon to be found together, and usually it is connected with the lower magics, the non-augmented ones, as you here say. But they *can* work together. Astarious has been a magic-using land for over five hundred years, but before that, there were more sorcerers." Sadness filled her face before she shook it off, and she peered into Nevaine's eyes. "Yes, I believe the ability is definitely there." She patted Nevaine's arm and turned for the door.

"I already asked my parents about training with you. They turned me down." Nevaine still wasn't certain if sorcery would work for her, but she hated having options taken away.

"Ah, but *I* didn't ask. Don't worry, I'll sort this out. Now, I'd like you to repeat that spell you did with the knives at least five times." She narrowed her eyes. "Without the anger." With a nod to Clait, she shuffled out of the stables.

"I don't even know how I did what I did—how can I replicate it? As for anger, it is going to be a very long time before I'm not furious." Just thinking about Sean brought her right back to wanting to kill something. Or at least hurt him badly. How had he hidden that he was engaged back in his homeland for that long? And why?

She stepped back to her area to throw and tried to focus on the target. And they wobbled so badly this time, two hit the wall instead of the target.

"That's just repeating what you did, before you did it right." Clait had returned to her hay bale to kibitz safely out of the range of any badly thrown knives.

"I don't know what I did to do it right. It wasn't right, actually, since apparently, I used magic instead of my physical knife-throwing skill. Or sorcery. Either way, it wasn't normal." She stalked over and pulled free the blades. She was also known as the most stubborn of the three sisters and wasn't backing down yet.

"But your normal skill with a blade is a reflection of your magic. And sorcery can be quite powerful even in small, untrained, amounts." Clait nodded.

"You know, when you sit there smug like that, you look like you're trying to be a wise old seer." The knives wobbled less this time.

"I *am* a wise seer." Clait poofed her fur up and extended her neck.

"Since when?"

"Who are you talking to?" Finnian stuck his head in the stable doors, then spotted Clait. Lizeth's husband was tall and slender, with shaggy dark-brown hair and a handsome face. He'd been a woodsman in the royal forest until he fell into Lizeth's Challenge. He still wandered the woods for an hour or two a day. "Ah, good to see you, Clait. Scruff is looking for you, by the way. He already had Tobias with him."

Clait jumped down from the bale. "That is probably not good. Keep practicing, and figure out what you did when it went right." She jogged off toward the palace.

Nevaine rubbed her eyes. The majority of times, her early morning workouts went unnoticed by others—and she liked it that way. This morning, when she really needed to be alone, she was anything but.

"Thank you for getting Clait. Give my love to Lizeth." She liked her brother-in-law, but just wanted to be alone.

"Actually, Gliandra said I should drop by to see you. It was more like an order, and she wouldn't say why. She dropped in to your parents' breakfast."

"That'll go over well." She sighed. Her father loved breakfast and especially spending private time with his wife. There would be no way Gliandra would get her way if she interrupted that special time.

"What will?" Finnian had been a newly hired woodsman when Nevaine first met him—one who inadvertently saved Lizeth and possibly the kingdom. The rough edges had been mostly worn off, and he looked far more like a prince than woodsman now, but there was still a wildness to him sometimes. However, he loved Lizeth to distraction. Something Nevaine hadn't realized she was envious of until now.

"Nothing. I need to practice." She gave him a tight nod and turned back to her target.

"Where's Sean? I wanted to get him to look at a wagon for me."

That simple question caused the tears to build up, and she dashed them away quickly. "No idea. Hopefully falling off a cliff somewhere." She wanted to tell her sisters when she was ready, but it all came out now.

Finnian came to her and gently turned her toward him. "He left? That doesn't sound like him. Something must have happened."

"Well, he fooled us all, okay?" She tried to step out of his embrace, but he held on. The compassion in his deep-brown eyes just made her cry harder. "Look, you were lucky—you fell for Lizeth and once she got to know you, she felt the same. Apparently, Sean had other plans once he got to know me. He was engaged in his homeland." She used her finger to stab Finnian in the chest. "Engaged!"

Finnian released her enough to grab the hand she was poking him with. "I don't believe that. Sean really cared about you. I know, trust me. Before you decided to be more than friends, he would spend nights at the pub complaining about his unrequited love and that he didn't know if he could stand being around you if you truly only wanted to stay friends." He used his thumb to wipe away a tear. "He was smitten."

"Yeah? Then explain this." She dug into her vest and pulled out the crumpled letter. She'd meant to destroy it, but some part of her kept hoping that there was something in it that she'd missed. Even though the small cottage he'd rented was completely cleared out when she ran there after getting this note. It had been slid under her bedroom door, although none of the guards recalled seeing Sean in the palace since the day before.

Finnian scowled as he read, re-read, and re-read the note a third time. "This isn't him. The writing is similar, but it's not *his* writing. Do you have anything else from him?"

"That's his signature, I know that." At this point, she wasn't sure if that was his writing or not—she wasn't functioning right.

"It could be, but the rest of the words…" He stopped and narrowed his eyes at the letter, then muttered a soft spell under his breath and flicked his fingers. The signature stayed but the rest of the words vanished. Then another series of words appeared. It was a letter to Sean's parents, one dated three months ago. Nothing of importance, aside from the fact he told them he'd fallen for Nevaine.

Nevaine read that part a few times. "How did you make that appear? How and why did someone take an old letter—if that's what this was—and trick me?" She snatched the letter and waved it in Finnian's face. "Where is he?"

"It was a spell of revealing. The paper was protected against magical searching, but not sorcery." He frowned. "Think about what you're doing in a few days. What would throw you off and possibly make you fail your Challenge?"

"You think someone convinced him to run away, saying he was already engaged just because of my Challenge?" That seemed to be stretching things. And if he'd been that weak-willed to be convinced to do such a thing, it was as bad as if he *was* engaged.

"No. I think someone kidnapped him; then, using sorcery, changed a letter they found, and most likely cleared out his home to make you fail your Challenge."

Chapter Two

Nevaine pulled back in surprise at his words. "Why? We already have an heir. Yes, we can rule with three queens and king consorts, but there doesn't need to be three." Part of her figured Finnian was doing this to make her feel better, but there was a seriousness to his gaze as he took back the letter.

"There are things that happen during a Challenge that could be more important than just determining who is fit to be an heir. And no, I can't say more. But we need to talk to your parents about this." He turned and left the stable.

Nevaine wanted to keep up target practice, just for the normalcy of routine if nothing else, but a part of her hoped he was right. She didn't want Sean kidnapped or possibly killed because of her. But if he hadn't run off to get married, she needed to find him.

She jogged alongside Finnian. As the shortest of the three sisters, she was used to keeping up with her much longer-legged sisters but Finnian's stride and pace were impressive and jogging was the only way not to fall behind. She wanted to ask more—about that bit of sorcery he'd used, for one thing—but she now felt that there were eyes watching them as they crossed the open space between the stables and the palace.

If someone had taken Sean, they likely were someone with access to the palace. Sean was a journeyman craftsman, apprenticed to the master blacksmith—he knew his weapons and would have been hard to take unawares. Or killed. She tamped that thought down immediately. He was alive—she knew it.

The guard at the entrance nodded to Finnian and gave a bow to Nevaine. "Your parents have called for you."

Nevaine knew it was most likely due to Gliandra's conversation with them, but this worked out well. "Thank you. That's where we're going."

Finnian slowed his pace as they headed for the throne room.

"They're probably still at breakfast. Gliandra would have kept them talking."

He nodded, then changed direction. There was something going on in his head, and he wasn't up to sharing it right now.

The door to her parents' private dining room was small and plain, and often overlooked—

which was the intention. A single guardswoman stood in front of it and bowed when she saw them. "That was fast. They just sent someone to get you. Both of you." She shrugged and swung open the door.

Nevaine saw that Gliandra had, in fact, interrupted breakfast as there were many untouched dishes on the table. And that the table was set for extra people besides her parents.

"Piallen went up to get Lizeth in her wheeled chair. She still isn't able to put any weight on her foot, and I don't want her trying." The king rose and motioned to two of the extra seats. "I know Nevaine didn't have breakfast yet, but I assume the same for you. Please, both of you, take some food."

Gliandra looked an odd combination of pleased and worried. But she did have some eggs and potatoes on her plate, so hopefully things weren't too bad. Or worse than what Nevaine already feared.

The queen watched them both carefully, then nodded. "It appears that you have news beyond what caused us to send for you. I'd like to wait until your sisters have come down before we discuss it."

Nevaine wasn't a big breakfast person, but she could tell that if she didn't at least make a show of it, her father would be upset. The world could be falling apart, and he would make sure his daughters ate first. She had nothing personally against breakfast, but she always wanted to get out doing things and it slowed her down.

"Easier to give in. They'll win anyway," she said as Finnian also hesitated before moving to sit. She took a bit of everything, then sat down with a cup of tea. That showed how thrown off she'd been by Sean's letter. She might not often eat breakfast, but she always drank tea in her rooms before starting her day. This morning, she hadn't.

The door opened again and Lizeth, with her left foot propped up, came wheeled in by Piallen. Her chair was elaborate and fit in the halls and corridors of the palace. When she'd first broken her foot, and complications meant it couldn't be completely healed by magic, Lizeth had been determined that she could push herself around with some spell songs. When she almost sang herself off a balcony, her parents drew the line. She had to have someone push her around now. Lizeth was as independent as the rest of them, so that didn't sit well.

Nevaine had seen her and Scruff in hushed conversations this week, and fussing with her wheeled chair. She'd bet that there would be a change soon.

Finnian rose and removed the chair next to him so Lizeth could be wheeled in. Piallen smiled as he took over her sister's chair and sat next to Nevaine.

The three sisters didn't look that similar: Lizeth was tall and blonde, Piallen had their mother's deep blue-black hair, and was even taller than Lizeth—she was also the most athletic of the three. Nevaine had medium blonde-brown hair and was shorter than everyone. Her late maternal grandmother had been tiny, so everyone said she took after her. Her lack of height didn't slow her down, even when she was a child.

The only thing all three sisters had in common were bright-blue eyes—those came from their mother. Piallen and Lizeth had been closer growing up, but that had shifted when Lizeth got married. All three were still close, but now it was more Piallen and Nevaine who confided in each other.

Finnian gathered enough food for three people and put it in front of Lizeth, along with an entire pot of tea.

Nevaine and Piallen shared a look and then both tilted their heads to stare at Lizeth. Lizeth and Finnian had been married over a year ago, long enough to start a family should they wish.

Lizeth had said she wanted to see more things and go more places before having a family, but until Nevaine and Piallen, or preferably both, successfully completed their Challenges and were officially confirmed as heirs, there was a line of succession issue.

Had Lizeth given in and gotten pregnant?

Lizeth looked to both of them, shook her head, rolled her eyes, and went back to eating.

Nevaine shrugged. It was Lizeth and Finnian's choice. Most likely he was just making sure she had enough food to heal. They'd been planning on a trip to the kingdom of Wasier, a land with massive mountains and thousand-year-old trees. Until Lizeth tripped over a rock while chasing flutterbys with a net and managed to break her foot in multiple places.

"I think Nevaine and Finnian should go first, then we'll tell you what news we have." Her father wasn't as jovial as her mother could be, but he was generally a happy man; he was just more subtle about it. Right now, he looked somber. He hadn't sent for them because he was planning on having Gliandra start training Nevaine in sorcery. Or at least, not only that.

Nevaine would have preferred to tell her sisters about Sean alone, but if it might be part of something larger, she had to let them all know now. She tried to keep emotion out of it as she ran down what had happened that morning. She then handed the letter to Finnian. "Can you make what was on there before visible again?"

Gliandra opened her mouth, then closed it. Nevaine watched her, but she was being as nonreactive as the king.

Finnian muttered a few words, then handed the note down to the king and queen.

"This is exceptionally disturbing, but you say this isn't his writing?" The queen looked ready to go find Sean herself if that wasn't the case.

"The original note, the document this one was copied onto, was a letter to his parents, one that was either not sent or taken before it could be sent. The date on the original letter was three months ago," Finnian said. "The changes were done with sorcery, not magic."

"Three months ago." The queen looked to her husband. "That was when the Laiandran ambassador arrived." Ambassador was a misnomer; he came to try to broker a deal, claimed a complete lack of involvement regarding the Stiklin invasion of the palace two years ago, and left a few weeks ago empty-handed. It was the first time since the ravine had appeared hundreds of years ago that they even attempted to send someone to discuss the issues between the two countries.

Nevaine had disliked the man from the start and now was kicking herself that she didn't investigate him further. "But why would someone from Laiandra want to go after Sean? He's not from our kingdom. He's not a royal. He's just a blacksmith. I don't get it." She really had a hard time believing that someone would go through all of this, and take Sean, just to sabotage her Challenge. An arcane ritual held on to out of habit by the royal family. Yes, it was ordained by the oracles, but they rarely got involved in anything anymore and their followers had been getting fewer.

Finnian's scowl was deep. He'd liked the Laiandran man even less than Nevaine, and he'd avoided him whenever possible.

Piallen looked around. "But their entire land is without magic or sorcery—it's their first law. How could he have changed the letter?"

She also had a pile of food—all self-obtained. But she was usually outside practicing archery, swordplay, and acrobatics the entire day. This was probably her second breakfast.

"Just because an empire claims to be one way, it doesn't mean that rule is enforced for everyone." The queen gave Finnian a sympathetic glance. "Having the common people not have access to magic or sorcery gives those in power who have it far more power. And while we do have magic sensors in most of the palace, we don't have sorcery sensors—the subtle differences could be a mistake on our part. Something Gliandra will help us correct."

The magic sensors were basic and usually only run when there was a large event, but they would have been used on all ambassadors. But they wouldn't have picked up a sorcerer.

Gliandra nodded. Nevaine could only recall a handful of times the sorceress came out of her cottage deep in the grigeen forest. But she looked quite at home right now and like she intended to be a more frequent visitor.

There wasn't going to be a resolution to the Sean disappearance this morning, but the king and queen would be sending their best trackers out.

Nevaine wanted to be involved. And was shot down.

"But I know him better than anyone. If he left on his own, I'll know where to find him."

"And that's why you won't be involved." Her father gave her a sad smile. "You still assume that he left on his own and would be approaching the search with that assumption. We will send someone to Hilath, but I don't think we'll find him there."

"Not to mention, you do have a small event to get ready for," Lizeth said. Lizeth's Challenge had started earlier than it was supposed to, and without ceremony. She ended up running into it with Scruff and Finnian when she was trying to lure the Stiklin out of the palace. She later said it was best that it happened that way. Which said a lot, since Lizeth loved ceremonies.

Nevaine didn't like ceremonies at all. "I'll be fine. Hisu has prepped me."

"But you need some sorcery training too. I apologize that we said no to training with Gliandra when you first asked. There were reasons, but they weren't as solid as appeared. But I now believe that you might need to train with her before you go." Her mother smiled. "And after you get back."

Nevaine wanted this Challenge to be over so she could hear about the ones faced by her father and Lizeth. Her mother knew, even though she hadn't gone through one herself, as she was a princess from another kingdom and was told once she married the king.

The grigeens knew—how, she wasn't sure. But Clait had always been extremely closed-mouthed every time Nevaine brought it up.

"If you don't want me roaming around tracking Sean, should I really be out in the forest training?" She knew the forest was safe, and part of her was curious about this sorcery ability she might have, but her parents' decree was annoying her.

Before anyone could respond, a rapid knocking came from the door. Piallen was closest to the door and jumped to her feet before her father or mother could say anything.

"Yes?" She kept her voice polite but she had her hand on the hilt of the large dagger she often wore. Her parents had banished her sword inside the palace for most occasions.

A wearied guardsman stood there. "Princess Piallen, might I enter? I have news for the king and queen."

Piallen looked over her shoulder at her parents. Both nodded but her father looked concerned.

Piallen stepped back and the guardsman came in.

"I have grievous news, Your Majesties. You were correct in suspecting something was afoot, but not what you thought. The cottages on either side of Sean were attacked last night. Two people were killed and the rest are unconscious from a spell of some kind. One that is not responding to the mages."

Chapter Three

Nevaine looked to her parents. "Were you investigating Sean?"

"Only after Gliandra told us he was missing. We didn't know of the letter and thought perhaps his neighbors could shed some light. I fear this reinforces that he might not have left voluntarily," the king said.

"Could Sean have done it before he left?" The guardsman blanched as Lizeth and Piallen glared at him. "Or perhaps he was the victim and to get him, the attackers had to silence the neighbors." He took a step back toward the door.

"I would like to see these victims." Gliandra got to her feet, holding tightly to her cane. "I might be able to see what the healer mages cannot."

"Agreed. I do believe that our blindness toward sorcery has led to some of the problems we are now facing." The king nodded to the guardsman. "Thank you for notifying us. You will, of course, keep all speculation away from the general public." At the guardsman's quick nod, the king gave a small smile. "Thank you. Please escort Lady Gliandra to the victims. Get them to the healing ward once she has cleared them of any dangerous spells. And keep guards at all three cottages until we can get more people out there." He meant more magical people—and from the way he nodded to Finnian, he also meant sorcerers now.

The kingdom of Astarious didn't have any rules, official or unofficial, about sorcerers, but it seemed to have very few living within its borders. Nevaine hadn't really thought about it until Finnian became her brother-in-law and she found almost a kinship to the sorcery he used.

Finnian rose after the guardsman and Gliandra left. "I would like to go see what I can find there."

Nevaine rose as well. "I would also. I know you don't want me on the trail of whoever led Sean away. But I might be able to pick up on things in the cottage. I'm afraid I wasn't very thorough when I found his cottage empty." Aside from throwing a broken stool against the wall in anger—she'd been thorough in that.

"Me also." Piallen also rose. "You don't know what different eyes will see." She used her father's own quote when he opened his mouth to protest.

He glanced to the queen, and they both nodded. "Agreed. Just be careful and don't get in the way of the mages." He nodded to Finnian. "Or sorcerers."

"I'll make sure they stay out of trouble." Lizeth smiled as she pushed her chair back from the table.

"Now, you can't go too." Her mother pointedly looked at her raised leg.

"It's my foot, not my brain. Or my spell singing." Lizeth folded her arms and glared universally around the room. "I'll take Scruff along and if there are any problems that I can't handle, or I'm incapacitated, he'll contact the other grigeens immediately." One advantage of being the official guardian of the grigeens was Lizeth could summon them all with a call.

"It seems I have little say." Her mother looked slightly pained. "Just stay out of trouble, please?"

Up until the mayhem with her Challenge, Lizeth had been the least likely sister to get into trouble of the three—that had changed when she got back. Most noticeably after her decree that royals didn't have to marry someone of royal or noble blood. It had taken the kingdom's nobles a few months to come to terms with that; then the most conniving of them started flinging their offspring at the remaining two princesses. Since both Nevaine and Piallen were usually heavily armed, that died down after a few weeks. However, that seemed to have started Lizeth on a path of changing things and going on adventures.

Lizeth grinned, and Finnian pushed her out of the room, with Nevaine and Piallen following.

Finnian and Piallen both quickly detoured to get their swords, then rejoined them.

"I know we'll find him; the best people are working on it," Lizeth said to Nevaine as she patted Finnian's hand as it settled on the back of her chair.

Nevaine nodded. "I was so sure that he'd abandoned me. Luckily, Finnian un-spelled that note." She was still trying to switch gears from fury at Sean to concern. Not that she didn't care about other people, but anger was more in her natural behavior zone.

"I thought things were good with you two?" Piallen held open the door to the outside.

"They are. Were. Whichever. That's why the letter caught me so off guard. Just to let the three of you know, if it does turn out—somehow—that he did run off to get married, I will be okay." She didn't add that they might want to stay clear of her practice range for a month or so.

Laughter came from down near her feet. "You are a horrible liar." Clait jogged alongside them with a quick nod to Scruff, who had silently climbed onto Lizeth's lap a moment before. "But I believe you would try to be okay." She wagged her white fluffy tail as she ran.

"Others from the pack are behind you, aren't they?" Scruff said from his lap spot, clearly too content to look back himself.

"Yep, just a dozen. There's something wrong, and old Liaf felt it in his bones this morning. There are grigeen patrols all over."

"What? Is it something connected to Sean being missing?" Nevaine knew Clait, and she was as unflappable as they came, but between her tail twitching, the tone of her voice, and the fact the grigeens were on patrol—she was concerned.

"It might not be related to that, or that could be one of the results." Clait shot a quick look toward Scruff, then shrugged. "It is hard to tell. We should all be on guard."

Nevaine scowled. Prior to the attack on the palace when Lizeth was a few days short of the supposed start of her Challenge, there had never been any oddities concerning it. Young royals went through the ceremony of blessing from the oracles. Then vanished for about a week—although Lizeth, Finnian, and Scruff were gone for four weeks—then most of them came back. Often muddy, dirty, but triumphant. They were then granted status of heir to the throne. History spoke of a few who never came back, but it was rare.

The attack on the palace seemed to have sped up Lizeth's Challenge, and the attackers—magic-destroying creatures called Stiklins—all vanished the moment she did. That had never been resolved, and the oracles had been cryptic, even to the king and queen.

And now this was happening right before Nevaine's Challenge. As Finnian had said, there was clearly something more to these Challenges than just proving the worth of a royal heir. Perhaps someone outside of Astarious had figured that out and was using it against the kingdom.

"And she's plotting something." Piallen walked to the other side of Nevaine as they went down the narrow roads of the village.

From the look on Piallen's face, she might have been talking to her for a bit. They were also far closer to Sean's cottage than she thought they should be, which meant she'd been lost in thought for too long.

"What? Sorry. I was thinking, not plotting." Nevaine shot her sister a glare. That she'd been deep enough in thought that she might have missed something one of them said was another issue. "I wish you could talk about your Challenge, Lizeth. Something has changed because of yours, and I have a feeling that others outside of Astarious are aware of it."

"You know we can't," Lizeth said. "But Finnian and I will discuss it with our parents and see if we can sort out what changed. Of course, there's always a chance that there was interference in past Challenges and no one recorded it."

"The secrets surrounding the Challenges might be our downfall." Nevaine paused and her hand dropped to her dagger as they came around the corner to the street Sean's cottage was on. "Aren't there supposed to be guards?" Sean's cottage was unguarded, and so were the two on either side. "And where's Gliandra?" There was something wrong, beyond the lack of guards, but it was a feeling, not anything logical. Something was out of balance and that pulled on Nevaine's magic.

Finnian and Piallen also drew weapons. Although both had magic—Piallen—and sorcery—Finnian—neither relied on it. They were both expert swordspeople and archers. Right now, the swords were out.

"There should be." Lizeth sang a spell song, then frowned when it bounced back to her. "Someone is magically shielding those three buildings." She took a deep breath and sang louder. This one sounded different—more aggressive—even to Nevaine. This time, a shimmer wavered over the three buildings, but her spell still didn't go through. Lizeth had come back from her Challenge with her spell-singing abilities weakened. Recovery was slow, but after two years she was finally almost back to normal.

That her spell song was blocked spoke of extremely powerful spells.

"I see a foot." Piallen pointed to an open doorway. All three sisters had extremely good eyesight, but Piallen's was the most acute. Nevaine would take her word that there was a foot and not a small rock sticking out over the threshold of the farthest cottage.

"One more try. Scruff, get ready to call in your people if needed." Lizeth sat up higher in her wheeled chair and sang loud and clear. Again, a slightly iridescent shield over the buildings wavered, and looked to be holding, then collapsed.

Nevaine wasn't sure what she'd been expecting to happen, but Gliandra tottering out from Sean's cottage without her cane was not it.

"Run! It will explode!" Gliandra yelled as she tried to run.

Finnian raced forward and picked up Gliandra, while Nevaine and Piallen ran to the other two cottages to look for anyone else. Lizeth sang a song of containment, and Scruff and Clait both gave chirping cries that were quickly answered and repeated by the dozen grigeens who had been following them from a distance.

Soon, more grigeens were echoing the call.

Nevaine charged to the first cottage, only to be pushed back by a pressure spell. She fought through it with far more trouble than should have been necessary. Her own magic didn't seem to be impacting the spell as it should. The owners of the cottage had been removed, hopefully already taken to the healers, but the two guards inside were both dead.

"What part of explosion do you people not understand?" Gliandra yelled out as she reached Lizeth and leaned on the wheeled chair as she moved her away.

"If there is anyone left alive, we have to get them out." Lizeth took a brief break in her singing, but so far nothing had changed.

Nevaine was about to run to Sean's cottage, when a blast of hot air shoved her backward. A moment later, all three buildings exploded.

Chapter Four

The world spun, and Nevaine couldn't hear anything except her pounding heartbeat. She'd thrown up a shield at the last moment but still took a few hits. And was now trapped in a mound of debris. Her shield had held, but the space around her was small and had little room for her to move. She tried to push the building pieces outward, but nothing budged. She closed her eyes and focused as Hisu had taught her. She needed to lift the rubble—balance the pieces of it and lift. Nothing fancy; just lift it. A simple spell.

The rocks and debris around her shifted and she thought for a moment they would move, but then nothing. She leaned back and tried to control her breathing. No light from outside most likely meant no air coming in. There was no way to know if her sisters were okay, or if anyone had a clue as to where she was. Her hearing was still thrown off by the explosion, so even if someone was yelling for her, she wouldn't know. She tried to lift the wreckage once more, but there was even less movement this time.

Panic was setting in. Even if there were someone out there looking for her, they'd have no idea where she was and might not find her until she'd run out of air. If someone wanted to mess her up for her Challenge, killing her was a bit extreme.

She turned a bit, and her dagger poked her in the side. Swearing at herself, she twisted enough to pull it out and started pounding on the building rubble. She needed to find where pieces abutted each other and use the dagger and her magic. She almost cried when her dagger struck a crack between two pieces of rock. She took as deep of a breath as she dared and focused on her lifting spell at the same time as she wedged her dagger into the space between two stones. The debris shifted, with more than a little crumbling down on her face, but there was now a pinprick of light.

And she heard distant voices yelling.

"Here! I'm here!" she yelled, and tried to widen the pinpoint of light. Scrambling sounds came all around her, and she feared that her shield was failing completely, but soon more daylight appeared. Then Clait's face looked in, nodded, and more scrabbling. There must have been a dozen grigeens digging her out.

Nevaine felt the remains of her shield spell fall just as a huge amount of debris was pulled away and the sky filled her vision. A group of grigeens looked in, then pulled back as a guard stepped forward and helped pull her out. He said something to her, but his voice sounded faint and she wasn't sure what he said. She shook her head and pointed to her ears.

He nodded and carried her free of the mess.

The area where the three cottages had stood looked like the old stories of wars Astarious used to have with Laiandra. Nothing remained but piles of rubble. Judging by the way the worst destruction was where Sean's cottage had been, it had been the primary target.

Spells to do something this large were difficult to master and would be hard to create without giving themselves away.

There were dozens of guards all looking carefully through the rubble. "Where are my sisters?" Nevaine looked around, but didn't see them, Finnian, nor Gliandra. A brief terror ripped through her at their absence.

This time the guard who'd helped her up spoke closer to her ear. "Princess Lizeth, her husband, and Lady Gliandra are safe, and have been taken back to the palace to have their injuries looked at." He paused. "At the king and queen's insistence. All of them wanted to stay, looking for you."

She could imagine. That's why there were so many guards. That was a partial relief. "Piallen? Where is she?"

"She took off running toward the forest right as the explosion hit." Scruff answered as he looked up. "People are looking for her, but haven't found her yet."

"I have to find her." Nevaine broke free of the guard who was holding her up, but almost crumpled to the ground. If he hadn't caught her, she would have. She felt numb, but looking down, she noticed a lot of blood coming from her left leg. She'd been hit with something as the buildings exploded. Once her adrenaline faded, she was going to be in a lot of pain.

She looked around. Guards and grigeens continued to move slowly through the piles. She'd been found, but there was no way to know who had been in the cottages when they exploded. "Clait, Scruff, can you send the grigeens to find her? Is Tobias here somewhere?"

"He already ran off after her." Clait lashed her tail. "We were focusing on you."

"I'll be fine, but I can't go after her. Please—find her."

Scruff and Clait shared a look, then both nodded.

"Get Princess Nevaine to the palace," Clait sternly told the guard; then she and Scruff raced off with a few dozen grigeens—the entire flock, it appeared—after them.

"I'm sorry, Your Highness, this might hurt." The guard tried to be gentle as he picked her up and slowly stepped across the rubble.

Nevaine gritted her teeth as each scrambling step he took jarred her leg. There was a good chance that whatever hit her leg was still inside.

The rest was a blur as a royal carriage that was waiting took her back to the palace. She managed to thank the guard who carried her, but she was seeing spots and the pain was getting worse.

The palace had double guards at every entrance. They quickly brought out a gurney to the carriage and got Nevaine into the royal healing ward.

Her mother was waiting and trying not to look worried—as usual, it didn't work. "Take her to the first room. I'll work on her myself." The queen's magic was primarily focused on healing, but she didn't use it much—unless it was her daughters. She'd been upset at herself that she hadn't been able to heal Lizeth's broken foot but looked grimly determined to not let that happen again.

"Are the others okay?" Nevaine focused on her mother's face as the movement from gurney to cot jarred her leg.

"Yes, only minor abrasions. Piallen is still missing." The clipped tone of her mother's voice was a massive indication of the level of worry she had for both of her younger daughters right now.

"Clait, Scruff, and a mass of grigeens went after her. They'll find her." Piallen had to be okay. If she ran for the forest, it was because she saw something. Along with being a talented archer and swordswoman, Piallen was an incredibly fast runner. She could have outrun the explosions.

"Good thinking." Her mother gave a small smile. "If anyone can catch that child, it will be the grigeens. Now, this isn't going to be pleasant. A shard of metal is in your left thigh." She handed her a glass. "Drink this. I will be as quick and gentle as I can."

"Does this mean my Challenge is off?" Not that she was that disappointed. Unlike Lizeth, being a queen never held that much interest for her. She took a sip of the drink. Yup—nasty. There had to be a rule among healers somewhere that all beverages related to the healing process had to taste vile. But she knew there weren't other options, so she slowly drank it.

"Oh, no." Her mother laughed. "You're not getting out of it that easily. This injury might cause a bit of pain from time to time until the scar tissue softens, but there is no reason that you can't go to your Challenge in two days."

Usually she followed up with, "It won't be that bad" when Nevaine protested about not wanting to have a Challenge. It hadn't gone unnoticed that since Lizeth had gotten back from her Challenge, the queen no longer said that.

Nevaine gulped down the rest of the drink and was unconscious within a few moments.

MURMURING AROUND HER as she woke gave her pause as she tried to figure out where she was and why so many people were with her. The bed was comfortable, but not her own. For one thing, the knife she kept under her pillow wasn't there and the room was far too bright.

"I think she's waking."

That was Lizeth—so probably things weren't too bad. Her sister was the emotional one and if bad things were happening, it would be clear in her voice.

A few more moments and everything came back to her. For someone who was used to waking up fully aware quickly, this dragging feeling from the medicine her mother gave her wasn't fun. Nevaine slowly opened her eyes, then put her hand over them. "Water? And it's too bright in here."

The lighting dimmed, and she felt herself being pushed into a sitting position with a mass of pillows behind her. And a lovely tall glass of water was put in her hand. By a slightly roughed-up looking Piallen.

"They found you." Nevaine finished the glass of water and held it out for more.

Piallen nodded. "Yes, and thank you for sending the grigeens after me." Her look was grim. "They almost got me."

"You haven't been clear about *who* almost got you, by the way," Lizeth muttered from her wheeled chair at the base of the cot.

"Because I wanted to tell Nevaine first. They're gone now, so going after them would be pointless." Piallen was rarely serious, but she was now. Her almost-black eyebrows pulled down low over her sharp blue eyes. "I thought I saw Sean right before the explosion. He was standing at the edge of the forest, watching. I took off after him, and he ran. Then the explosions happened, and I almost caught him. A bunch of Laiandran thugs then jumped me. Or tried to. Two won't be going after anyone again. The three remaining were all injured when they vanished."

"Vanished?" Finnian asked from the corner.

Once the second glass of water cleared the last of the cobwebs from her mind, Nevaine noticed that the room was more than crowded. Her parents, both sisters, Finnian, and Gliandra were all standing there.

She wasn't sure she liked the idea of all of them waiting around watching her drool in her sleep.

"Yes, vanished. Right before my eyes. The grigeens came charging into the area and a whirling circle opened up behind the attackers. The living ones grabbed their dead, and they raced through the circle. I tried to follow but it vanished before I got to it. Cowards." Pi-allen always chose physical fighting over using magic, and them refusing to continue the fight and fleeing clearly didn't sit well with her. "If the grigeens knew what it was, none of them are speaking, even Tobias. They made sure I was escorted back here, then all raced off to the forest."

"Sean?" Nevaine was surprised at her feelings as she asked about him. But she needed to know. The bit about the thugs and some magic circle was disturbing too, but Sean was the first thing out of her mouth.

"After I initially saw him, or someone I thought was him," she scowled, "I didn't see him again. He wasn't with the Laiandrans, nor did he go through whatever that thing was with them."

"Are there such things as magic portals, and, if so, why hasn't anyone told me about them?" Nevaine did a lot of studying of magic, but that was something she'd never read about. She would have focused her studies on them if she had.

Lizeth and Finnian shared a concerned look but neither said anything. They'd seen something like that, and it must have been during the Challenge—so they couldn't talk about it except to the king and queen. Who were also sharing glances.

"There might not be magic spells for them, but there are sorcery incantations that can do that," Gliandra said from the corner. She was the only one seated but she looked pale. "They haven't been around in hundreds of years and take sorcerers of great power to do them. Are you certain they were Laiandrans?"

Piallen shrugged. "They were dressed as their guards do, but I suppose anyone could copy their clothing. Do you think they're launching another attack?"

"Or someone wants us to think they are." Finnian shook his head. "I have no love for the land of my birth or the empire behind it, but how hard would it be for someone to copy their clothing? That ambassador who was here had four guards with him at all times. Dozens of people would have seen their uniform."

"That's a good point. And there are other kingdoms, such as Northalian, who have a stronger base of sorcery and have been difficult the past few years," the king said. They'd had some issues with Northalian two years ago. They ended up coming to nothing, but Northalian was significantly smaller than Astarious and if they attacked, it wouldn't be directly.

The queen turned to Gliandra and Finnian. "Would there be any residue for you to sense? It's been a few hours but it might give us something to work on."

Both shrugged, but Finnian deferred to Gliandra, who finally nodded. "We might? To be honest, it's been so long since I've been around any sorcery beyond my own, I'm not certain. But if Princess Piallen is able to take us there, I believe we should try."

Nevaine stretched her injured leg. It was stiff, but no pain came. "I'd like to go as well. If Sean, or someone pretending to be him, was in the woods, they might still be around." She pushed herself up and swung her legs over the edge. "See? All better." She grinned at her mother.

Her mother frowned back. "Just because you can move doesn't mean you should go out wandering the forest. They know what Sean looks like."

Nevaine opened her mouth to argue but her father stepped in. "I think she needs to go. The Challenge is not only a way to determine royal heirs, it's also a rite of adulthood. She'll be twenty-one soon. As an adult, we can't stop her from what she strongly feels she needs to do." He winked at her. "Well, we can stop you as your king and queen, but not as your parents."

Nevaine nodded. "I feel strongly about this. Very." She wasn't lying; she was now even more confused about Sean than before. But she added emphasis to make her point. She needed to go out there.

"I will personally be responsible for her safety." Finnian pulled himself up to his full impressive height before giving a small bow to the king and queen.

The king laughed and shook his head. "Good on you to try, son, but the only one responsible for Nevaine since she was old enough to wield a knife has been Nevaine. I recommend she changes out of the healing robes first, however. All of you be careful and take any of the grigeens who will go with you. If they've called a council, they might not send anyone when you call, but try anyway. I'll send guards as well."

"As long as they stay outside the forest once we enter it." Gliandra had been lost in her own thoughts from the look on her face, but shook her head at his last words. "The grigeens won't interfere with the search, but the guards would just by being there."

Piallen helped Nevaine escape, and they went to her rooms.

"Are you sure it was Sean?" Nevaine wasn't moving quickly but the stiffness would fade.

"It really looked like him. I'm sorry." Piallen sounded more upset about it than Nevaine.

Although Nevaine still wasn't sure what to think. "But he outran *you*?" Even with a lead, that was hard to believe. She'd never challenged Sean to a race, but few could beat Piallen.

"I know. Do you think it was a spell?" Piallen asked.

Nevaine opened the door to her room. When Lizeth had gotten married and she and Finnian moved to their own spacious chamber elsewhere in the palace, Nevaine had been offered Lizeth's old suite of rooms as the next oldest. She'd declined. She liked her smaller, cozy chambers—she had everything exactly where she wanted it.

"I think since we know sorcery was used for that portal thing, that's a valid thought. But Sean doesn't have magic."

"And we don't look for sorcery in the kingdom. Yet," Piallen said as she waited in the front room for Nevaine to change. "I have nothing against sorcerers, but I think we need to watch out for them. If Sean was a sorcerer, no one except Gliandra would probably pick it out. Finnian is still learning to be a sorcerer himself and might not have noticed."

Nevaine put on her hunting outfit, complete with her boot knives, throwing knives, and a pair of daggers. She contemplated adding her sword, but she was better with smaller blades and with Finnian and Piallen along, they had enough swords.

She came out to find Piallen watching her carefully. "Are you sure you have enough weapons? There's little chance we'll find those people who attacked me." She wasn't doing a good job in squashing her smirk.

"One can never have too many weapons, little sister." Nevaine held her head high and tried to look snooty. "It would be bad form to find oneself in a situation where one did not have the appropriate knives!" She was doing her best impersonation of Lady Viloan, the one who'd been tasked to teach all three sisters proper decorum and etiquette. She called Lizeth a massive success, but Nevaine and Pi-allen fell into the failure range. Neither could really be bothered, as Nevaine spent her time working on her knife throwing and magic learning, and Piallen just couldn't be kept inside long enough for proper training on which silverware to use first at a formal func-tion—or anything else, for that matter.

Lady Viloan had retired to the country when Piallen turned fourteen, saying she'd done what she could for them all.

"Garrote?" Piallen nodded.

"Three. Again, can you ever have too many? They're quite handy for other things, you know."

Piallen arched an eyebrow.

"Well, you could use one to snare an animal, go fishing, hang up your laundry. So many options." Nevaine smiled and led the way out of her room.

"The question is, are all of those weapons for the attackers, who most likely are wherever they came from by now, or Sean?"

Nevaine kept walking to stay a bit ahead of Piallen so she couldn't see her face. "Both? Who knows? First, I think Sean might be *the one*, then he betrayed me, then he's a victim. Now? I have no idea. But better to be prepared for the worst." She patted her daggers. Not that she'd necessarily kill him if it turned out he did betray her. But she might accidentally wound him while bringing him in to face the king and queen.

Finnian and Gliandra were waiting in the main foyer of the palace when they came up.

Gliandra nodded and leaned on her cane. "We get four guards, who after much pushing on my part, will stay outside the forest upon our arrival. Clait, Scruff, and Tobias are breaking free of whatever the rest are meeting about and will join us at the forest's edge."

"Any idea what their meeting is about?" Nevaine asked as they went outside and were flanked by the silent guards. There had been more interaction with the grigeens since Scruff had declared Lizeth the guardian of the grigeens, a position not held for hundreds of years. But many of their ways were still a mystery.

"Our visitors would be my guess." Finnian shook his head. "I really hope this wasn't because of that Laiandran ambassador." Finnian had refused to meet with him, even though the man had made numerous attempts. Scruff had to chase him off at one point.

"Ah, but you made a good point. There are other lands who look with greed upon Astarious, not as powerful as we, but they might be looking for ways around that. As the king said, Northalian is a prime candidate, in my opinion." Gliandra was using her cane, but it seemed like she did better on the uneven ground of the rough path leading to the woods than she did in the palace.

"Here is where I saw the person who looked like Sean." Piallen halted at the edge of the woods. "He was standing right by that tree, watching what was going on at the cottages."

"What was he wearing?" Nevaine surveyed the area and looked back to where the guards and workers were removing the last of the rubble from the cottages into carts. This would have been the perfect spot to watch it all. And he would be in the trees just enough to not be seen by anyone aside from Piallen.

Finnian pulled back, and even Gliandra looked at her in question.

"Just humor me. What was he wearing?" She knew with everything that had gone on, most people wouldn't recall clothing they saw for a split second—she also knew that her little sister would.

Piallen closed her eyes briefly, then nodded and opened them again. "Dark clothing. Loose dark tunic over a brown undershirt, black leggings. Nothing I've noticed him wearing before."

"That doesn't sound like anything he ever wore, but could be blacksmith clothes?" Nevaine now realized that he usually changed before they met after his training at the smithy. And that she'd only seen him at the blacksmith once. She shook her head. "I should have gone to the smithy this morning, but I was too upset. After this, if we don't find him, we need to speak to blacksmith Gjal. He worked closely with Sean and might give us more insight." She'd been hoping that the clothing would have helped more—either something he wore regularly or something extremely noticeable as not him. This hadn't been as helpful as she'd wished.

Scruff, Clait, and Tobias showed up then. They wouldn't say anything about what their people were discussing, but were there to help figure out what happened.

"Okay, so where did he go?" Finnian had been one of the local woodsmen until he literally fell in with Lizeth and Scruff on her Challenge. He might live in the palace now, but he still spent time stalking around the forests surrounding the palace. Between him and the three grigeens, anything odd in the forest would be noticed.

"This way." Piallen led through on an old path. Nevaine brought up the rear, carefully watching both Finnian and Gliandra as they slowly moved forward. Finnian was looking at the ground, not as helpful as a few dozen grigeens running through had churned things up. He'd nod every once in a while, but didn't say anything. Gliandra was moving slowly, but not due to needing her cane. She was almost smelling everything as they passed and her free hand did some interesting moves. She also appeared to be reciting incantations as they went, but her voice was so low Nevaine couldn't sort them out.

Nevaine wasn't as woods savvy as the others, but she didn't see anything that helped. A few broken tree branches where the trail had thinned out even further, but that was it. A coldness came up from behind her and at first, she thought it was just a switch in weather. Spring could be a fickle thing in Astarious. Then it felt sharper. She reached out with a small spell, she didn't want to disrupt what Gliandra was doing, but there was an unhealthy edge to the cold.

The wind grew worse and lifted her up. Nevaine often preferred her knives and daggers over using magic—she liked studying it better than its application. But knives wouldn't work against a wind spell. And this was a nasty one.

Chapter Five

Weather was a delicate and dangerous thing to try to control, and few mages who tried it more than once survived, as it could turn back on them. She didn't know anyone in Astarious who could create something like this. Her magical strength was in balancing—or in this case, unbalancing. She sent a spell to destabilize the wind and was immediately dropped as the shards of cold air went shooting off. Whoever created the spell hadn't had as much control over it as they should.

The others all spun as she dropped to the ground, the impact sending shooting pain up her injured left leg even though she'd tried to cushion her fall. She was on her feet by the time they got to her.

"I'm fine. My leg just didn't appreciate that landing. Didn't any of you feel that wind spell?" They'd kept walking when she'd been lifted up and, considering their abilities, that alone was odd.

"What wind spell?" Gliandra looked around as if the person who cast it was hiding nearby.

"A nasty one. Sharp cold, grabbed me and lifted me a few feet up before it dropped me when I broke the spell itself." She rubbed her arms as the residual cold finally left them. It was bad enough that someone was flinging that type of spell around, far worse that she was the only one who noticed. Had she not been able to break it, would she have just been stolen by the wind before the others even noticed she was gone?

Could that be what happened to Sean? This was not good.

Gliandra stepped back to where Nevaine stood and muttered a few magic words. The rocks along that part of the trail glowed, and her spell words became darker. She waved Finnian over.

"Tell me what you notice, but use your sorcery, not your wood sense."

He scowled but came back, along with all three grigeens. They didn't say anything, but all three were also frowning at the softly glowing rocks.

"Ignore my spell. Listen for yourself—what do you feel?"

He closed his eyes and took a deep breath, then pulled back with a start. "This entire path is covered by a sorcery spell. And not a nice one. It feels like it's been here for a while and aimed at specific people." He looked to Piallen. "Why didn't she trigger it when she came through before?"

Gliandra let the glow drop but nodded. "Good question as yes, this spell was set for any of the royal family."

Piallen turned red. "I've had a problem with leaking magic ever since I can remember. It just slips out of me. It's better now, but my tutor, Miake, made me always keep a short containment spell running. It doesn't draw much power, but it does keep me from leaking." She held up a necklace with a tiny golden acorn on it. "This was given to me as a child."

Tobias stepped forward, nodding slowly. "It's just a simple cantrip, but it could be enough to have confused that sorcery—especially if it targeted the royals' magic and not their blood."

"Which would be trickier, to be honest." Gliandra shook her head. "This is not good, not good at all. I'd say we should go back immediately, but the grigeens have said you two princesses are most stubborn." She nodded to Finnian. "They believe the same of you."

Scruff sniffed the formerly glowing rocks. "Now that we know what to smell for, we should be able to avoid any more traps. We'll lead, if no one minds." It wasn't a question as he and the other two were quickly bounding in the direction Piallen had been leading.

She shrugged and took off after them. "They did find me fairly easily when I was fighting off those attackers."

The slow pace of before was gone, and Nevaine kept her magic, as well as one of her daggers, at the ready.

The grigeens stopped at a small clearing. It was clearly the site of a fight, and Piallen nodded. "This was it. I was winning, but if they could make something like that portal, it might not have stayed that way." She smiled at the grigeens. "Excellent timing on you and your people's part."

All three of the grigeens smiled and bowed. Their long canines made a friendly smile impossible, but they tried.

Gliandra stepped forward slowly, still moving her fingers and muttering words. She got to the far end of the clearing and turned. "Piallen and grigeens, please step back out of the clearing. I want this to be some training for both of our potential sorcerers." She nodded to Nevaine and Finnian. "Reach out with your sorcery, not your magic, Nevaine. What do you both feel here?"

Nevaine didn't step forward at first. While she might like to learn more about sorcery and see if it could be worked into her own magic, she didn't know that now was the time.

"Yes, it is." Gliandra laughed as she watched Nevaine's face. "I didn't read your mind, child; you just have an expressive face. Magic and sorcery can be difficult to work together in the same person. You were born with magic and the potential for sorcery." She smiled. "There are few who have both and can master both. I think you are stubborn enough to be one of them. But, it's never too early to start. Now, what do you sense?"

Finnian had been walking around the edge of the clearing slowly and was doing some of the same small hand gestures Gliandra had done.

Nevaine hadn't been taught those, but she still closed her eyes and walked to the center of the clearing. She turned slowly, tamping down her magic when it tried to help. "There. There's a huge hole...a void...right there." She opened her eyes. She was pointing at an extremely roughed-up edge of the clearing, but it looked intact. There wasn't a hole she could see. Until she closed her eyes again. "A gray whirling void, right there."

"I feel it too." Finnian was closer to it, and she could see it pulling on him. He must not have been able to see it doing that and started to move closer.

Gliandra shouted a warning as Nevaine tackled Finnian before he could go too close. He was a good foot taller than her, but the advantage of having to hold her own against two much taller sisters was that she knew where to hit tall people to take them down.

"Everyone back! It's active!" Gliandra and Piallen ran to Nevaine and Finnian and helped pull them farther away.

The three grigeens, with Clait in the lead, ran toward the void.

"No! Clait, you have to get back here!" Nevaine didn't believe in boogeymen or monsters but there was something vile trying to come through that void.

Clait flicked her tail, letting Nevaine know she heard her, but wasn't going to stop. All three grigeens halted a few feet from the void. Nevaine closed her eyes to make sure it was still open—yup. And the three grigeens glowed in front of the darkness. She opened her eyes but it was just the three normal grigeens and an empty clearing.

"Tobias! Stop!" Piallen couldn't see what the others could, but she knew her grigeen friend was in danger. She also looked ready to run and grab him.

Nevaine put out her hand and held her sister's arm. "We can't."

The grigeens started chittering in their native tongue, and the trees around the clearing began to shake.

"Stay where you are. This is beyond our understanding, and we could mess things up." Gliandra held up her cane to reinforce her words.

The three grigeens went totally still. All three were actively sending spells toward the void. It wasn't magic per se, more of a combination of magic, sorcery, and something else.

The void fought back but was already shrinking. Then it slammed shut, flinging all three grigeens backward.

Nevaine opened her eyes and ran to Clait. "Are you okay? Speak to me!" Clait's eyes were closed, and her tiny body was limp. Piallen and Finnian ran to the other two—who also looked limp.

"Clait!" Nevaine closed her eyes. Maybe if something had come through that void before it shut, she could pull it out of Clait. Clait's body was dark at first, then began to glow.

"Open your eyes. I'm fine. Just took the wind out of me for a bit." Clait looked to where the other two grigeens were likewise stirring. "All of us, it looks like." She got to her feet and stalked over to where the void had been. Her fur raised and her tail was seriously poofed. "And good riddance! We know of you now...stay where you belong!" She spat at the ground, turned, and kicked with her back legs as if burying something, and came back to Nevaine.

Scruff and Tobias got up as well, but didn't yell at the empty area. They did spit and kick at it, though.

"What was it? And if you three can close it, why was it left open?" Nevaine hadn't seen anything but the void, but the wrongness coming from it left her colder than the wind spell had.

"The one those people used before was shut down when we left," Clait said. "But they didn't shut it down correctly and unfortunately none of us checked." If furry faces could blush, the tone of her voice indicated that she would be. They'd had almost the entire grigeen pack out here, and they'd missed something major.

Something that was a complete mystery to Nevaine.

"What was behind it?" Gliandra looked as concerned as the grigeens. Finnian looked upset but not at the same level. Like

Nevaine, he probably only sensed *something* had been there, but not what. Piallen kept looking around with her hand on her sword.

"Something took over their portal." Clait kept lashing her tail and didn't look like she wanted to continue talking about it. That was worrying. Clait could be sarcastic and snarky, but she was usually also extremely calm and chatty. She wasn't either right now.

"It was a darkness unlike we'd ever seen, even me." Scruff was older than the other two, and one of the eldest of the pack of grigeens. His tail wasn't lashing but he looked upset. "We've shut it down, but the area is broken. Whoever pushed through might be able to again."

Nevaine tried to sort it out. "So, someone opened a portal to here, tried to grab Piallen, might have taken Sean, and were chased off when your pack arrived. And something else just tried to come through the remains of that portal?" She put the emphasis on *things*. Whatever had been there was gone, but she wasn't going to forget that feeling for a long time. "Was it connected to whoever set that weather spell?"

Gliandra continued to watch the grigeens, but shook her head. "Two different groups are what I sense. I'd say the weather spell was from the Laiandrans, or whoever they really were, and was a trap set for Piallen. What just occurred from that abandoned portal was something else."

"The trap was for Piallen? Why not me? If their hypothetical goal is to stop me from successfully completing my Challenge, wouldn't taking me out be the easiest way?"

"It would. So, whatever they are doing must be aimed at causing you to *fail* your Challenge, which is different than not starting it. Think about it. First, they take your boyfriend, then go after your sister." Clait nodded as she shook off her fear and started pacing. "They couldn't go after Lizeth as she is mostly confined to the palace—and is more powerful than either of you two. For now." She gave an odd tilt of her head as she studied Nevaine, then shook it off. "Removing and possibly threatening those you care about would make it hard for you to complete whatever is before you."

Chapter Six

There was little more to do out here. However, Finnian insisted he was going to speak to the head woodsman and get some of the foresters to come walk through this area. At the very least they'd block off this section until the king and queen could get more mages out to clear it completely. And dismantle that weather spell.

They left the four guards who'd been waiting for them at the entrance of the trail until the foresters could come out.

There was still no resolution to whether Piallen had seen the real Sean, or part of a trap to capture Piallen. Either way, it appeared that the goal had been to lure her into the weather spell.

The grigeens chittered between themselves, then took off to go tell their pack what had happened. Nevaine hoped that Clait would come back to the palace afterward and give her some insight into what they felt and how they shut that void down. Since Piallen couldn't sense or see the void like the rest could, she couldn't say whether it was the same as the portal she saw.

Nevaine had a feeling they weren't at all the same. The void was dark and cold, and would be hard to forget.

Finnian had already taken off when Nevaine recalled the reaction both he and Lizeth had at the mention of the portal. It must have been something that happened during Lizeth's Challenge, but at the very least they needed to be asked about the void. If she and Finnian couldn't speak to her about it at all, hopefully she could compare notes via their parents.

"You did well." Gliandra had come up alongside Nevaine as they headed toward the edge of the woods. "I believe you will make a great sorceress."

"Thank you, I guess. What was that back there?"

Gliandra was silent for a few steps. "It was part of the void between worlds." She waved her free hand. "It's difficult to explain without a few days and a dozen pots of tea. But it is a place beyond our world. Powerful sorcerers who worked with wizards a thousand years ago had the ability to create such portals to travel wherever they wanted immediately. They weren't often used, however, because of the sheer amount of power they took—and the danger of them exploding on the user. But that was long ago. The wizards are gone, and no one remaining has close to that power now. Or so it was thought." She shook her head.

"My theory, in brief form, is that whoever opened that portal lacked the true power needed to stabilize it and cracked the wall separating the universes in their attempt. When they shut it down, or so they thought, something tried to come through the crack."

Nevaine wasn't sure what that meant, but the implication wasn't good. Someone having the ability to open that portal thing was scary—but someone with the knowledge but not the power to do it right sounded worse. Magic was far more dangerous for the untaught powerful person than it was for a well taught but lesser powered one. She assumed that sorcery was the same.

"I need to go shoot something." Piallen looked twitchy. Her reaction to stress was to work out until she dropped. Her hand kept reaching back for her bow, and she looked ready to bolt.

"I don't think you should be away from the palace. If someone tried to use you to mess up my Challenge, you're still at risk until I leave." Nevaine knew she needed both her sisters with her before she left. And she needed them to be safe.

She normally wasn't a clingy type, but this was unnerving her. Knowing that was apparently the point just made her angry.

Tobias and three unknown grigeens came scurrying out of the shrubs next to the path. "We will watch her. Never fear, the grigeens will not let anything happen to any member of the royal family. Four have also been dispatched to keep an eye on young Finnian, as he also tends to roam about." Tobias was a large grigeen and rather round. And he was one of the gentlest of them all. But right now, his grin was more than a bit on the feral side.

There was no doubt that anyone or anything that went after Piallen or Finnian would have their hands full of angry grigeens. Not to mention the grigeens managed to shut down that horrible void thing, which spoke of more magic than they let on.

Nevaine nodded. "Just keep her out of trouble." Then she faced Piallen. "And no running after things without the grigeens." Admonishing her not to run after things would be pointless, but at least hopefully she'd pause and take the four grigeens with her.

Piallen was already jogging off toward her archery targets, but waved as she and her four grigeen escorts took off.

Nevaine and Gliandra turned off toward the palace. "Can you speak to my parents about the Challenges?"

Gliandra laughed. "I'm not a royal, and I'm not even an Astariousian. Although I've lived here long enough to be one now, I suppose. But no, I can't talk of the Challenges."

"I think there was a portal of some kind in Lizeth's Challenge. She and Finnian shared a look when it was brought up."

"You caught that too? I noticed it, but aside from a few odd visits from the oracles when I first moved here fifty years ago, I'm not involved in any Challenge talk." She smiled. "And no, I can't bring up what the oracles spoke to me about. However, clearly there was something in Lizeth's Challenge that involved the portals in some form. I can bring *that* up to your parents, if by some chance they missed Lizeth's and Finnian's reactions."

Good point. Her parents were pretty observant. Nevaine dropped her pace to match Gliandra's—noticeably slower than how she'd walked in the woods—and let her thoughts drift. One thing about the mess of today: it kept her from worrying about the Challenge.

"Why are you afraid of sorcery? I won't be offended, but it was on your face."

Nevaine blinked when Gliandra's comment pulled her out of her thoughts. "What? I was the one who asked my parents to let me train with you. Why would I do that if I was afraid of it?"

"You asked them on a whim and from the side of knowledge for knowledge's sake—not to actually practice it. People are born with magical potential, and to a more subtle extreme, the same is true of sorcery. But there are fewer people with the potential for sorcery, and many lands, like this one, have far more mages and magic users than sorcerers." She paused and waited until Nevaine did so as well and had turned back to her. "You not only have the ability for sorcery, you are also a powerful magic user—as I said, a rare combination. And yet, part of you fears it."

"I don't fear it. I'm just not sure how much practice I can apply to it. It is true that my initial interest was more academic than practical, but I'm not sure how far beyond that I could have time for."

Gliandra tilted her head. "You don't want to be different from your sisters. Neither of them have even the slightest potential for sorcery." Her smile was sad.

"What? No, I don't need to be like them. It's fine, we're all different." Nevaine turned away, more upset at herself than at Gliandra's questions. She could deny it to others but she knew it was there. Both Lizeth and Piallen stood out more than Nevaine—and had since they were kids. They were tall and gregarious. Nevaine had always been small and preferred her own company. But surely that wouldn't make her want to avoid sorcery? "I don't know." She sighed and ran her fingers through her hair. "Maybe you're right? However, I don't think this is the time to start figuring out my head. Second-guessing oneself during a Challenge has led to not-so-great outcomes in the past. Or so I've been cryptically told."

"Excellent point, and I do apologize. However, I would like to get you started on a few small spells before you go. Are you free right now? Rather, after we report back to your parents, since the others have vanished?"

Nevaine nodded. "Maybe just a few simple spells—ones that I might be able to use on my Challenge. Let's go speak to my parents."

They had to wait a few minutes since both the queen and king were in meetings with councilors. But both came out of their separate offices to go to the larger one to hear what Nevaine and Gliandra had to report. Clait came racing in just as the guard was shutting the door.

"I am sorry about being late. Those meetings go on forever." She jumped up on a chair next to Nevaine, delicately curled her tail around her feet, and looked around the room.

The king smiled to Clait, then nodded to Nevaine and Gliandra. "You appear to have much news. Please, do go on."

"Before we do, you might want to call up some extra mages," Nevaine said. "It will make more sense once we tell you our tale, but getting powerful magic users out in that part of the forest will be crucial. We left the four guards who came with us at the start of the trail, so it should be easy to find."

"And my people will lead them to the two areas of trouble." Clait nodded.

The king and queen both narrowed their eyes, but called for a runner to gather the five strongest mages in the kingdom. "It will take them an hour to gather. Now, what are we gathering them for?"

Nevaine, Gliandra, and Clait all shared what happened, from the wind spell that tried to grab Nevaine, to the void.

"And you saw this void as well?" the queen asked Nevaine, since that had been part of Gliandra's tale.

"I did. With Gliandra's assistance, I was able to use sorcery to see the void. It was real and terrifying." She rubbed her arms at the chill the memory brought.

"This is extremely bad timing, but I'm beginning to believe there are things afoot with our Challenges. Don't tell Piallen until we sort it out, but we might have to make changes." The king shook his head. "But nothing bad has ever happened before a Challenge. During, sometimes, but not before. At least not before Lizeth's. And now yours?"

Nevaine wasn't sure how to respond to that. The Challenges had to be started before the royal's twenty-first birthday. Tradition put it a few days before it to give the Challenger as much time to train as possible. Maybe they could move Piallen's Challenge up a bit if it was true that it was being used against the kingdom? If she were ready, that was. Obviously, since Nevaine's own twenty-first birthday was in three days, there wasn't much they could do to change hers.

"Can you reach the oracles? They need to be aware of this." Gliandra kept her voice soft.

Clait nodded in agreement. "My people are of the same assessment. We have a different relationship with the oracles than you. We can't reach them—only when they come to us. But if you have any way to do so, you might want to. Lizeth's situation before she left was worrying, but for it to happen to Nevaine as well is exceedingly problematic."

"Was there any sign of Sean?" Her mother's voice dropped, and her glorious blue eyes were sympathetic.

"No, and there's no way to know whether or not it was he who Piallen saw. And if it was him, he was taken by the same thugs that attacked Piallen. Was anything found in the destroyed cottages?" She changed the subject. She needed more information before she sorted out how she felt about Sean, who might have betrayed her, might be injured, or might be clear across the world, dragged through that portal.

"Ah, that was something you missed while you were unconscious as your mother repaired your injuries." Gliandra nodded. "Might I?" She turned to the king and queen.

"By all means."

"When I got to the cottages, before the rest of you, I found that the guards on watch, six fine men and women, had been knocked out. Not killed, and I believe they will recover?" At the nods from the king and queen, she continued. "I then sensed a spell, a nasty one that I haven't seen in ages. That's when I came running out to warn you all and everything exploded." She pursed her lips. "It seemed more exciting at the time."

"Since then, we've had mage alchemists going over the remains. There's very little in clues left behind. Our best guess is that whoever kidnapped Sean feared they left a clue, and came back to take care of it," the king said.

"Then why knock out or kill the neighbors if they were blowing it up anyway?" Nevaine was trying to make sense of things, but so far that wasn't happening.

Clait lashed her tail a few times. "I would guess that they first took care of the neighbors, so none of them could go for help. They then abducted Sean, got the fake note to you, and dragged him into the forest, where the portal was waiting. At some point, Sean said or did something that made them think he'd left clues behind. They snuck back and set the explosion spell." She shook her head. "Disgusting cowards, all of them."

"Could that be what happened?" Nevaine looked around the room. "It's all speculation at this point though, isn't it? Until we find Sean, or those people who jumped Piallen, we have no idea." For someone who loved knowledge and the gaining of said knowledge, this was a horrible situation. Nevaine valued understanding the world almost as much as she did a good knife. And right now, she didn't even know what had happened to the man she might have been falling in love with.

Clait reached over with a thick paw and patted Nevaine's arm. If anyone understood her, it was Clait.

The queen caught the movement and gave Nevaine a sympathetic smile. "I think we have enough information to get the mages started on searching the forest. You should go rest." She paused when she saw Nevaine's face. "Or work on some spells. Inside the palace. Yes, others around you have been targeted, but your Challenge is in two days."

"I was thinking we would keep the ceremony small," the king added. "I had already limited the invitation list; it will be reduced further and we will state it is due to attempts on both your and Piallen's lives."

"But I didn't think I was the target of that wind spell. I mean, I could have been. But it had been there for a while—Piallen was probably the target for that one." She didn't mind it being a smaller group; she just didn't want people fawning over her.

The queen nodded. "That could be, but it sounds better if we have two daughters, particularly the Challenger, at risk when we have to insult numerous fussy nobles."

"Now that that's settled, do you have any way of contacting the oracles to let them know what's been going on?" Gliandra asked.

Nevaine had never seen or heard the oracles, but she'd done every bit of research she could on them when she was growing up. Ancient genderless beings, they had once been worshipped as deities. That ended centuries ago, but they still appeared to help guide Astarious during hard times. Once the wars had ended, and Astarious was still standing, they prepared the first royal of the new era to go forth into a Challenge.

He vanished into thin air in front of his parents and assembled nobles. Then reappeared on a farm almost on the edge of the kingdom a week later. He said he was forbidden from telling anyone, even the king and queen, where he'd gone or what had happened. But the oracles declared him fit to be heir in front of the entire kingdom.

Aside from the Challenges, and visits with the grigeens, the oracles weren't seen or heard from anymore.

But Nevaine agreed that they needed to know what had happened today.

The king and queen looked to each other. "We normally don't, aside from the day of the Challenge, and that might be too late. We will attempt to reach them."

Nevaine really wanted to go practice her knife throwing, or even archery. But as much as she wanted that outlet, thinking of someone stalking her meant she needed to *not* do what she'd normally do. "I'll be training in sorcery, it seems." She tilted her head toward Gliandra.

"Excellent. Normally I would have you come out to my cottage, but I think it's best we all stay in here." She looked up to the king and queen as she got to her feet. "Do you have a spare magic dueling room we could use?"

"Dueling? Probably safer, actually. Yes, the chamber at the entrance to the bottom level is fully magic shielded, even against sorcery. But I'd like Nevaine to stay for a bit. Clait? Could you run and get someone to bring Lizeth down here?"

Gliandra gave a small smile. "I'll get things ready, and will see you in the chamber." She bowed to the king and queen, then she and Clait left.

"Do you need something? Why did you want me to stay?" Nevaine asked.

"Just to see how you were holding up." Her mother rose and engulfed her in a hug, then held her out in front of her. "Such a fierce soul in such a tiny form. That's what they said when you were born."

A brief shadow of sadness crossed her face. "We thought we were going to lose you."

Nevaine normally would push her mother away and discount the words. She'd been hearing how she was so small at birth that she almost didn't survive since she was six. But right now, it felt good to be in her mother's embrace. "I know," she said softly.

"We also wanted you to stay to be here while we try to reach the oracles. Lizeth has had some contact with them, and we're hoping she can do so again." Her father hugged her as well.

From the look on his face, "contact" was a weaker term than whatever he was talking about. But Nevaine was surprised that she was being included, as whatever happened must have been during Lizeth's Challenge. She opened her mouth to question it, then instead just shut it and settled back into her seat. There was a chance that some information about Lizeth's Challenge would come out and be helpful during her own.

Honestly, Nevaine hadn't been concerned about the Challenge until this afternoon. Confidence was vital for both weapon and magic fighting, and right now her confidence was a bit rocky. The people behind this might not have succeeded in grabbing Piallen, but they possibly grabbed Sean, and they did mess with Nevaine's head.

"Now, what is going on inside that head?" Lizeth asked as a guard wheeled her into the room, bowed, then left.

"Good to see you too." Nevaine got up and hugged her sister to offset her sarcastic-sounding automatic reply.

Clait returned to the chair she'd had before but didn't say anything.

Lizeth pulled back with a questioning look—hugs weren't Nevaine's normal behavior. "Are you sure you're okay? You did have a building drop on you."

Nevaine laughed and went back to her seat. "And you don't even know what happened in the forest. But, yes, I'll be fine. Besides, haven't you always said my head is harder than stone?"

Lizeth rolled her eyes and nodded. "I am glad to be right in this case."

"There have been a number of events," the king said. "We will fill you in on all of them. But for now, we're asking you two to stay in the palace. Finnian as well once he finishes working with the head forester."

"Not Piallen?"

The queen gave a chuckle. "Do you think short of locking her in her room that we could get her to stay in?"

"Scruff came by to check in. She now has ten grigeens watching her now. Six she doesn't know about. And agreed, you'd have to lock her up." Lizeth looked to Nevaine. "So, is this a pep talk for my little sister?"

"Not really." Nevaine grinned. "More like we need your help."

"Yes, what she said." Their mother looked between the two. Lizeth and Piallen had always been closer to each other than to Nevaine. Not that they all didn't love each other—they did—but Nevaine was sometimes the odd girl out. Which only increased her naturally sarcastic tendencies.

"Without disclosing important details from your Challenge, we're hoping that you can reach the oracles for us." The king quickly filled Lizeth in on what had taken place in the forest.

"Scruff touched on parts of it when he came through to make sure I'd stay put, but bypassed the whole void-of-death issue." The scowl she wore said that she'd be talking to him about the omission.

"I'm sure he meant well," her mother said.

"I did seem to have more contact with the oracles than what I read in prior Challenges when I returned. And yes, Piallen's description of the portal does sound like one we came across during my

Challenge. But there wasn't a void attached to it, or anything else really. It was more like an odd roadway to cross a long distance." She glanced over to Nevaine. "And nope, until you come back from yours, I can't tell you more than that."

"Could you try to reach the oracles now?" the king asked.

Lizeth shrugged. "I can try. I'm not sure if they will listen."

Clait jumped from her chair to Lizeth's lap. "We grigeens have a different relationship with them. Let me help. Close your eyes and focus on when you've dealt with them before."

Lizeth shrugged and closed her eyes just as Clait did.

The silence was starting to get disturbing, when Lizeth opened her eyes. Or a better description would be that someone looked out through her eyes.

Her blue eyes were now almost white.

Chapter Seven

Nevaine jumped out of her chair, two small knives already in her hands.

But Clait hadn't gotten off of Lizeth, nor even opened her eyes. In fact, she seemed to be purring.

"It is good to know you are prepared with steel, but you should also be ready with magic or you won't be coming back." The voice came from Lizeth's mouth but it wasn't hers. "We don't have time to be here like this—it is too exposed for us. But know that thanks to our vessel, we have the information that is needed. In light of these recent attacks, we will move up your Challenge to dawn tomorrow. Be prepared." Lizeth gave somber nods to the king and queen, then collapsed.

Nevaine grabbed Lizeth and Clait before either could tumble out of Lizeth's wheeled chair.

Both blinked and shook their heads but managed to stay upright.

Nevaine watched them carefully. "Was that an oracle?" She had to admit that was an impressive trick, even if it was brief. Maybe when she got back from her own Challenge, she could call up an oracle like that. There were a lot of things she'd like to ask them. Sadly, most of her books had little information on them.

Lizeth rubbed the side of her head and accepted the glass of water that their mother brought her. "I feel like the weight of the world just dropped by my head for a visit. But yes, that was an oracle. They didn't seem to take up so much room in my head...before."

Nevaine hadn't missed the change of words or the quick glance in her direction.

"They now know, so we'd better hustle to get this one ready." Clait jumped off Lizeth's lap and headed for the door.

"I'll let Gliandra know my training will have to wait until I get back." Nevaine hadn't wanted pomp around her Challenge and bumping it up by a day would definitely take care of that. Most nobles couldn't move that quickly, even if they were told immediately.

"I think you should still train for a bit. At least get a few small sorcery spells stored in that incredible brain of yours." The queen glanced to the king, and he nodded in agreement.

"But we have so much to do to get her ready." Lizeth looked around the room, then sighed. "Fine. I was hoping for some fancy event to offset the lack of it before my Challenge. Can I at least meet you in an hour or so to pick out clothes?"

Nevaine laughed. Unlike Lizeth, she didn't notice her clothing much, but she'd like to spend some time with her sister.

"How about two hours of sorcery training, then we have Margie send up a feast to Nevaine's rooms, and the three of you spend time sorting things out," the queen said.

"That sounds wonderful." Nevaine didn't usually spend much time socializing, even with her sisters, but she found the idea of it comforting right now. "Maybe our grigeens would like to join?" They did what they wanted to do, but she wanted to make sure that Clait knew she'd be welcome.

"I believe that would be lovely." Clait jumped off her chair and walked to the door. "I'll tell Scruff and Tobias, then meet you in the magic training room." Nevaine opened the door and Clait left. She was flapping her tail but it was her thoughtful swish.

"I'll go work with Margie on all matter of foodstuffs." Lizeth smiled at Nevaine as the guard who'd wheel her in returned to take her back out. "Come hungry."

Nevaine waited until they shut the door again, then ran and hugged both of her parents. She knew they thought something was horribly wrong when she pulled back and saw their faces.

"I'm fine. And I *will* be fine." She looked between them. "I just realized how lucky I've been and how grateful I am for you both."

Her father looked proud; her mother was a bit weepy. Nevaine squeezed them both once more. "You've raised me well; I will be okay." Before they could respond, and possibly make *her* weepy, she ran from the room.

One thing about whoever was trying to mess things up: it was making her more emotional. Anger and annoyance were often her go-to emotions, but there were more floating around now. In her head, she was also going through what she was going to do to the people behind this—especially if Sean was an innocent victim. Nevaine was a thinker, but she was also very good with knives and other assorted weapons. Whoever was behind this would regret interfering in her life.

Clait was sitting outside the dueling chamber as Nevaine got to the bottom level. Long ago, these had been dungeons, but eventually modern thought kicked in and it was determined that they were archaic. Prisoners of any sort were now kept in a modern jail on the edge of town. The former dungeons were used for exercise, weapons training, and contemplative thought—rarely all at once, however.

"Took you long enough. I thought I might have to go hunt you down." Clait turned and went into the room before Nevaine could respond.

"It's only been a few minutes. You are so—" Her words were cut off as a larganian rambler charged toward her as she entered the room. Huge, dark-green, armor-plated animals with not a lot of brains but enough bulk to simply run their enemies over—and not found anywhere within a hundred miles of the edge of the kingdom. Her hand dropped to her dagger, but then her mind grabbed a spell.

One that Hisu had recently taught her. The animal flew in the air and spun. Lizeth had a song spell that was similar but this one gave more control over the object.

Or would have, if it had been real.

She knew it wasn't but her mind had automatically gone to that spell. The rambler dissolved in midair and reformed into a giant, ancient, and very annoyed-looking bird of prey. It screeched and dove for her as Nevaine flung an anti-magic spell at it.

She wasn't as good at fighting magic with magic as she was fighting off a physical attack, but the spell held and the hunting bird dissolved and didn't come back as anything else.

"Too slow. You could have been completely torn apart by the time you used the right spell," Gliandra said from a corner of the room. "Why did you use the first spell?"

Nevaine put away her dagger as her cheeks went warm. "I reacted to the rambler as real—not as a magical distraction." Novice mistake, and one she was honestly surprised she made. Gliandra was right: had this been a real attack, Nevaine might have been killed.

"And you're already kicking yourself. As you should. But that points out that you'd be a good candidate for sorcery. It's more automatic. It takes more effort in the beginning to memorize the bits and bobs, but then it will become instinct in a fighting situation—accurate instinct not based on your assumption of the situation. The hardest part for most sorcerers is the memorizing part. But you have a very inquisitive mind—you're designed for sorcery." Her nod and smile were smug.

"So, you'll teach me these sorceries? By tomorrow?"

"Sadly, no. Even you wouldn't be able to obtain, process, memorize, and utilize the works in time for something large like a spelled rambler coming at you. However, I can give you training in a few small sorceries during this first session." She paused and pulled a slim blue book out of her vest. "And give you a sorcery incantation book that you can work on during your Challenge."

That was one of the things that had sparked Nevaine's interest in sorcery in the first place—the fabled incantation books. There were rumored to be over a hundred but only someone studying sorcery could read them. The books in the libraries only had general information on sorcery, nothing of the actual spells or incantations themselves. She took the book gently and fought the urge to immediately sit down and read it from cover to cover.

Gliandra laughed. "If you weren't destined to be a queen of the realm, you would have made an amazing librarian. The incantations in that book will make more sense after our training today. Keep the book safe, read it when you can, and read it thoroughly. One small incorrect emphasis on a word and you could destroy the entire spell. Or yourself. Or nearby kingdoms." She gave a tight smile. "Just be careful."

Nevaine patted the book and tucked it into her own vest. "Understood. Where do we start?"

The training was more physical than magic lessons had been, almost like she was learning knife work all over again, with a side of long-distance running. Too bad that Piallen had no sorcery potential; she would have excelled at the physicality of sorcery training.

When Gliandra finally called a break, Nevaine slumped against a wall in exhaustion. "Is it always going to be this hard? I'm all for hard work, but this is draining." She finished three glasses of water before she finally felt okay.

"Not always. This is the introduction that all other sorceries will build on. Sorcery builds upon prior knowledge and spells in a way magic doesn't. That's one of the reasons you might be able to become an amazing sorceress—your natural ability to balance and process information. But you also have a problem that most sorcerers don't have—you're also a user of powerful augmented magics. There's basically a fight going on inside you. The vast majority of sorcerers don't have any magic ability, and the few who do have only small non-augmented magic skills. There are very few who can control both." She nodded slowly. "If this succeeds, you will be the first royal sorceress-augmented mage in history. You could be extremely powerful."

Nevaine narrowed her eyes. There was an invisible *but* there. "Or?"

"Or completely destroy yourself as two major magic systems fight each other and literally rip you apart from within." She gave a weak smile.

"You aren't the best at sugarcoating things." Clait had silently watched from the corner but came forward now. Her tail lashed.

"Better to get the truth of it out than cover things with lies and have the child die. Are you ready to help now?" If Gliandra was upset at Clait's criticism, she gave no sign.

"I was waiting for you to explain things to Nevaine first." Clait shook her head and turned to Nevaine. "Sometimes people who live in the woods forget how to interact with others."

"I interact just fine, you fluffy troublemaker." Gliandra laughed. Considering that she socialized far more with the grigeens than with anyone in the palace, they both had valid points.

Both of them paused, then Clait opened the door, looked down the hall, then came back and shut it again. "It's clear. Do you want to tell her, or shall I?"

Nevaine was still exhausted but she'd rather go through another round of sorcery training than deal with more mysteries. She found that she was far less fond of them when they were directly related to people she cared about. "Tell me what?" She folded her arms and glared at them.

"It's not bad. It's just sort of skirting the rules. But I believe it's needed," Gliandra said.

"And there has been precedent," Clait added with a few more lashes of her tail.

Nevaine tilted her head back and took a few deep breaths. "What?"

"Clait should go with you on your Challenge. I believe your parents would agree, but putting them in that spot of doing so could make things worse."

"No one can go with a Challenger. Lizeth got away with it because apparently the oracles decided Finnian and Scruff needed to be along. But I can't ask others to join me, nor, if you recall when my sister came back, can anyone offer to come with me." After confirming that Lizeth hadn't lost her standing as heir due to her unexpected traveling companions, her parents made it clear that Nevaine and Piallen wouldn't be allowed the same option.

"I think we were always supposed to go along. Why else have grigeens assigned to each royal at birth? Not all of my people agree, but they are waiting for guidance from the oracles."

"Which means you shouldn't go along. I don't know how I feel about being a queen—never really thought about it much. But not only could you being along stop that from happening, you might also mess up other things within the Challenge." Nevaine held up her hand before Clait could argue. "You wouldn't do it intentionally. But from what I can tell of the vague Challenge descriptions they let us non-Challenged folks read, the Challenges are extremely balanced. Lizeth's worked because the oracles pulled in Scruff and Finnian—she didn't realize it but her Challenge was designed with them included. Mine wouldn't be."

"That you know of." Clait shook her head. As usual, that move left her looking like a light gray-white owl. "I was along for that oracle visit through Lizeth—the oracles had something more to say but it was cut off."

"Seriously? Less than a day before my Challenge starts and now we're questioning the oracles?" Nevaine got to her feet. "I can't take the risk that going against them could cause failure of the Challenge or something more horrific. Lizeth can't talk about her Challenge, but I caught the basics of it—something extremely serious was on the line. We always thought these Challenges were simply a rite of passage, but what if they're more?"

"That's why I think Clait should join you." Gliandra became serious. "There has never been interference with the start of a Challenge—not since they first began. But Lizeth's was fraught with troubles. Troubles that vanished when she left. You have had a lot of issues just in this one day. I think Clait needs to run through some sorcery-assisted incantations in the hour we have left and go with you."

"Grigeens know sorcery?" Nevaine knew the furry creatures had their own magic but it was vaguely defined in any books she could find. And none of the grigeens would speak of it.

"We have our own magical system. But we are all able to pick up at least supportive amounts of sorcery. Some refuse to learn, like Scruff, but I am more than willing to learn to make a connection and assist a sorceress." She gave her version of a smile.

Nevaine ran her fingers through her hair. "Fine. We train. But, if the oracles want you with me, they will have to find a way to make it clear—themselves. Otherwise, you stay here. Agreed?" Considering how hard it could be to get a hold of the oracles, and the fact that they'd already appeared once, Nevaine wasn't too concerned about them showing up and allowing Clait to join her.

"Agreed." Clait scowled and lashed her tail.

"I think it would be a mistake. The oracles might not be able to make their opinion known before tomorrow, but agreed." Gliandra nodded. "Now let's work on some assisted incantations."

If possible, Nevaine was even more fatigued at the end of the second hour than she had been at the end of the first. The assisted part of these incantations was to increase the power and focusing behind them—but it meant more strength and control on Nevaine's end. Clait helped but not with the power needed.

"You're heavy," Nevaine said after gulping down some more water.

"I'll have you know I'm quite trim." Clait didn't look ruffled by the exercises at all. Not a single piece of fur was out of place.

"You know what I mean. Magically." Nevaine turned toward Gliandra. "I noticed that my spells were stronger and tighter, but accommodating Clait is brutal. If we were in a serious fight, I wouldn't have to wait for the enemy to kill me—I'd drop dead of exhaustion."

"That will change as you get more used to sorcery—and your magic stops trying to help. You'll have to decide in a fraction of a second whether to use mundane weapons, magic, or sorcery in a fighting situation. The magic has been with you since birth and eventually will work with the sorcery. But right now, they can't function together."

Nevaine was too tired to respond. This issue would probably be moot—if Clait couldn't come with her on her Challenge, then at least that would get rid of some magical weight. It did feel like there had been a fight of some sort inside her as she fought off the swarm of spells Gliandra flung at her. Most of them Nevaine had never heard of before.

Clait marched over to where Nevaine slumped against the wall and shook her head. "Get up. We have just enough time for you to get showered before your sisters arrive."

Gliandra smiled. "Have a wonderful time, young ones. I'm taking a guest room in the palace, but will see you at dawn before you leave." She paused, almost to the door. "You did extremely well, by the way. Still miles to go, but a good start." Then she left.

Nevaine got to her feet slowly. Might need a long shower to get all of these kinks out.

Clait ran to the door. "Get ready. I have a few things to check in with the pack about. See you soon." With a flick of her tail, she jogged off, leaving Nevaine to hobble down the hallway alone.

She was lost in thought, and trying to keep her body from stiffening up after that workout, and so hadn't noticed there was anyone in the hallway with her.

Until she was grabbed from behind and had a spelled bag dropped over her head. The magical bag kicked in before she could draw air to yell, let alone grab any of her weapons. Then everything went dark.

Chapter Eight

Nevaine struggled as she woke up. The spelled bag had been removed, but there was now a gag over her mouth and her hands were tied behind her to the chair she was sitting on.

She was in a small, dark room not much larger than a walk-in closet, and whoever was with her was out of her range of sight.

"I'm sorry. I tried what I could do to stop this from happening, but you can't be allowed to complete your Challenge." Sean stepped into view as he spoke, his light-blue eyes almost looking gray in the dim light of the room. His black hair was tousled and there were bruises on his face and what she could see of his arms. "It's too dangerous for you to go."

Nevaine couldn't talk but mumbled every swearword she knew behind her gag. She'd actually been worried for that lying rat? And he was *behind* the problems and now had kidnapped her? Her magic needed external words, even just muttered under her breath. However, sorcery could work with finger movements.

Her hands weren't tied well enough to keep her fingers from moving. She closed her eyes and thought of the gestures for a simple sorcery incantation—about all she knew, but this should work.

Sean was flung up against the wall hard enough to make him wince and knock the air out of him.

"What...ow." He dropped to the floor, caught his breath, and stood up. "Not sure how you did that, but don't. I'm trying to save your life. If you go on that Challenge, you will die."

Nevaine narrowed her eyes and flung him at another wall.

"Stop it!" He got to his feet faster this time. "I am trying to save you. They want to kill you and will do it during the Challenge."

Nevaine shrugged and shook her head.

"Who are they? Good question. I believe it's a group of Laiandrans and Northalians. That was just going by the accents I heard when they grabbed me. They planned an attack right around the time of your Challenge, something about things being less defined?" He ran his fingers through his hair. "Sorry, my Laiandran is a bit rusty. But then it looked like that wouldn't happen, your folks stopped them somehow, so now the plan is to follow you on the Challenge and kill you. Somehow that will give them power. Over something. It wasn't clear." He frowned. "They might actually just need to capture you; you apparently have something they need. But I couldn't get more than that." He looked down at her as if she could tell him what it was with her gag on. "I can't take the gag off. You're a strong magic user, not to mention that while your voice isn't as loud as your older sister, you'd still be able to get guards down here." He swung a second chair around to face her and sat down. "I don't know what to do."

Nevaine studied him. He had the same boyish charm that had caught her attention in the marketplace a few months ago. He was selling wares from the blacksmith and didn't realize who she was. Wearing a tight undershirt with a heavy leather apron over it at the time, he was noticed by pretty much every woman and a few men who walked by his booth. Most of the people who worked in the smithy were large and bulky. Sean was a little taller than Piallen, and had a lean, muscular build as opposed to a bulky one. His face was beautiful; rugged, but beautiful. Not a phrase used about men very often, but with piercing blue eyes, high cheekbones, and black hair—he was stunning.

When not grimy from the forge or in the act of kidnapping her.

How could she have been so wrong about him? She wasn't one to just fall for the first good-looking man she met. All of her boyfriends when she was younger had been students, academics, book people. Sean was definitely not. He wasn't stupid at all, but was more a hands-on learning guy. And she was naturally suspicious of pretty much everyone, yet had fallen for him after just a few trips to the market. Stupid.

"Did you just growl at me?" He leaned away from her.

She hadn't meant to, but it was warranted. She needed to figure out how to use one of the non-verbal incantations to get the ties off her hands. First, she was punching that stunning, albeit roughed-up face; then she'd bind him with magic. She really wished to do far more to him, but she wanted him to stand trial for kidnapping and whatever else he'd done, not be in a hospital.

"Look, it's just a few more minutes. We're close to dawn. When the oracles try to send you, and you're in this shielded and non-traceable location, the Challenge will be withdrawn. And *they'll* have no reason to kill you."

He looked to say more, but Nevaine's fog-filled mind finally caught up with his words—it was almost morning? She'd been down here all night? Everyone must be frantic.

She was furious.

She moved her fingers as much as she could, flinging small sorceries until the ropes were destroyed and fell off. She took her gag off first, then punched Sean. She reached for her weapons, but then saw the collection of everything she'd had on her in the corner. She dove for them and grabbed everything. Then she ran for the door, only to have Sean seize her from behind. He might not be bulky, but there were some serious muscles in his arms from the smithy. He held her tight.

"I know you and I are through; I don't blame you at all, but I can't let them kill you. Just a few more minutes."

Nevaine kicked back as hard as she could and pulled open the door. She started yelling as she ran up the stairs two at a time, throwing back a knife that only barely missed his shoulder when he got too close. There were two guards at the top of the stairs, but she ran past them. "Stop him!"

She kept running but glanced back to see Sean still behind her and the guards standing frozen in place. Damn it—another lie. He had magic or sorcery.

She picked up speed as she ran for the ballroom and slammed through the doors. Her parents were there, along with her sisters, Finnian, and a dozen or so grigeens—they all looked sad, then shocked as she ran in. The clock was striking six as she ran through the arch meant for her Challenge. Clait ran through at the same time. The world spun, and she had the sensation of being flung out somewhere. Clait was next to her and looked as out of it as she felt.

A chime rang in her head and a light voice followed, also in her head. *"You have begun your Challenge. Be fleet of mind, gentle of foot, and strong of heart. Blessings of the oracles are upon you."*

That was good and bad. At least she'd made it through in time, but she had no idea where she was.

A body landed on her legs as she realized they were in the middle of a grassy field somewhere. Sean was unconscious, but he'd made it through as well and was laying partially on her.

Nevaine kicked him off her. "Damn it—how did he come through? How did *you* come through?" She shifted her look to Clait.

"It's good to see you, too." Clait licked a paw, then ran toward her and jumped in Nevaine's arms. "We were so worried for you! What happened, and why is your boyfriend here?"

"He is not my boyfriend or anything else, except a future prisoner of our kingdom. He grabbed me right after you left our workout." She scowled. "With a highly illegal spell bag." She filled Clait in on what happened. She'd expected Clait to go add some more bruises to the unconscious man, but instead she jumped down and rolled him over.

"He's been beaten repeatedly. And then healed." She scowled as she sniffed him more closely. "And beaten again. I don't understand what he meant about them trying to kill you if you went through the start of your Challenge, though. Nor how he reeks of both magic and sorcery and yet I never noticed it before." Her tail partially poofed in annoyance.

"You shouldn't have come through with me. Now things might not only get messed up, but you could die along with me, if his warnings were correct." Nevaine looked down at her tiny friend. "But part of me is glad you're here. This is not how I expected my Challenge to begin."

"We thought you'd been taken through one of those portals—every magic user aside from the royal family is out searching the woods for you or a new portal, including Gliandra." She looked down at Sean. "Let's see if we can wake him up—maybe he has answers since he felt going on the Challenge was a death sentence."

Nevaine looked around. "Wherever we are." She wasn't sure what she'd been expecting and had hoped that spending some girl time with Lizeth and Piallen the night before her Challenge would give her a clue—that didn't happen. But wherever they were, it wasn't in Astarious anymore. Or at least nowhere she'd seen or heard of in their kingdom.

The field they were in looked normal, until she realized that there were blades of dark-purple grass along with the normal green grass. And the trees at the edge of the field looked oddly short and long-limbed. From what she could see, they appeared to have branches covered in long thorns and tiny purple leaves.

There was little more she could see as a fog covered everything a few feet past the trees. She shook her head and looked back to Sean.

While Clair had been concerned when she examined him initially, she was rougher as she shook him. "Get up. Now. I know you hear me." She shook him again.

Nevaine was about to help when his eyes flew open and he winced. "Where am I?"

"On my Challenge. Which you shouldn't be, for a large number of reasons. What were you thinking?" She raised her left hand and arcs of electricity crackled around it and started reaching out toward Sean. That was new, but not unlike what she'd used to destroy her ties earlier. She shook her hand and the arcs vanished. It was one of the few sorcery incantations she'd tried during her practice but couldn't get right. Apparently, she'd somehow figured it out.

"I was trying to stop you." He looked over to Clait. "You made it as well? At least I guess we can all die together." He dropped his hand over his eyes.

"You almost made me miss my Challenge. You might have disrupted it so badly, that you could have destroyed it. Do you know what that means?"

He held his hand higher so it still shaded his eyes, but he could look at her. "Yes. That you might live after all. I'm not going to try to justify my actions—you will die on this Challenge, as it was originally set up. Maybe Clait and I can stop that from happening, maybe we can't. But the only thing I regret is that I couldn't stop you from going. I would do everything I did again in a heartbeat."

Clait and Nevaine shared a look and then walked away from Sean. He wasn't going anywhere right now.

"Any idea where we are, or if this is where my Challenge was supposed to be?" Nevaine looked around. "Aside from the weird fog, it kinda looks like the farmlands near Koria."

Clait pawed at one of the purple strands of grass.

"Okay, aside from the purple grass and those trees. How am I supposed to know what the Challenge is? Shouldn't I have been given notes or a book?" She patted herself down and sighed in relief. At least Gliandra's book was still with her.

"I think a major part of the Challenge is for the young royals to sort things out with just their skills and their minds." Clait tilted her head. "Although a thin guidebook would be handy. I have no idea what to expect either. We grigeens have a different relationship with the oracles than your people do, but even for us their motivations are a mystery. I think this is still going to be something you'll have to work through."

"Without any other books." Nevaine gave a slight shudder at that idea. Even in her training stable, she had piles of books tucked behind the hay bales. She also had books all over her suite of rooms in the palace, and one of the main reasons that she had turned down Lizeth's old room was that she'd built so many book cubby-holes into her own.

Sean groaned, then slowly rolled to his feet. "Bigger question. Do you want me to stay, knowing that I'll do whatever I need to do to save you, or do you just want me to wander these strange lands for-ever alone?"

Nevaine sighed. "You'd probably just follow us if I send you off, wouldn't you?"

"Probably." His grin was deadly. "And I was the best seeker when my brothers and I played hide-and-seek."

"Okay. In part because I got the idea that when Lizeth went on her excursion, she felt it was important that Scruff and Finnian stayed with her. She couldn't say why, though." Nevaine looked up. "Something's wrong with the sky. It's acting like it's late afternoon and we just got here. Clait? Do you sense a storm?" Storms could be deadly in the open lands—they'd need to find shelter.

Clait sniffed the air, and her tail started lashing. "No. But it *is* late afternoon. We went through the arch at six in the morning and landed here hours, many hours, later. I don't like it. But I don't think we should be out in the open like this." She started jogging toward the closest clump of trees.

"If this is my Challenge, shouldn't I sort out where we go?"

Clait stopped and turned over her shoulder. "Where do you think we should go?"

Nevaine looked around. The clumps of trees all looked the same, but the one Clait was heading toward was closer. "Fine, that one. But look for some place we can find shelter. It might feel like a normal storm to you, but something is wrong."

Sean jogged up alongside them. "The weather is changing—maybe not yet, but it is. Not good for anyone to be out."

Clait was tiny, but she could move faster than most humans when she wanted. And right now, she wanted to move.

It only took a few minutes to get to the weird trees. They provided shelter by the sheer numbers of them as they went farther back inside the tree line. They all looked for anything like a trail, but hadn't found anything when a crack of lightning and rolling thunder immediately after filled the darkening field behind them.

They all turned to watch as the purple grasses collected the lightning as tiny arcs all fed down to them.

"That better not happen to these purple leaves." Clait stared at the mass of trees around them.

Sean's eyes got wide, and he shook his head. "No."

"No? Did they rattle too many things when they beat you up? Don't you dare slip into shock—we are *not* lugging you around wherever we go." Nevaine agreed that the lightning wasn't normal and even less normal was the way it was almost feeding the grasses. But Sean was so disturbed that his breathing became shallow.

Then he dropped to the ground and sat staring out at the field. "It can't be."

Clait was closer to eye level with him now, so she stomped up and peered into his eyes. "What? You can't just sit there looking like the world is ending and not tell us. Especially since you were the one who kept saying someone was going to try to kill Nevaine on this trip."

He shook his head but didn't get to his feet. "I'm sorry. I just figured out the only place we can be. I've never seen it...well, when I was a baby I did. But I've heard of those fields—and it's a very good thing we left them." He looked up to Nevaine. "Somehow, we're in the Offialian Empire. Thousands of miles and a massive sea away from your kingdom. Those fields? Remnants of sorcerer battles a hundred years ago. The sorcerers are gone, but the killing strikes from those grasses aren't."

Chapter Nine

"The syth fields?" Nevaine looked closer at the grass—it was moving as if sentient. There weren't many books available in Astarious about the Offialian Empire—three, to be exact...and she had copies of them. But they didn't contain a lot of useful information beyond things like the syth fields. The Offialian Empire was massive and unknown, as they'd shut all of their borders decades ago. It was also on the far side of the massive Algarien Ocean that few people even tried to cross.

Very little information got out. And even fewer people.

She narrowed her eyes. "You're saying that you're Offialian? I thought you said you were from Hilath?"

Sean ran his hands through his hair, which didn't fix it much. "My family is from Jilve, a small town on the western edge of the Offialian Empire. My parents fled across the Algarien Ocean on a rickety ship with fifteen other families when I was a baby to escape the oppression and constant warfare. A seer had told them they would have five strong boys—and all would die fighting for the empire before we were twenty. I was the first, and they fled after the seer's report. Only three families survived that trip, and all of them scattered as soon as they reached land—less likely for anyone to connect them to the empire if found." He flashed his smile. "If it helps, I grew up in Hilath."

"I wonder if we were pulled here because of your tie to the empire," Clait said and then turned back to Nevaine. "This really might not be your Challenge but could be the death of all of us. The Offialian Empire doesn't like strangers any more than it likes deserters."

"I would never have brought us here—never. My parents didn't talk a lot about the empire or their lives here, but the few stories they told were horrifying."

Nevaine looked at the lightning still bouncing around the field, then sat down next to him. She was suddenly exhausted, and going deeper into the trees without a plan—since they now knew where they were—was a bad idea. "Any idea how long that will go on?"

He shrugged. "Maybe an hour? The stories about them weren't good. The empire used to take prisoners out to the fields, tie them up, and leave them there. Between the lightning and the grasses, they were slowly and painfully killed."

"That's horrible." Clait lashed her tail.

"It's a horrible empire. My parents knew that their odds of surviving the ocean voyage were slim, and worse with a baby, but they knew staying wasn't an option."

Nevaine really looked at his bruises. They were already healing even though they'd looked fresh when she first saw him, but it was clear they'd been rough. "Who did that and when? And why?"

"The who are the Laiandran spies who found out who and what I was. And knew that you and I were involved."

They hadn't been totally secretive about dating but kept it fairly covert. It wouldn't be unheard of for someone to try to take advantage of someone close to the throne. Before Lizeth's decree that royals didn't have to marry other royals, it was easier to pick out the troublemakers since there had to be royal blood somewhere in the suitor's line.

Nevaine was the first to openly date a commoner after the age of twenty. "Laiandran spies? Who? Are they inside the palace?" Not that it mattered, as there was no way she could warn her family about them from halfway across the world.

"I couldn't tell you, to be honest. They made sure to keep me tied up and blindfolded when they grabbed me. They're who I stole that bag from that I used on you. Sorry about that. They first thought they could use me to get to you and kept beating me to make me give in and work with them. Then, something changed. They blew up my house and set a trap for you or your sisters. They went from trying to get an in with you, to trying to throw you off so much that you'd fail your Challenge. An hour before I escaped, they mentioned a few times, when they thought they were out of hearing range, that you wouldn't be coming back from your Challenge. That's when I escaped."

"How did you escape, might I ask?" Clait was back to annoyance and tail lashing. "Also, it appears that you have kept certain talents hidden. Shouldn't you have been able to simply escape? It's not easy to keep a mage or sorcerer contained if you don't realize what they are."

Clait had a good point. He'd used magic against the guards when he chased her. If no one knew he was a magic user, he should have been able to escape long before he did. Nevaine watched him carefully for any tells of lying.

"I am a fully trained battlemage and a level-three sorcerer." He shrugged. "Sorry, your people don't have sorcerers, not really. Your friend Gliandra is a level ten, a few steps below the highest levels. Finnian is about a four or five. I'm at the lower end but can still use sorcery if magic doesn't work. My parents feared the Offialian Empire would come looking for us, and trained my brothers and me in magic or sorcery, whichever we had the potential for. I'm the only one who has both." He gave a shake of his head. "As for why I didn't escape, I wanted to find out why a bunch of Laiandrans were slinking around Astarious, stalking a very lovely princess. I intended to stop them once I'd learned what I could, but that didn't work out as planned."

"You might have messed up my Challenge and somehow pulled us here. And for what? Did you get any useful information?"

Nevaine really wasn't sure what she thought about him. His bruises were fading even faster, which supported him being a trained battlemage. Her parents were looking at that training for Piallen based on her skills, but were worried about her focusing on the magic aspect. One of the essential components of battlemage training was that they could self-heal. Not immediately, and not a fatal injury, but they could get back into a fight much faster than other magic users.

"I learned that you and your Challenge are something the Laiandrans feared so much that they set loose some of their few magic users to sneak into your land. Those secret ones that the empire denies having. They created a portal to grab Piallen, hoping both her and my disappearances would stop you. I'm glad they couldn't catch her."

"She had some help on that," Clait said smugly. She was still watching him closely but her tail was still.

"I gathered. My parents are fascinated by your people, by the way. The few packs of grigeens that live here are wild and avoid people. Unless, of course, someone wanders too close to their dens. Those people don't come back."

Clait's eyes went wide. "There are grigeens here? My people have been missing for a few hundred years—my pack is the last known one and probably only still in place because of the Astarious royals. Think before you speak—are you certain that your parents spoke of grigeens in the present? As in twenty years ago?"

"Twenty-three years ago was when we left, but yes, at that time there were feral packs. My parents were surprised that there were none in Hilath, but warned me when I moved to Astarious to be wary of them."

"This changes things. We have to find them." Clait didn't look like she was accepting anything other than a confirmation.

"We can try, but I have no idea how we'd find them—it sounds like they stayed well hidden." Nevaine looked to Sean, and he nodded.

"That could be your Challenge." Clait held up a tiny paw. "No, I'm not just trying to convince you that we need to do this—but we do. The loss of grigeens in the rest of the world has had major negative repercussions. We work with magic; build it, transform it. We do the same with nature." She pointed out toward the still crackling fields. "My people might be here, but they have either forgotten who they are or they aren't allowed to do what they need to. That would never be here if my people were free to do what they are supposed to do."

"She's right," Sean said. "My parents brought what old books they could when they fled. My brothers didn't read them much, but I broke my leg as a kid one summer and was bored, so I went through a few. There has been a serious decline in the natural order of things here since the grigeens went feral. Things like that field and worse. And from what I read, I don't think the grigeens went feral by choice." He looked carefully at Clait.

"We wouldn't have. Something drove the ones who live here into hiding—maybe the same thing that made the rest of my people vanish." She frantically cleaned a paw—usually more a sign of thinking and agitation than an actual dirty paw.

Nevaine noticed that when asked about others of their kind, none of the grigeens said they were dead—just that they were missing. She'd never wanted to ask further as it was thought to be a cultural coping mechanism. But it might matter now. She wasn't sure if there was a correlation between her Challenge and the grigeen situation, but she needed to get all the information they had to figure it out. "How do you know your people are missing?"

"And not simply dead?" Clait gave a sad smile. "A question that has been asked for a long time. My people realized that our pack was the last of our kind—which happened three hundred years ago and is a long, sad story for another time. But we reached out to the oracles and to the seers of distant lands. They couldn't find them. Even the oracles simply said they were missing. Not dead. Never dead. But gone. My people have worked hard to find out what happened but for obvious reasons, we don't want to go far from our protected woods."

"Those woods are protected? I played in them as a kid—I never noticed a magic shield." The grigeen woods were a small portion of a much larger forest that was protected by the royal family. But Nevaine gathered the protection that Clait spoke of was something more.

"It is an old spell, one tied to the trees themselves; it protects us and gives comfort. That's why Gliandra built her cottage there fifty years ago. Her heart was weary, and she appealed to our leaders to stay there."

Nevaine watched as the lightning started slowing down and the grasses sent up fewer responding arcs. Not only would such a thing be horrific as a killing ground for an evil empire, but animals could be caught in it. All because of unchecked magic users and no grigeen protection. She nodded. "I have no idea what my Challenge is, if we're where we're supposed to be, or what it will take to find and help these grigeens, but I think we have to try."

"Agreed." Sean looked up as both turned to him. "Hey, I got broken ribs trying to find out why the Laiandrans wanted to stop you from completing your Challenge. At the very least, I get a small say in what we do."

Nevaine shook her head. "And how long did those ribs stay broken?"

He shrugged. "Ten minutes, but they still hurt when it happened."

"I, of course, strongly agree. Just seeing new grigeens, meeting them…" Clait shook her head. "It would mean a lot."

"We won't be able to take them back with us though, you know that, right? I'm not even sure how we'll get back, but I don't think a bunch of grigeens could make the trip."

"Agreed." Clait grinned. "But there are other ways."

Sean got to his feet but then looked past Nevaine. "What are those?" He pointed to three packs sitting against a tree. Ones Nevaine knew hadn't been there when they ran into the forest.

Nevaine grinned and ran over. One of the few things she'd been able to glean about the Challenge was supplies. The Challenges were created by the oracles, but they didn't want the royals to die due to lack of food or basic supplies. So, packs were sent. The fact that there were two full-sized packs and a grigeen-sized one told Nevaine that the oracles were aware of and approved of her companions. And that whatever the Challenge was—this was the right place.

"Wait! You don't know what those are!" Sean jumped to his feet and tried to stop her, but she already had the first one in her hands.

"Actually, these are a good sign." She held up a man's shirt, then tossed the pack to Sean.

Clait came over, chittering, and pawed through her pack. "This is wonderful! The oracles have blessed us." She pulled out a small apple and started munching.

Sean stood there for a few moments watching them look through their packs, then shrugged and started going through his. "They gave me some small explosives?" He peered closer at four thin objects. "Yup, that's what they are. Not helpful for blowing up anything large, but you never know when you might need them." He tucked them back in his pack.

Nevaine had managed to piece together that the packs existed through reading a few carefully expunged versions of Challenges that she picked out of royal autobiographies, but she had really been hoping for some secret book telling her what she needed to know. Even a pamphlet. Nope. The pack was well stocked with dried food, clothing, and a water bag. One that looked odd. She held it up, took a few sips, and watched as the water in the almost translucent bag refilled.

"Okay, that's new. They refill on their own. Do you each have one?" She shook the bag toward the other two. Sean held up one identical to hers, and Clait held up a smaller one and a small bowl. Grigeens could use bottles, but it was awkward. The tiny bowl would be easier for her.

"I have to say, I like these oracles." Sean was holding up a pair of black leather pants and a rustic black tunic. He looked down at his own clothes. "There's a subtle difference in the styling—I certainly don't recall what clothes looked like here, but I'd say we should change to blend in better."

Nevaine looked at her outfits. They were far more rustic than her own well-tailored clothes. If they'd been similar to her own clothing she'd say to hold off, but there was enough difference that the odds were they needed to swap.

She pulled everything out, picked a shirt and pants, then piled them back in. The packs didn't look large enough to hold everything. Probably some sort of spell, like the water bottles. "No books or weapons though." She gave a sigh.

Sean tilted his head. "You have five knives, two daggers, and two garrotes, I know—I took them off you once I tied you up. You need more?"

"You can never have too many weapons." Nevaine felt a pang at her words—the same ones that she'd jokingly said to her sisters just the day before. She hoped the Laiandrans were wrong and she found her way back to them. "Oh, and I do have a total of six knives and three garrotes. No, I won't tell you where the extras are."

They took turns going deeper into the woods and changing. She had to admit that all black did suit Sean. His blue eyes almost glowed.

"Why are you scowling? Do the clothes not fit?" Sean twisted around, trying to look at himself.

She wasn't going to tell him they fit far too well. But that wasn't what was making her scowl. "They're fine. But right after those spies blew up your house, Piallen chased what she thought was you through a magical trap and was ambushed in front of the Laiandrans' portal. She said that you were wearing something like that, which was why I figured it wasn't really you."

He gave a crooked grin. "You've memorized all of my clothes?"

"No. Don't get that look, mister. I'm still not sure how I feel about you. But I am observant of everyone around me—that is not something you would normally wear."

Clait walked around him slowly. "It does seem to work for you, though. You look quite roguish."

"Thank you." His smile dropped. "While I am a battlemage, I'd still feel better with some actual physical weapons. Unlike you, I have none. I think a nice sword would lend this rogue look some teeth." He did a fast spin that made Nevaine and Clait laugh.

Nevaine shook her head. Damn him. This wasn't the time or place to decide if her initial feelings about him were right or wrong. He wasn't really who she thought he was and that bothered her. She'd deal with that once they got back. Right now, they just needed to survive and figure out her Challenge.

"We have no map; I don't see any towns or even villages out here. I'm not sure where we can find a sword—or a clue as to my Challenge." She held up her hand as Clait opened her mouth. "Beyond contacting the feral grigeens. I'm honestly not sure where to go."

"Being as that, even though the lightning storm is gone, we are still perilously close to nightfall, I'd say we go farther into the woods and rest." Clait studied the trees for a moment. "I wouldn't suggest a fire of any sort, however. The trees are feral also."

Nevaine looked to see if Clait was joking, but she wasn't smiling. She was also staring with a lot of focus at one of the trees. "Are you talking to it?"

"Not really talking, but we are communicating in a fashion. It has been so long since one of my people has come this way, the tree was confused." Clait grinned. "But it remembers us now. It recommends that we go farther into their woods, where a small cave sits. They are expecting a rainy night after the lightning storm."

"I'd rather not be in the rain. Not sure about leather pants and all," Sean said. "As for fire." He snapped his fingers and a flicker of light appeared in his hand, then increased and kept a steady glow. "These won't keep us warm, but we won't have a problem with light."

Nevaine studied the light. "Is that sorcery? It has a different feel."

"Yup. And each sorcerer or sorceress will have a slightly different feel to their spells. It's one of the ways that sorcery is different from magic. It's not a one size fits all. I could teach this one to you. It's not difficult."

"I'd like that, thank you. Gliandra gave me a small sorcery book. I will need to go over it as well. Maybe you could help me with any questions."

Sean laughed. "Is it an addiction? This obsession with books?"

"I like knowledge, and books are the best places to get that. Sadly, I am not to go to university for advanced study." A few weeks ago, she had told him of her wish to go away for school after she completed her Challenge. She hadn't had a chance to tell him that her parents denied her again.

Clait took the lead and stalked through the woods but kept quiet. She'd heard all about Nevaine's attempts and denials.

"I'm sorry. I know it meant a lot to you. I'd say try again, but if the Laiandrans are up to something, you probably shouldn't leave Astarious. Especially once you're an heir to the throne."

Nevaine shot him an evil look, then sighed. "I want to disagree, but you and my parents might be right. The Laiandrans haven't done anything in over three hundred years. But those Stiklins that invaded the palace two years ago must have been from them. And now with them trying to disrupt my Challenge? Something isn't right."

"They know, thanks to that massive ravine, that they can't do a full-scale attack on your kingdom. And, even though they do have secret magic users, they have chased out or killed most magically or sorcery-inclined people in their land—whereas your kingdom is well magicked."

Nevaine stepped over a tree root as they walked through the woods. "True, but if they are finding ways around it... Gah! I hate cowards almost more than the willfully ignorant."

"That's my feisty princess." Sean smiled and looked ready to say more, but stayed silent.

"I believe we should get to the cave in a few—" Clait cut herself off and jumped a few feet in the air as an arrow hit the ground right where she had been.

Chapter Ten

Nevaine had knives in both hands. Sean had dropped his light but had his hand curled, ready for a spell. Clait chittered as three men and two women, guards of some sort from the look of them, stepped forward.

It was still light enough that Nevaine could easily see the desperation in their faces. She wouldn't hesitate to kill someone threatening those she cared about, but these five looked like they had little choice. She'd try not to kill them if she could.

"Give us those packs, your weapons, and that furry one, and we won't hurt you." The leader was tall and once was probably in fighting form—he wasn't any more. His uniform was torn and stained and he looked gaunt, not naturally thin.

"Actually, I was just going to say if you all step aside and get that archer hiding back there to drop their bow, we won't hurt you." Nevaine beat Sean to the punch in responding, but he grinned and the spell he was holding in his hand crackled.

"I'd listen to her; you really don't want to see what she can do with those knives. Or any of the weapons she has." He flexed his arm and a bolt of light shot out of his open hand and past the people facing them. A scream and a thud followed. "Your archer shouldn't be dead—unless they landed wrong. But I can't speak for the rest of you, if you don't stand down."

Nevaine gestured with her hand, still holding her knife. And a small wind pushed back the three closest attackers. "I've had an overall horrible day, and you look like things aren't going so great for you. What say you let us go? And we just pretend this never happened?"

"We can't. Haven't had food in a week. Can't go back to town." The leader sounded far more desperate than before. "They will find us. Need to get out of here." His words were halting now. A rustle came from behind him and the others, but none of them turned around. "It's too late." His voice was soft as the sword he held fell from his fingers.

Clait started pushing at Nevaine. "We have to get out of here—now!"

All five people facing them froze and looked up into the darkening sky. Then they jerked sharply and tumbled to the ground.

Sean grabbed Nevaine's hand and started running. "We need distance—lots of distance. How much information did those trees give you about the area?"

Clait dodged around them and took the lead. "Enough to get us from here—they'll help what they can, but they're now afraid of those people. They say they've changed."

"They have. One of the lovely stories I read about my former homeland is what happens to deserters of the military. Those people must have been desperate, but they should have focused on getting farther away from where they had been stationed." He looked over to Nevaine but hadn't dropped her hand. "They're all dead now and will be coming back as zombies to hunt us. Providing they don't all kill each other first. It's how the kingdom punishes deserters."

Nevaine had nothing to contribute so she just ran faster—and also didn't let go of his hand. Clait led them through a twisting maze of trees.

At first, Nevaine thought they'd made it—the only sounds were them, and all three were trying to run as quietly as possible. Then she heard crashing and odd grunts behind them.

"At least two are after us. We won't be able to outrun them. The zombie spell will give them speed and strength they didn't have in life." Sean didn't slow down but he was looking for options.

Like her sisters, Nevaine had exceptional eyesight and saw the boulder up ahead before he did. "There's a defensive place up ahead."

She tugged on his arm and all three changed direction toward it. They got to it and had just scrambled up to the top, when the leader and one of the women stumbled into the clearing. Their faces were pale, jaws were slack, and their eyes had gone white—they also moved in a jerking fashion. The spell that killed them obviously animated their bodies, but it didn't have a lot of control.

The boulder they were on was really a massive rock pile with only one way up in the back. Nevaine hoped that if these two were as brain-dead as the stories implied, they wouldn't walk around the boulders, looking for a way up.

"Those things shouldn't be moving." Clait stood atop one of the smaller boulders and swished her tail so fast that it almost seemed to vanish. "What is this place that uses such dark arts?"

"I told you it was a horrible empire. I should have thought of this when I figured out they were deserters—all military are faced with this if they try to escape. That was another reason my parents wanted to leave before I turned a year old." Sean's face was grim as he looked down at the lumbering zombies.

"They recruit one-year-olds? To fight?" Nevaine found the zombies perversely fascinating from a scientific standpoint —if she ignored the fact they had once been living people. But making babies join the military was unheard of.

"To train. If it is determined that a baby will be on the military path, they are taken from their parents on their first birthday. The military is all they'll know."

Nevaine shuddered. The cheerful and confident man who Sean had become would have never existed had his parents not fled. "This empire is atrocious." Nevaine calmed herself and pulled in a tricky spell. The zombies weren't able to get them up here, but they also couldn't get down with them down there. "I can set them free." She said it softly, but Clait heard her.

"It would be a blessing. Let their souls rest. Concentrate." In the past two years, Clait had often hung around during Nevaine's magic training with Hisu. She knew which spell Nevaine was thinking about.

It was a potentially messy spell and one Hisu hadn't taught her until last year. Even then, he acted as if it was an "in theory only" spell and not really one to be used. Mostly because a situation where it would be helpful was almost unheard of. But Nevaine liked the more esoteric spells, so he taught it to her.

Its goal was to separate the soul from the body.

Sean watched her questioningly, but didn't say anything.

Nevaine watched as the two former military personnel stumbled about the base of their boulders. She'd have to do it one at a time and hope she had enough magic for both. It was a balancing of sorts, and one of the reasons Hisu felt she might master the spell. She would balance the body against the soul, and then let the soul go free.

The really only practical use was to help mortally injured and suffering people. The two below her were even more than that.

Clait went to Sean. She kept her voice low, but not low enough. "Stand back, but be ready to grab her if she falls."

"I *can* hear you. Thanks for the vote of confidence. But yes, please don't step in unless I fall. Hopefully not down these boulders." She took a step back. She needed to maintain visual contact with the zombies, but there was a chance she could collapse and she would rather not drop on them.

"I'll just be waiting." Sean held his crackling sorcery in his left hand, but stayed where he was.

Nevaine nodded and began gathering the spell. It was odd to switch back to magic after working on sorcery for a few hours, but eventually she centered herself. She focused on the leader as he was easier to see. Keeping her eyes on him, she went inside him and searched for his soul.

Not an easy thing under the best circumstances and while Nevaine loved a challenge, she'd almost given up on learning this spell when Hisu was teaching it to her. It involved a massive amount of balancing and even though that was where her strength was, it was so delicate she almost gave up.

It was worse this time. The soul was an intangible thing, but this spell changed that, making it something that could be seen and moved. However, there was little of it left in this man, even when she could see it.

She fought to stay in the spell and not throw up as she realized what had been done to him. Whoever attacked these people had not only killed them and turned them into mindless killers, but they were using their souls to build their own powers—and destroying the souls while they did it. With a deep breath to calm her terror, Nevaine magically took hold of the shriveling soul, quickly balanced it, and set it free.

She stumbled, and Sean was at her side as the man below them let out a long sigh and dropped to the ground.

Sean held her up. "You don't look good. I'm not sure what you did, but it took too much out of you. We can get away from that one—her leg is twisted." He nodded down toward the other zombie. She was limping in a circle as her left leg wasn't working right.

"I can't leave her. What those sorcerers did...it was horrific. Hold me up if you need to, but I have to help her." Nevaine didn't wait for his response but went back into her spell. It was easier this time as she knew what to expect, but it was also harder as whoever was behind the zombies knew what she was doing. And they were fighting back.

The battle to free the woman's soul was rough, but eventually it was free.

And Nevaine collapsed completely into Sean's arms. "She's free." She smiled, then the world went black.

RUSTLING SOUNDS MADE when people were trying to be quiet but not completely succeeding were the first thing Nevaine heard. She kept her eyes closed and her breathing steady to mimic sleep as she focused on recalling where she was and who might be around her.

"She will be okay. Whatever that spell was, it just took a lot out of her."

Male voice...Sean.

With that hint, all of the pieces fell into place. Along with a horrible feeling. "I'm going to be sick." She opened her eyes and tried to roll off what she was lying on but she was on a pile of blankets on a hard floor.

Clait was at her side with a flat piece of fabric immediately. Once Nevaine was through being ill, Clait carried it out of the cave.

"Feeling better?" Sean dropped down next to her and handed her a water bag. The cave was sparsely lit with the small glows that he'd created in the forest.

Nevaine wiped her mouth and gratefully took the bag. Luckily, she hadn't had much to eat, but it still wasn't fun to throw up. "I will be. Did the woman collapse?" She'd passed out before she saw it, but she'd hoped they wouldn't have come here if the zombie was still roaming around.

"Yes. I don't know what that spell you used was, but both of them were allowed to die." Sean's face went serious. "Promise me that if I am ever changed like that, you'll do the same? Or if I'm injured with no hope of survival? The sorcerers in this empire have some horrific spells—even worse than the zombie one."

"That won't happen..." Nevaine stopped when she saw his eyes. He was terrified. "Fine. While I don't believe that will happen, I promise that I will do my best to set your soul free." She stretched her neck to get some of the stiffness out. That spell had made every joint in her body ache. She really hoped she'd never have to cast it again. Ever.

Sean let out a low whistle. "That's really what your spell did? I couldn't sense anything beyond some extremely heavy magic."

"Yes. It was one of the most recent full spells that Hisu taught me. One he never thought I'd use." She shook her head. "Whatever sorcerer or sorceress who set that spell on those people was feeding off their souls. I'm not sure to what end, but it was horrifying."

"Both bodies turned to dust as we were getting off the boulders, probably part of the spells," Clait said. "The trees weren't happy, but not shocked. It must happen fairly often."

Nevaine let the shudder that comment caused go through her. Part of the Challenge—again, at least from what she'd pulled out of vague journal entries—was to see the world in new ways. This wasn't what she'd expected.

"Okay, so hopefully you won't need to do that again, because you didn't look good at all. But at least we weren't torn apart. We're in this cave thanks to Clait's tree friends, and we can rest and start anew in the morning." Sean sounded chipper, and was carefully ignoring his earlier request for her to set his soul free if needed, but his deep blue eyes were still somber.

Nevaine ignored it for now. He knew more of this kingdom than she did, and from what she'd seen so far, they had serious reasons to worry. If he wanted to present a happy front, she wasn't going to argue. At least right now.

They put together a rough meal of dried meat, fruit, travel bread, and water as Sean added a few more glowing lights around the cave. Nevaine found she was far hungrier than she'd expected given her stomach issue earlier, but she wasn't going to argue. She felt two sets of eyes on her as she reached for her third helping.

"Sorry, but if you'll both recall, someone grabbed me before dinner last night. Or whenever it was."

"I will never argue with a woman who eats," Sean said. "And it appears, that while not exciting food, the bags of food are spelled to refill as well. At least the oracles are making sure we have basic supplies."

Clait nodded as she put her things back into her own pack. "Agreed, but that is a hint. I believe they only do what they feel they need to give the Challenger a greater chance at completing their task. That they provided both refillable food and water might not be a good sign."

"And one we aren't going to think about right now." Nevaine flashed a smile at Clait's look of surprise. Nevaine's normal stance was to look for the bad first. "I have a feeling we'll have enough things to worry about on this trip without adding overly concerned oracles. Although, I still say if they were truly worried, they would have given us weapons and books."

Sean and Clait shared a look.

"What? Did something appear while I was out?" She started to reach for her pack.

"Now, it might not have come from the oracles, but when we found this cave there were a pair of swords." Sean held up his hands. "But they could have come from anywhere."

Nevaine tilted her head back. It was helpful that the oracles were trying to keep them from dying, but it would be more so if they would just pop up and talk to Nevaine about what she needed to do.

"The oracles must have believed you would be needing them." Clait glared at Sean. "I have other concerns, though. You've been awfully secretive about things such as your having magic and sorcery. That should be addressed."

Nevaine folded her arms and nodded. "What she just said."

Sean laughed. "Why didn't I tell you about my magic and sorcery?" He shrugged. "I figured every guy would be trying to impress you with his magical abilities. I wanted to win you without that." He sounded very honest in that last sentence.

Nevaine looked away. She didn't know if knowing about his abilities would have changed how she felt about him. But it was still hard that he didn't feel comfortable telling her after they'd been involved for a few months. "You should have told me."

"Would it have made a difference?"

"I don't know, but now how can I be sure you're who I thought you were?" She held up her hand as he looked ready to respond. "This isn't the time or place to sort it out. Let's leave whatever might have been between us in Astarious until we're back there. We need to focus on staying alive and getting home."

He flinched at the comment, but stepped back. "Agreed. One of the first lessons for battlemages is to focus on the task. I can do that."

Clait looked between the two of them and gave a massive yawn. "It's been a long day, and I think we need rest. The closest that the trees could direct us to the feral grigeens is a two-day trip." She frowned. "And not all of it is the woods. Unless we walk far around, we will have to skirt a village, maybe two." She shook her head. "These trees are even harder to understand than those at home."

Nevaine took the common sense, and the point that she and Sean did need to back off, as words of wisdom. "Agreed. Plus, I'm still feeling the reaction from that spell."

"I'll keep first watch; I don't need much sleep." Sean took some blankets and put together a seating spot just inside the entrance of the cave.

Clait looked up as she dragged a blanket near Nevaine and made a nest out of it. "The trees said this was a safe place. They watch over it, but they implied other powers did as well. Sean's parents might have stayed here when they were escaping—it's got a history of being a safe shelter."

"The oracles?" Nevaine tried reaching out, but if the oracles were here in some way, she couldn't tell.

"Not sure. The trees are odd, as I've said. But it wasn't a hostile feeling, so I believe we're safe." She stretched and curled into her nest. "I think all of us need to sleep. Sean, put out those lights and turn that seat into a bed."

Nevaine held back her laugh as Sean bowed to Clait and did as commanded. She feared that sleep might be hard to catch, even though she knew she needed it. Her mind was always active and the last few hours had given it a lot to process. But surprisingly, she dropped off to sleep almost immediately.

Unfortunately.

Chapter Eleven

The moment Nevaine fell asleep was when the demons came. They might not be real demons, and part of her knew they were only in her head, but they chilled her soul. They were chasing her through the palace back home: a combination of Stiklins, Lotha, and Tullary—the last two creatures she'd read about from countries so far from Astarious, that she never feared meeting them. But they felt far too real right now.

She screamed in her dream, but the palace was empty and looked like it had been abandoned years ago. The sounds of fighting came from the damaged walls around her as she tried to outrun the monsters.

Strong hands grabbed her, trying to shake her to death. Then a pair of tiny paws slapped her cheeks.

"Snap out of it!" Clait's voice was a lifeline and pulled Nevaine back to their cave.

She grabbed Sean's hands where he held her shoulders. "I'm fine. Fine." She took a deep breath to chase out the last of the chills. She wasn't a stranger to nightmares and the like—again, a problem of her extremely active mind—but this one felt far too real. "Just a nightmare." Maybe if she said it enough, she'd believe it. From their looks, the other two weren't sure.

"You do realize that when you were setting those souls free, the sorcerers controlling them could have latched onto you?" Sean sat back on his heels and shook his head. "You didn't show any signs of possession when you woke up before, so I figured you were safe. But maybe they got a hook into your mind?"

Nevaine rubbed her face to get the last vestiges of the nightmare out. "I thought you hadn't heard of the spell I used?"

"I haven't, but I have heard of the one that turned those guards into undead killers. And the people behind *that* spell are powerful and evil." He pulled up one of his little lights and moved it near her face. "Let me look at you closely while you tell us what you just went through."

Nevaine turned to Clait. "Tell him that I always have nightmares. That's all it was. I think I'd have noticed if something had gotten into my head."

"This felt different." Clait's tail twitched. "I sat through your nightmares as a child—I know what they felt like. This one wasn't the same. But I can't say what it is, either. My magic is more focused on nature, not people."

"Go ahead, then. Check in my head while I tell you about my nightmare." She tilted her head toward Sean. "Wait, just what will you be checking? I don't want you roaming around my mind." She didn't know if he could do that, but she really didn't want him anywhere near her confused thoughts about him.

Sean laughed but his dark-blue eyes were still serious. "I don't have the ability to read your thoughts—any of them. I'm looking for small triggers as you speak. It's hard to explain, but if there was sorcery involved, it will give out sparks, for want of a better word, as you talk of the images you saw. Now, where were you?"

Even though it had felt far longer in her mind, telling Sean and Clait the events from her nightmare only took a few minutes. At first, Sean was calmly listening while looking slightly over her head. Then when the sounds of battle outside the abandoned palace started, he scowled and bit off a few harsh sounding words of sorcery and appeared to be grabbing invisible things out of the air around her.

Nevaine would have thought he was just making things up as she couldn't see anything, but she could hear a faint sizzle each time his fingers closed on each other. Something was there.

"That was it. Then you two woke me up." She watched Sean carefully as he sat back.

"There is something there, but I don't think it was a work of sorcery, or magic...it was something else." He shook his head. "Someone or something wanted you to see those images. They were planted in your mind. That's all I could gather."

"So, every time I sleep, that's going to happen? I'd say that's an issue."

"I don't think so. But I'm not sure." Sean looked to Clait. "What did you sense? I know you said your magic was more focused on nature, but you do pick up on other things. I've seen you."

"Aren't you the sneaky one," Clait said. "I felt a presence...I think that was from the oracles."

Nevaine had wanted guidance, but soul-crushing nightmares wasn't how she wanted it. "Again, is this going to happen every time I fall asleep? And I thought the oracles weren't supposed to step in. Nor are they known to be anywhere within the Offialian Empire and haven't been an influence here in hundreds of years. Yet, they not only gave us packs, but weapons, and are now adding disturbing nightmares. I don't get what's going on." She shared her glare with both of them.

Clait responded first. "The oracles work in odd ways, which we don't always fully understand. They might not be found in many lands now, but a thousand years ago they were everywhere."

"Maybe the dream was how they can reach you without bending their own rules too much. Perhaps ask them not to do it every night." Sean was clueless, but trying to be helpful.

Nevaine yawned in spite of herself. "Well, I'm not sure what they were trying to communicate beyond scaring me. And that worked. But I'm now exhausted." She turned to Clait. "Wake me if I scream again, or we get invaded. Otherwise, let me sleep."

Clait nodded and turned to Sean. "She sometimes mutters in her sleep. Just ignore it."

"Good to know." Sean's grin was almost back to its normal state.

Nevaine fought another yawn, then dropped back into her blankets and was out.

No nightmares this time, no dreams at all—or, if she had them, she didn't recall them. But she did wake to an incredibly odd smell. "Is that grilled fish?" Not what she expected to smell for a number of reasons, but it was distinctive.

Sean and Clait were near the mouth of the cave, hunched over a small fire.

And three large fish that were sizzling away.

"Where did they come from? And I thought we couldn't use fire." It was an odd breakfast food, but she had to admit they smelled wonderful once she adjusted to the startling aroma.

"The trees told me we could gather broken branches from the ground as long as the fire stayed in the cave. They also told me where a small pond was that had too many fish. So, we're helping them out." Clait nodded to where another bunch of fish sat on an odd rock.

"Are they cooking on that too?" It looked like a normal rock...granted, one that was about three feet around. But there were thin tendrils of smoke coming from the darkening fish.

"Drying." Sean grinned. "I adapted a spell to speed up drying them out. They won't taste as good as fresh, but will supplement what food we have in the bags. There were a lot of fish in that pond."

Nevaine nodded, but wasn't sure how she felt. Astarious was a landlocked kingdom, but did import fish. She liked it as a special treat, and the ones he was grilling smelled good. But she had a feeling that her opinion would change after a few days of eating them.

Sean divided up the grilled fish and started eating.

"No more dreams?" Clait asked around a mouthful of fish. A rumbling purr as she ate showed how happy she was about the fish.

"None. Aren't you afraid of choking on a bone, eating it that fast?" Nevaine took a bite of hers, avoiding the small bones. It was tasty, but Clait was eating like it was the first food she'd had in years.

"Nope. My people started out living in coastal parts of the world. Our throats and gullets have a special way of breaking down the bones. Oh, how I miss fish." She licked her lips and went for more.

"You've never mentioned it. We do have it in the kingdom sometimes, you know."

"Yes, yes. But if those of us who frequent the palace get some, it wouldn't be fair to the rest of the pack who didn't."

"I promise when we get back, I'll make sure that we import enough fish for all of your people. Maybe every few months?" Nevaine had no idea how much fish a pack of grigeens could eat; she hadn't even known about them being coastal originally—and that really should have been in a book somewhere. But it was the least she could do for what the grigeens had done for the royals over the years.

A low rumbling went through the ground at her feet, and Nevaine's first thought was she was having another reaction from her spell yesterday. Then she saw both Clait and Sean react. It lasted long enough for all three to step out of the cave in case it decided to collapse on them, then stopped.

The birds that had been heard earlier became silent during the rumble. And stayed that way.

"What was that? An earthquake?" Astarious didn't really have them often. The last had been when Nevaine was four and in a wading pool. She thought the water sloshing around was fun—her nannies did not and scooped her out immediately.

Clait stomped around as if she heard something in the ground as they went back into the cave. Then she tilted her head back as if smelling something. Then shook her head. "I don't think so. The rocks in this cave say it wasn't them. It was something unnatural."

"You can speak to the rocks? Why didn't you ever tell me?" Nevaine looked down at her lifelong friend. So many adventures missed when she was young.

"One, you don't need to know everything, even though you believe you do." She softened the comment with a smile. "And two, I'm relatively young for my people, and my powers have been growing in the last twenty years."

"I thought you were over a hundred years old?" Nevaine had always seen Clait as a wise old person.

"I am. One hundred and thirty-two now. That's akin to thirty in your much shorter human lives. Our magic grows as we age." She shrugged. "Anyway, *that* wasn't natural."

"I'd say something exploded somewhere not far from here." Sean frowned as he quickly started packing. "We probably should get moving."

"If something is out there blowing things up, wouldn't it make more sense to hide for a while longer?" Nevaine wasn't one for hiding usually but she hadn't had a real chance to look through Gliandra's spell book. She already had it out.

"Normally, I would say yes, but that felt awfully close and was probably magic-based. I am a battlemage, but one of me against a bunch of them would be suicide. Better we keep moving. If they trap us here, we're as good as dead." He'd packed all of his things and even wrapped the dried fish in a cloth and stuffed it in his pack. He then broke up the remains of their fire and did his best to hide that anyone had been there.

The swords they'd found both came with belts and sheaths. That one was a larger belt and the other fit Nevaine perfectly wasn't lost on any of them as she buckled hers on. While not as good with the sword as Piallen, she could still use it if she ran out of knives. Her magic wasn't as powerful as her sister, Lizeth's, but she could still pull up some defensive spells.

Clait smiled. "I know what you were thinking. And that book might be more of a danger to be read than left hidden in this place. You'll have time for it later."

Nevaine scowled. Clait had grown up with her and could read her like a favorite, well-worn book. "Fine." She slipped the book back into her pack.

Sean and Clait both paused at the entrance to the cave and waited silently as they studied the forest around them. Nevaine was about to push them both when they nodded to each other and went down the thin path leading from the cave.

"Just listening for any changes in the forest." Clait jogged in-between Sean and Nevaine as they made their way down to the forest floor.

"I was listening for the more human and magical kind," Sean said. "There was definitely something blown up but it came from the east. Luckily, our direction is toward the west." He looked back to Clait. "Aren't you the one leading us?"

"I figured I'd wait until we were at the bottom in case anything large and dangerous wanted to jump out." Clait gave one of her fang-filled grins as she dodged around Sean when they hit the trail. "Better you face them than me, battlemage."

Nevaine followed between and a bit behind them; watching their dynamics was interesting. It hadn't been that Clait had ever said she didn't like Sean, nor even implied it. But she'd always been aloof about him. That was changing, but she wasn't sure if they were becoming friends, or Clait was sizing him up as a potential enemy.

Which was okay—Nevaine still wasn't sure about him herself.

The forest seemed quieter than before: not silent, but muted. Most likely due to them walking through it. When Nevaine did go out into nature, it was usually to escape some other task so she could read. Sadly, she was usually more focused on her books than on the beauty around her.

Luckily, both Clait and Sean seemed quite able to read the forest around them, so she focused on following them. The trees changed from the thorny purple ones to larger, more normal-looking pines. It was almost easy to believe that she was back home, heading out to a picnic.

Then the ground shook again, and she stumbled.

Unlike the slow rumble of before, this one was a single sharp jolt. Both Sean and Clait were almost knocked off their feet as well.

Sean turned back. "Are you okay?"

"I'm okay; earthquake or...?"

Clait frowned. "That was an earthquake. But I believe it was a reaction to whatever happened before."

"Earthquakes react?" Nevaine wasn't sure about that.

"Yes, when provoked enough. I wonder if what happened earlier was intended to cause the later reaction. There will be more, trust me." She picked up her pace.

Nevaine jogged to Sean. "You think someone intended to cause earthquakes? For what reason? I get that the first one might have been a magic-fueled explosion, but wouldn't that have been to destroy something, not set off random earthquakes?"

He frowned. "Unless they aren't random. I don't feel nature the way Clait does, but there are a lot of nature-inspired spells within the realm of sorcery."

Clait kept moving but gave a sharp twitch to her tail. "Abominations of the natural world, you mean. They can be found in old magic spell books as well, but sorcery seems to use them more often. The portal they used to try to grab Piallen, for instance. It was taken from a naturally occurring sinkhole. They mutated it to create those horrific portals." The shudder she gave rippled through her fur.

They continued on in silence. Nevaine was trying to tune in to the world around her. There were things to learn outside of books. The air was cool but had a slight tinge of warmth to it; the smell of the pines also carried a hint of...smoke. "Does anyone else smell smoke? Or...is that brimstone?" The stronger it got, she realized it didn't smell like burning trees, which was a very good thing considering where they were, but it seemed out of place. It smelled like rotten eggs.

Sean and Clait both paused. Sean reacted first, and grabbed Nevaine's hand and picked up Clait as he raced down a side trail. "If you know any shield spells, put them up now!" He started uttering a spell under his breath as he ran.

Chapter Twelve

"I can run faster than you, you know." Clait squirmed out of his grasp and took off down the trail.

Nevaine had no idea what she was shielding against, but put up the only one she knew. It balanced a series of small shield blocks into a much stronger whole. The stink of rotting eggs was stronger and dark-blue lightning crackles were arcing through the trees behind them.

"On my count of three, drop to the ground—both of you." Sean didn't yell, but his voice was pitched to carry to the two of them. "One...two...three!" He released Nevaine's hand and spun as she and Clait both rolled to ground. He flung a spell, then dove down as well.

A wall of dark-blue arcs amid a cloud of yellow slammed over them and vanished.

Nevaine stayed down, but looked around, waiting for another of whatever that was. "I give up. What was that?"

Clait shook her fur and cleaned a few spots. "I've never heard of such a thing." Cleaning for grigeens was constant, like the cats they partially resembled. But it was also used as a cover in awkward or frightening situations—in this case, Clait looked extremely rattled but didn't want to show it. So, she cleaned.

"It was an old spell, an ancient one. Magic-based. I don't know that it was actually targeted at us, though." Sean sat up but didn't get to his feet. "It might have been triggered by that earthquake."

"Or the explosions which set off the earthquake? How old was the spell, and how can you tell?" Nevaine felt magic lashing through the air above them as whatever that had been raced past. But she couldn't tell more from it beyond that it was magic and that most likely it would have killed them had it hit them.

"Ah, the quirks of battlemage training. Battle grounds are often laced with spells. So, if you advance and captured the enemy's ground, you needed to search for hidden spells. It seems that the same battlegrounds were often used, so there could be extremely old spells left behind. Knowing how old they were, or least a general idea of it, helped counteract them."

"How would we have counteracted that one?" The hair on Nevaine's arms was still raised.

"You wouldn't. It was slowed with age, and you tipped us off by smelling the sulfur, but normally it would have immediately decimated the first lines of an approaching army."

All three of them were silent, and Clait kept cleaning.

"Is it safe to move on? Do we need to change direction?" Nevaine was trying to pick up on any unusual scents or sounds, but she was second-guessing everything. The forest around them was still silent and the only smell now was the faint scent of pine. Hisu used to have her run through a brief breathing exercise if she got too wound up over something, so she tried it now.

"I think so. I'll be honest, this area is really disturbing. It seems like there are a lot of traps here." Sean noticeably had not gotten to his feet yet.

Clait finally stopped cleaning, shook her fur, and raised her head to sniff. Her pointed nose twitched as it tested the air, then she finally looked to Nevaine. "I think whatever that was has completely passed."

Sean jumped to his feet and held a hand out to Nevaine. "We might as well keep moving. If that was aimed specifically at us, hopefully it will take awhile for them to realize that it missed."

Nevaine took his hand and got up. She adjusted her sword; that was one thing she was not used to—running or diving to the ground wearing one—and it showed in this case. She was lucky she hadn't damaged it or herself when she dove for the dirt. Sean hadn't seemed put out about it at all. Maybe if Piallen did go through the battlemage training, Nevaine could tag along and pick up some pointers. Just in case there was some other time she was racing around in strange woods with a sword on.

Clait sniffed a few more times, then led the way back toward their original trail.

"So, you didn't really leave me a letter saying you were off to get married to a fiancée back in Hilath?" Nevaine winced when the words came out as they started walking. She'd intended to sort things out in a more appropriate place and time—like back in the palace.

"What?" Sean was behind her but she could hear his facial expression in his voice. "Where did that come from? Damn it, I knew they did something. The last thing I recalled before they put that bag over my head was them going through my papers. Considering that I had nothing of importance, it seemed odd. You didn't believe it, did you?"

"I did." Nevaine didn't turn around. "Sorry, but it was your signature."

"And you're suspicious of everyone." There was a layer of accusation there. "Wouldn't you have known that I wouldn't do that? Have I once mentioned a fiancée or girlfriend?"

There was a lot of hurt there, which was one of the reasons she hadn't meant to mention it while out here in enemy territory and while having deadly spells flung at them.

"I have to be suspicious. It comes with being a royal." Nevaine bit her lip. Flinging around her status wasn't her thing at all. She ran her fingers through her hair as she turned back to him. "I'm sorry. But it seemed that we might have had something, then that happened right before my Challenge. I had to question it. Us."

He looked down at her. The hurt was still there, but something else was as well. "I understand. I wish you'd trusted me, *us*, enough to question it, but I understand." He touched the side of her face and looked ready to kiss her, then instead stepped back. "I'll keep you safe for your Challenge and help get us home, if I can. Then, if you want, I will leave Astarious." He shook his head as she started to speak. "Not now. Emotions aren't good in life-or-death situations. Rule one of the battlemage creed." His crooked smile didn't have much happiness behind it—but he was trying.

"Agreed." She wanted to say more but wasn't sure how it would come out. He had a point; she didn't trust him enough when faced with evidence of betrayal. That didn't bode well for them as a couple. Nevaine focused on shoving whatever her feelings about him were aside—she knew this wasn't the place, but she was used to dealing with issues immediately. Or as Clait would sometimes say, rashly.

She turned back to Clait. "On our way? I promise to hold off from outbursts. At least until we're home."

Clait watched them both with narrowed eyes, then spun and continued trotting down the trail.

Since being silent on the trail was probably a good thing, plus she had no idea what to say to Sean, she kept her mouth shut. He had an expressive face and the hurt in his eyes was real. She believed him about not having a fiancée—now. But the fact that he'd hidden his powers, and considering how strong battlemages were—it took a lot of effort on his part—did still raise questions. Did she know who he really was? She'd been close to seriously falling for him when everything went sideways. But was it really him she cared about, or just who he pretended to be? Her foot hit a rock and the resulting stumble shook her out of her thoughts. Another reason not to think about him or them.

Clait continued on, tilting her head up to sniff the air from time to time but appearing to know where she was going. A quick glance back showed that Sean was doing his version of the same as he watched the forest around them.

Nevaine decided to distract herself with some of the sorcery spells that Gliandra had taught her. She'd only gone through a few in the book, but one advantage of spending a lot of time reading: she processed information exceedingly fast.

The first spell was a defensive one, and particularly appropriate for this time. One of the surface differences between magic and sorcery was how they came about. Sorcery used spell words and sometimes finger movements. Aside from magic that was based on an action—like Lizeth's spell songs—most magic came from inside the person. Nevaine's magic was almost a series of balancing spell parts on top of each other. She could combine established spells into a single more powerful one as long as she balanced them correctly. Because she read so much, she had a lot of spells to work with. There were few in the augmented magic world who had her skill with spell balancing.

In a way, sorcery did the same balancing. The words of the spell, the movement of the fingers, and the intention of the sorcerer all combined to make a spell of sorcery. Which could be why it appeared she had a talent for it.

This spell required a constant low-level chant, but the words weren't in a language she knew. That was a question for Gliandra—did the language matter? If not, she'd look to getting the spells translated. Through her own magic, knowing what the intention was helped create the proper balance. The same could be true with sorcery.

This spell would build a low-level field of protection around the spell caster. It wouldn't stop swords, arrows, or knives, but it would seriously slow down, and eventually hold, any lower-level magics. But if someone like a fully trained battlemage came at her, and this spell was her only defense, it would slow the battlemage down—but not stop him.

She wasn't specifically thinking of how to stop Sean, but he was a good benchmark. Sometimes slowing an opponent down allowed for an attack of one's own.

"Your pronunciation is off." Sean had gotten closer behind her than she noticed. "The 'ah' at the end needs to be more drawn out. Once you know the spells well, you can work on lowering your volume. If I were fighting you, I would have come up with five ways to take down your spell just from the words you used."

"Good to know." Nevaine grinned. She wasn't upset about being corrected; her goal had always been to understand things. Unlike Lizeth, who got annoyed whenever she didn't get something right on the first try.

The forest was thinning out, and grasses and small flowers started appearing in the larger patches of sunlight. If she ignored the fact that this was her Challenge and wasn't sure what she was supposed to be doing, it was a lovely day—all she needed was a nice pile of books and a place to read and it would be perfect. Now that no zombies, spell traps, or earthquakes were trying to kill them. She held her breath as that thought came. She wasn't superstitious, really, but she didn't want to tempt things by pointing out, even in her own head, that things were good at this exact moment.

A light filled her eyes, blinding her, and she tried to throw a blocking spell, but then she dropped to her knees. She could see the forest around her and Clair and Sean running toward her, but it was faint, like a veil of gauze had dropped over all of her senses.

"An unusual start to a Challenge, but he is supposed to be here, just as you and she are." The voice echoing in her head was really a collection of voices—odd but melded together almost seamlessly. *"You have a specific goal in this Challenge. To find and release the golden grigeen. Your little friend can help, but you have to rely on your own senses and abilities to get there. The going will be difficult and all of you*

might die in the effort. But the effort must be made. Be fleet of mind, gentle of foot, and strong of heart. Blessings of the oracles be upon you."

There was a slight pressure change in her head, and reality snapped back into focus. Sean and Clait had just reached her—even though they'd been close by—when the oracles left. Nevaine let out a long breath but remained seated. Her head was spinning from the visit and from the words. The golden grigeen was a myth that down-on-their-luck treasure hunters went after. No one agreed to as to what kingdom or empire it was supposed to actually be in. But the implication had been that it was worth all three of them dying to get.

"Were you hit?" Sean dropped next to her as he kept watch around them. One hand was already flickering in a spell formation.

"I'm fine. A bit…disoriented. But fine." Nevaine looked to Clait. "I had a visit from the oracles."

Clait's eyes widened, and she sat down hard. "That's unusual. What did they say that you can share with us?"

Nevaine figured Clait meant that could be said in front of Sean, but was trying to be nice about it. For good or ill, they were all in this together. The man might die on this adventure; he should at least be involved in what it was. "They said it was an unusual Challenge, so it fits. We have a target, something we have to be willing to die to get free." *Might as well just blurt it.* "The golden grigeen."

Sean laughed, then stopped when he saw Nevaine wasn't joining in.

Clait tilted her head and narrowed her eyes. "That's a myth to trick the greedy. It doesn't exist. Are you certain that's what they said?"

Interesting response, since most grigeens, Clait included, were exceedingly fond of anything gold.

"Very." Nevaine got to her feet and dusted herself off. "They said you're both supposed to be here, that's what we need to find, and that we all could die. Not a fun one-sided conversation but at least we have a goal now." She didn't add that they hadn't given a single clue as to how to find this thing, but that would be obvious soon. If she had access to the palace library, she could likely narrow down the presumed location for it.

"That was short and useless." Sean pushed away a clump of hair that had fallen over his eyes. "Although, nice to know that my diving after you as you went through the portal was a valid idea. Not fond of the dying part, though."

"I still don't understand why they are sending us hunting for that useless, made-up relic. My people have never believed it was real." The fur along Clait's back was raised, and her tail was doing short, sharp twitches.

Nevaine watched her furry friend. She was really upset. "What is it supposed to do? All missing relics need to be a power of something."

"Not this one. It's repugnant. The oracles are wrong. Maybe it was a trick and the real Challenge is hidden in their words." Clait's eyes were starting to get glassy, and she looked frantic. "That's it, yes, of course."

Nevaine picked Clait up and looked into her face. "Why are you so upset about this?"

"It's a trick. Simply a trick. We have to stay away from the tricks." She was almost frothing.

Sean reached out to her. "There's a spell on her, but not one from here." He leaned forward and whispered, "Golden grigeen."

Clait's tail lashed and her claws extended.

"It's attached to the name." Nevaine looked closer at Clait. He was right; a faint magical overlay was on her. One that hadn't been noticeable until triggered by the words *golden grigeen*. She focused on the spell but it was so old, she had no idea how to deal with it. It probably wouldn't kill Clait, but it could incapacitate her. She was heading toward a state of shock as it was.

Nevaine grabbed a magic spell she knew—this wasn't the time to experiment with sorcery—it was simple, but should work. A variation of the spell blocks she'd used as a child. These were smaller but could block against specific things. Such as a pair of words. She didn't want to block the words completely; like it or not, Clait was most likely going to be needed to find the object. But enough to make it an annoyance rather than something that would make her slip away like this.

Clait blinked as whatever spell had been shutting her down was pushed back. "That was not nice." The way she was glaring around, Nevaine thought she might be talking about her spell blocks. "That spell...not yours...the one that made me upset about that *term*, it was made by one of our people." She licked her lips and scowled. "By a few of our people. The first one I sensed was Eroth, our pack leader. Can't zero in on who else was involved. But I will. They have some serious explaining to do."

"So, we can mention the golden grigeen without you getting ready to pass out?" Nevaine watched Clait carefully as she said it but aside from a twitch in her left eye, she seemed fine.

"Yes, but can we just call it the object? I'm not sure why the oracles want us to find something that might not exist and has been rumored to be in every country in the world—yet never found—but they did. Calling it the object will help me a lot."

"These oracles, they don't play tricks, right? I've heard of the object as well but it's made of fool's gold and is a joke." Sean caught himself right before he said *golden grigeen*.

"They don't, but judging by Clait's reaction, I'd say the oracles know more about the object than they told me. Why make her so intently disregard the rumors of that thing? Even with my spell on her, Clait still thinks it's a useless quest."

Clait wrinkled her nose in annoyance. "You're right. There's no reason for me to be angry about this. Aside from the whole we-might-all-die issue." She waved her paw. "I'm not being sarcastic. I'm serious. Even before the life-and-death issue, I was furious and wanted to discount the entire idea. Not good. A spell of this caliber would have been on all of our pack. Which explains why we never even mention that thing. Which means someone doesn't want us to find it, which means that we should." Clait paced in a tight circle as she spoke.

Sean raised his left eyebrow as he watched her while her muttering dropped below normal hearing. "Does she do this often? Or is it from the spell they put on her?"

"It's just her. She'll keep twisting the words until she sorts it out. But I don't know that out here in the open is a great place for introspection. Unless it's about where we should go to hunt this thing down." Nevaine looked up as the bushes around them started to move. "And if these are friend or foe." Her hand dropped to a throwing knife and the other hand held a small blast spell as the rustling came closer.

Chapter Thirteen

Clait stopped trying to walk a hole in the trail and rose up on her back legs, sniffing. Sean slowly rose to his feet from where he'd dropped down next to her and had his hand on the hilt of his sword. The shuffling in the bushes grew louder, but nothing showed itself.

Some animals did hunt in packs and would circle their prey like this, but anything that would feel bold enough to face the three of them, and be a threat, probably wouldn't be this small.

Clait gave a high-pitched trilling cry and the rustling around them stopped. Then she shouted what sounded like random noises, but were probably words.

Still nothing came out of the shrubbery, but a voice. "We speak your tongue." A bit stilted but in clear Common.

"I figured you were uneducated and without honor since you snuck up upon us instead of presenting yourselves."

There was such a level of snobbery in her voice and bearing that Nevaine wondered if she'd been taking lessons from Lizeth. Lizeth wasn't truly a snob, but she could channel that attitude better than Nevaine or Piallen.

The large bush in front of them rustled, then a stocky and bedraggled-looking grigeen stomped out. His fur was a deep red, but white flecks on his face showed his age. He came out on all fours and stopped a foot away from Nevaine.

Clait walked around her to stand in front. "Who are you?"

Nevaine hid her smile. She knew that Clait was bursting with excitement to see another grigeen, but she was holding it in well. Also, she was a stickler for etiquette and these new grigeens had broken some social rules.

"I am called Onlian. I lead the hunts for my pack. I don't know you; you are not from any of the local packs."

At the word *packs*, Clait's tail twitched so much it looked ready to lift off. But she kept her voice steady. "I am called Clait. My companions and I have traveled far and are on a quest. My pack is distant, and you would not have heard of us. How many packs live in this land?"

Onlian waved his paw and twenty more grigeen came out of the shrubs. They all looked like they were sizing things up for a fight.

Nevaine held up the hand she held the magic spell in. "This is great, but I really don't want to have to spell these grigeens into the next village over." Onlian seemed focused on Clait as they sized each other up, but the rest of them watched her and Sean.

Onlian turned to Nevaine and Sean. "They are with you? Humans and grigeen do not mingle in this land. You truly are from somewhere distant." He chittered something to a smaller black-furred grigeen, who then took off into the forest, with four others running directly behind. "This is not a good place to talk. We came seeking whoever sent that killer ground cloud. Although you are traveling with two human magic users, they don't smell like the spell caster. Follow us, but stay silent."

Clait looked to Nevaine and when she nodded, jogged after Onlian. The rest of his group of grigeens fanned out alongside them throughout the forest.

Sean stayed silent as he brought up the rear but Nevaine could almost feel his questioning of what they were doing. She was thinking it as well. But, even before her odd drop-by visit from the oracles, they were intending on finding the local grigeens. Now they found them, but had a bigger task. She didn't think these wild grigeens would have the same reaction to the words *golden grigeen* as Clait. It seemed like a specific spell, not something genetic. But she wasn't going to try just yet.

Just seeing grigeens that weren't from the palace woods was fascinating. She'd never really thought about why there were no more grigeens in the world, beyond a scientific inquiry and the reality that the rest of them were probably dead no matter what the local ones believed. But watching these new grigeens around her changed her mind.

"This will do. Come into our circle and be protected." Onlian stepped back in front of a massive stone arch. There were more ruins beyond it, but they hadn't been noticeable until they got here.

Clait nodded and passed under the arch—then vanished. Nevaine ran after her and came out in a clearing filled with grigeens. Sean was on her heels and swore lightly as he shook a spell he'd been holding out of his hand. The rest of the grigeens who'd been following alongside them jogged in.

Onlian came in last and bowed low to a huge brown and white grigeen sitting on a pile of rocks in the corner. That Nevaine hadn't even noticed them before spoke of magic. Not to mention that from outside these ruins, the place looked empty and abandoned. Lots of magic.

"These are the ones who caused that spell?" The voice was deep and extremely annoyed. "I don't recognize you." That was directed at Clait, and the fur on her back rose a bit in response.

"I don't believe they set the spell; its smell is not upon them. The grigeen is called Clait and is from far away. I would present the other two to you, but I do not know what names the humans use." He made *humans* sound like a swearword, and Nevaine refrained from stating that he hadn't asked.

"Please present yourselves, humans." The older grigeen nodded. "I am Zila, and I rule these lands."

Nevaine stepped forward. "I am Nevaine and count Clait as my family and companion." It was an old fashion claim of clan, but seemed fitting in this case. The small smile Clait flashed her indicated she'd been right.

Sean also stepped forward. "I am Sean, and for what it's worth, my life is forfeit to theirs."

Zila nodded and tilted his head. "You would die to protect a grigeen?"

"Yes. Without hesitation." Sean stood stiff, his hands locked behind his back and staring straight ahead.

"And both of the humans are also extremely far from home. Interesting. Why are you here? Certainly not simply to speak to old and forgotten grigeens in the forest?"

Nevaine wasn't sure if he was speaking to her and Sean or not.

Clait rose on her back legs and sat on her haunches. "We have come just for that. Aside from my pack in a far distant land, there are no more known grigeens in the world. All of the packs vanished hundreds of years ago after a great battle."

The muttering that came from all around them pointed out that there were a lot more grigeens in this area than could be seen.

Zila raised one massive dark-brown paw. "Peace. This is grievous news if true. I don't doubt you, guest Clait, but I would verify your words for the satisfaction of my people."

Clait bristled slightly but nodded. A small light-gray grigeen came up to her. They briefly touched noses, then at Clait's nod, the smaller grigeen closed their eyes and held one paw out.

After a few silent moments, the smaller one opened their eyes. "She is speaking the truth. Our people are no longer known in other lands. Her entire pack is in agreement of this belief." The higher-pitched voice indicated a female, but unless they identified themselves, it was difficult to tell gender. At least for humans; Nevaine was sure the grigeens could tell.

"And there is no knowledge of how this happened or why they were killed?"

"We don't believe they were killed. There has been evidence that they vanished, not died."

"The oracles took them." Zila's tail whipped about. "They are not to be trusted."

"My people, and the humans who protect us, all believe the oracles are good. What makes you say otherwise?" Clait was honestly looking for answers, but there was a sharp tone in her voice that didn't bode well.

Zila looked toward Nevaine and Sean, then went ahead. "The oracles destroyed us. We were a powerful people once and lived in the cities among humans. But, with the humans' help, the oracles attacked us. Dwindling our numbers and chasing us into the forests."

"How long ago was that?" Nevaine knew the vanishing of the grigeens was usually just a vague time of a few hundred years ago—but she'd tracked the time down through study. It was five hundred years and seven months ago.

"Many, many years."

"Five hundred?"

Zila pulled back and narrowed his eyes. "That is what our records keepers say. How do you know if you aren't working with the oracles?"

This was going to be tricky. She didn't want to lie to them; having the local grigeens on their side was much better than being hunted by them as they looked for the golden grigeen. But that meant admitting to her connection with the oracles. And for that matter, the connection of Clait's pack with them. Clait looked to her and nodded.

"We work closely with the oracles and always have. But they don't control us." She held up her hand as the grigeens around them started chittering aggressively. "They are not evil. They are guides only, but saved Clait's pack when the others vanished. Which was five hundred years ago and seven months. The same time that your people were chased into the wilds."

The chittering grew louder, and Zila's ears went flat. He finally spoke. "How do you know these things and yet deny that the oracles are controlling you?"

"Books." Nevaine folded her arms. "Although I still haven't found what happened to the grigeens worldwide, I have tracked down when it happened through reading books."

"And that coincides with what my pack has passed down. The oracles brought us to Nevaine's ancestors long ago; we protect their royal children, and the kingdom protects the pack." If Clait was disturbed by the chitters around them, she gave no sign.

"We will need to have a council to discuss this news, and your association with beings who have been our enemy for hundreds of years. Do not leave, nor think of using magic to escape this place. It will fold back upon you." Zila didn't wait for a response but was already climbing down the back of his rock pile when the small black grigeen who'd left them earlier came racing in. They looked roughed up and their eyes were wide.

"We found the humans who set the spell. They grabbed the others with me and locked them up. They are coming this way."

Zila shook his head. "This place is unbroken and will remain that way. We will discuss sending people to free our brethren, but there is no fear of us falling under attack." He was smug and his opinion was clearly reflected in the furry faces around them. Most likely this place had held for hundreds of years.

"But have any magic users made a concentrated attack?" Sean looked around the ruins and shook his head. "Hiding you from people who aren't looking to attack you isn't the same as hiding you from magic users strong enough to set off that spell we felt."

"You are safe here as well. The protections of our ancestors will save us all. We must stay hidden." Zila sounded less confident and also less likely to be sending out a rescue for the captured grigeens.

Clait looked around. "This is what you have become? You blame the oracles for chasing you out into the wild forest, but maybe they were trying to save you? And now all you want to do is hide? You are not of my people." She turned, stomped to the entrance, and then nodded to Nevaine and Sean. "Coming with me?"

Nevaine and Sean joined her. The spell keeping this place hidden was visible up close but Nevaine was sure she couldn't see anything that would stop them from leaving.

Clait dug in her back feet and flung dirt behind her. Judging by the snarls from the other grigeens, that move was almost worse than Clait's words.

"You will not be allowed to leave!" Zila had gotten back up on his throne of rocks and motioned to Onlian to move after them.

Clait didn't turn but pitched her voice to carry. "Watch us. Not only will we leave, we will rescue your missing people." She dropped her voice. "I don't see a spell blocking us."

Sean grinned. "Nope." But he held a nice big crackling spell bubble in his hand as he stepped through. Nevaine shook her head—*show-off*—then followed him, with Clait jogging alongside her. Onlian and a few others moved after them as they went through, but without serious intention and they stopped before they got to the passageway.

"Not a single spell to stop us—he lied." Sean released the spell he'd held and turned toward Clait. "So which way do we go?" He didn't even question that they were going to free the captured grigeens.

Nevaine looked back but, as before, the ruins looked empty. Then the small black grigeen came out. Followed by Onlian and a dozen more.

"You would help our people without being one of them?" On-lian peered up at both Sean and Nevaine. "And not one of our pack?" He dropped his gaze to Clait.

"Where we come from, we don't stand by and let innocent be-ings be taken," Nevaine responded. "I'm assuming that those who took them have done so before?"

Onlian nodded. "And we never see them again. But I've gotten near the village before. I believe bad things happen to those who are taken."

"How long has Zila refused to go after them?" Clait had calmed down—a little. But there was still a snarl in her voice when she said Zila's name.

Nevaine understood where it was coming from. Even as children, she and her sisters were taught to protect their people. And this con-cept was reinforced by the grigeens in their lives.

"We've never gone after them. Even before Zila. I'm Halui, by the way." The small black one nodded. "I fought hard to keep my friends from capture—we all did. Knowing that no one would come for us." She smiled to Clait. "Thank you for standing up."

Clait nodded. "Now, which way?"

Halui took the lead, with Onlian and the rest of the rebel grigeens right behind. Clait stayed up near Onlian while Sean and Nevaine kept the rear covered. The grigeens were all softly chatting while they walked, so they weren't worried about their enemy being too close.

"Do you have the slightest idea what we might be up against? And I thought that spell that almost got us had been triggered and was old?"

"No more idea than you have. As for that spell, it was old. It was triggered, but I believe someone used a lot of magic to release it. But I'm going on a gut feeling." He nodded to the grigeens ahead of them. "And the fact that they sensed the magic user. Since the original caster should be long dead, based on the age I felt, someone had to have used magic to trigger it."

"Good points." Nevaine studied him as they ran. He was a fighter but was also smart and compassionate. Damn it. That combination was more dangerous to her than his good looks.

"What are you scowling about?"

She schooled her face into a neutral smile. He was observant as well. "No reason. Just thinking some heavy thoughts that will have to wait until we get back home."

"If we get back home." He shrugged. "I'm not trying to be pessimistic, but if the oracles said we might die, I believe them. But we will go down fighting."

"And having a battlemage along isn't a bad thing. That's most likely why they included you in my Challenge. You do realize that by jumping in after me like you did, you should have been killed, right?"

"I could handle those guards."

"Nope, you should have been killed by the spell surrounding the pathway. After Lizeth went through her Challenge with Finnian and Scruff, sensors were put up. The oracles reinforced them." She laughed and shook her head. "Which should have been when I realized that you were supposed to be along for this."

"Had I known about that...I still would have taken the chance." His grin dropped. "But the oracles' warning does reinforce why I tried to stop you from coming."

"You had little to base that on and almost cost me my Challenge." Nevaine shook her head. "I appreciate you trying to save me, but did you think maybe those people who grabbed you meant something else? Or were aware that you heard them, and were setting you up to destabilize my Challenge?" She watched him carefully. He'd risked everything to try to save her—but that could have been helping the people against them.

He shrugged. "I didn't have a lot of time, to be honest. But they sounded like they were trying not to speak loud enough for me to hear. I have excellent hearing, and I *might* have been augmenting it with sorcery once I heard your name."

"Did *they* know you were a magic user?" She was still annoyed about that issue. She was exceedingly observant—usually—even a high-level battlemage should have found it hard to hide from her. Which he obviously did. Nice to know a handsome face and broad chest could befuddle her powers of observation so easily. She could hear Lizeth's laughter in her head.

"No one in Astarious should have figured it out. And I'd think if they did, they would have done a better job of keeping me contained." He glanced over at her. "I had been wondering how I was going to handle the whole mage-sorcerer issue with you, and everyone else I've been around these last few months. I actually finished my apprenticeship with the blacksmith a month ago, and was supposed to head home a few days after that. But the beautiful princess made leaving impossible." He flashed a massive grin.

"You have another one hanging around?" She laughed, then narrowed her eyes. "You told me that you had another year of study. On the first day we met."

"There's only one princess for me, but she's a handful." His smile now had a sadness to it. He wasn't sure how she felt about him, and she agreed. "As for the first day, I believe in long-term planning."

"Yet you had no idea how you were going to deal with telling me and others that you were a fully trained battlemage? Those aren't common, in case you hadn't noticed."

"Yeah, I hadn't thought that far ahead." He froze and stopped speaking as the grigeens all came to a stop.

There was nothing around them that Nevaine could see, but she sent out a searching spell. It was a basic, non-augmented type of magic spell, but it worked well to track down magic. It was one of the first non-augmented spells all three sisters had been taught. The spell coming their way was so subtle, that even with her spell, she almost didn't catch it. From the frown on Sean's face, it had almost slipped by him as well. It would wind its way into the minds of everyone it touched, then simply put them to sleep. The good thing was that it wasn't strong and relied on a gradual buildup.

"Do you want to counteract it, or me?" Sean already had a spell forming, but at least he was polite enough to ask.

"Age before beauty, good sir." Nevaine winked as she said it. She was almost twenty-one; he was twenty-four. And if she was honest, he was almost as pretty as she was. She'd never seen him in fancy clothes, but she had a feeling he would be hazardous to anyone around if he dressed up. He was dangerously attractive just looking scruffy.

Sean gave a sideways head tilt at her comment, muttered a few words, flicked the fingers on his right hand, and released his spell.

Nevaine waited as the spell trying to stop them slowed down, and then crumbled. Many of the grigeens were on their back legs, sniffing and nodding.

"Well done," Clait called back as they started walking again.

They were moving faster but still kept to their chittering conversation. To be fair, that sleep spell was usually used when there was a concern someone might be coming but no idea from where. It might not have been aimed at anyone specifically.

"Was that a magic and sorcery combination?" His words and small hand movements used to disperse the spell were sorcery, but she'd also felt magic in the mix. Having one person strong in both was uncommon but not as rare as merging the two into a single functioning spell.

Sean flushed. "Yeah. Weird, I know. I started with sorcery training as a kid, but then found battle magic, so I switched over. I have a tendency to create my own mismatched spells. Used to drive both my sorcery teacher and my magic instructor crazy. But it works, and I don't do it all the time. Heavier or more dangerous spells will almost always tap into the battle magic side."

"That is weird, just have to say it. But if it works, it works." Nevaine's own way of balancing spells was considered unorthodox also, but they worked for her. "What is the difference between battle magic and regular magic?"

"It's complicated, but on a basic level, battle magic is rougher, stronger, and more violent. Anyone with enough magical ability, stubbornness, and a quick mind can eventually master battle magic. They just like to make it sound secretive and elitist."

"Piallen might start the battlemage training for her last two pre-Challenge years. She meets those criteria."

"She would make a good one. You would as well, you know. You're not too old to start the training." He drifted closer as they walked, and she had to look up to see if he was joking or not.

There were a lot of things in his dark-blue eyes but joking wasn't one of them. Silence fell before she could respond, and the grigeen all pulled in closer to each other and slowed down. They'd been walking for a while but she hadn't seen any signs of human civilization. Most towns or villages had people who lived farther out, farmers and the like. There had been nothing but more old forest.

Clait came jogging back as the group came to a halt again. "The town is only two miles from here. They want to wait until it gets closer to dark before we go in." Her tail flipping back and forth indicated she wasn't happy.

"Then why did we leave when we did? I thought time was important here?" Nevaine agreed that while she and Sean could go into town unquestioned, a pack of fifteen or so grigeens would be noticed. Especially if there had been actions against them that were accepted by the town in general.

"That is what I would like to know." Clait looked over her shoulder at the silent grigeens. "To be fair, they've not attempted this in hundreds of years. They hide from the humans and don't try to rescue the captured. They once tried to rescue kidnapped grigeens and the outcome was horrific. Half of their original pack were killed."

Chapter Fourteen

The silence after that statement remained until Sean broke it. "I could go ahead and see what the town is like." He looked farther down the trail.

"*We* could go." Nevaine weighted the first word, then looked down to Clait. "Sean and I, not you."

Neither Sean nor Clait looked happy, but for different reasons. Nevaine pointed to Sean. "Look, you're not going off to play hero, or whatever you're thinking, alone. You and I will do recon and come back." Then she looked to Clait. "Seriously? You want to go into a town that seems to do evil things to your people, without a clue as to what's actually going on there? Not to mention, someone who knows Sean and me needs to stay out here and rescue us if things go wrong." She ignored Sean's look at her words. She didn't think that would be the case either, but it would help Clait. She needed to stay out here with the rest of the grigeens.

"I can help scout." Clait wasn't giving up.

"You could end up being grabbed and risking us being exposed." Nevaine didn't want to point that out, but she would say whatever she needed to in order to keep Clait out of this, or at least out until they knew what they were facing. If they all needed to go in, fine, and—like it or not—the oracles did say any or all of them could die on this Challenge. But she wanted to hold that off as long as possible. She softened her voice. "You can't always protect me."

Clait furiously cleaned a front leg, then looked up. "Fine, I will stay here. But that town is close enough that if you both aren't back here by nightfall, we're coming after you."

If the town was as close as they implied, and they couldn't get there, run a quick surveillance, and get back before nightfall, the odds were good that they would already be dead. But Nevaine nodded.

Halui trotted over, her sleek black fur making her hard to see in the dark forest. "The trail will branch off in a short while, maybe ten minutes at your pace. Take the new path to your right. It will circle the town partially and lead you to a lesser-known entrance." She tilted her head. "You should both be able to pass as swords-for-hire, but she needs gloves. Her hands are too smooth for a swordswoman."

Nevaine nodded and brought out a thin pair that had been stuffed in her pack. It was a good point and something she hadn't thought of. "Where would we have been coming from at the direction we'll be approaching?"

"Licthei. It's not big, but many for-hire jobs for the humans go through there. If asked, say you're heading north to the Pantiar Mountains. That should stop the questions."

Sean had taken off his pack to adjust a few things, then put it back on. "What's the name of the town we're going to?"

Halui gave a soft laugh. "That would help, would it not? It's called Wath. Not large or powerful, but it's in the center of things in this part of the empire. Safe journey. And again, thank you. We haven't thought of humans as anything but enemies for many generations." She gave a nod and slipped back up front.

Clait watched her go. "They've been through a lot, and I don't agree with that Zila person, but I hope we can help them." She looked up as Nevaine kept watching her. "And yes, I meant it when I said I would stay here until nightfall. Now go scout and be nosy humans." She made a shooing motion with her paw.

Sean nodded and headed down the trail with Nevaine alongside him.

"Did any of those names sound familiar?" She shook her head. "Not from when you were here as a baby, but from reading your parents' books. Which I would love to borrow sometime, by the way."

He laughed. "We might be able to make that happen at some point, providing we don't die and can get back to our side of the ocean. As for familiar, not the towns, but the Pantiar Mountains are. People will probably stop bugging us once we mention them because they're pretty awful—or at least they were when the books my parents have were written. They had been seats of power of the prior rulers of this land, long before the Offialian took over. There had been some nasty battles there, both sorcery- and weapons-based. There are supposedly pockets of deadly relics and killer spells floating around the range."

"Not a fun place to visit." Nevaine shook her head as a few things connected. "But unfortunately, a perfect place for a mythological statue we're supposed to find."

They reached the branch in the path, sooner than Halui had said, but she was guessing at how fast they walked. It was small where it met the first path, then widened out as they went farther. Now they could see small farms. None of them were large or looked prosperous, but they were clearly working farms.

Nevaine grabbed Sean's wrist. "What kind of names are common here?"

"Good point. Sean is extremely common; I don't know that Nevaine is. Not to mention if we run across someone who is familiar with distant royals? Might need to change it. Neva is common, and close enough that you'll answer to it."

"I can do that. And if you see me taking my gloves off, say something. Maybe a skin issue that makes me keep them on." Most likely no one would question them, but it was always better to have a story ready. Made for less fumbles if it was needed at some point. She didn't have pampered princess hands, but knife throwing didn't build up calluses like sword practice would.

Sean nodded, and they approached a low wall and battered wooden gate that circled the edge of a town. Considering that the wall was only four feet high and the gate looked like a strong breeze would destroy it, she wasn't sure what the purpose was.

Then she got a closer look at the wall. The edges were rough and pieces had been hacked away. "This used to be a proper city wall—why'd they start taking it down?"

Sean looked around the small buildings inside the wall. "For building materials. It wasn't just the horrors of the Offialian Empire that made my parents flee—it was the poverty. These walls were probably built a few hundred years ago. As defense they still wouldn't have been great, but as housing material?" He shrugged.

Nevaine looked at the buildings and their hobbled-together appearance. The better-quality bricks were clearly from the wall. Not good that the locals had to do that to survive, but it reinforced the little she knew about the Offialian Empire. They were huge, powerful, and didn't care about their people. She took a deep breath as they walked toward the main entrance. The gate they'd first walked by was closed, but not too far ahead was a larger gate—which maintained more of its original wall—that had two thin-looking guards in front of it. They appeared to simply be watching people passing through, but did stop a group of young toughs. She couldn't hear what was asked, but they let them go by.

Sean slowed down and roughed up his hair. "Let me do most of the talking. And grimace a lot. Pretend someone interrupted your reading."

"I don't grimace." She caught his lifted eyebrow. "Okay, yes, sometimes. But if I'm reading, people should leave me alone." She easily channeled that level of annoyance at getting deep in a great book and have someone interrupt her. She'd come within seconds of spelling Lady Dalip into the abyss once, when she'd hunted Nevaine down to complain about something a few months ago. That was a great grimacing moment.

The guards looked ready to let them pass, then seemed to have noticed their swords and stepped over just a bit in front of Sean and Nevaine.

"Purpose here?" The first guard who spoke was a woman, and she was the same height as Nevaine—however, the scars on her face and her solid muscles said she'd proven herself a fighter.

"We've got a contract." Sean dropped his voice in a nice impersonation of the blacksmith back home. "Pantiar Mountains. Just stopping for supplies. Don't plan on staying." He looked around the village behind the guards as if he'd just seen it and discounted it.

The second guard, a massive man who'd clearly strayed from fighting and into drinking, leaned forward and carefully looked at both of them. "Aye, they look dumb enough to go up there."

The woman nodded and both guards stepped out of their way. "Try not to die too soon up there. If it's below halfway, we have to send folks up for your bodies."

Nevaine gave them her best grimace, and Sean nodded. They both kept quiet until they'd merged with the crowds in the marketplace and the guards were far behind them.

"I really hope we're wrong about where we might have to go for that statue." Nevaine kept her voice low as she glanced around the crowds. The clothing that she and Sean wore was basic enough that they didn't stand out as outsiders, but the quality of theirs was much better. Hopefully, if anyone noticed, they would simply believe that she and Sean were just very good at what they did and didn't see them as rich marks to go after.

"Me too." He kept watching everything but didn't look happy. "This would have been my life. Actually, I doubt I would have made it to being this old. Most fighters hit the front lines at age fifteen. Few see sixteen."

"Who are they fighting against?" Nevaine spared a glare for a merchant who started to approach them. He backed off immediately.

She knew that the massive Algarien Ocean blocked them, at least for now, from invading Astarious or any of the kingdoms on the other side. But she didn't have any books on what other kingdoms or empires were over here.

"Everyone else on this side." Sean shook his head. "I don't know now, as my information is twenty-three years out of date. But when my parents left, the empire was in a constant state of expansion. I doubt that has changed, or this town and the guards would be in better shape."

Nevaine nodded and continued looking around them. That was tricky in a market area as staring too long at any one person or vendor cart would make them swarm forward to try to sell her things. She hated that in the markets back home. It would be worse here.

So far, no grigeens. Also, no pelts, which made her feel much better. But still didn't give her a clue as to what these people were using the captured grigeens for.

"Make way!" A voice bellowing behind them made all of the merchants and customers shut up and run to the sides of the road.

She and Sean stepped behind a merchant cart. Better to see without being seen. The man who'd yelled was huge, and wore little clothing beyond chains and a few leather pieces to keep him decent. He had a long whip and used it to chase back anyone who'd not cleared the area well enough.

More chains clanked behind him, and at first she couldn't see what it was. Then she saw the grigeens. Dozens of them, all chained together. Their fur was matted and they looked half starved. One of them stumbled and a whip crack from the back of the group got it back up and in line.

"What are they doing to them?" Nevaine was fighting to keep from racing out there and blasting the grigeens free. She knew this needed planning, but right now she was all emotion.

"They don't have much magic energy." Sean narrowed his eyes as he watched the grigeens pass by and down a side road. "The guards are somehow suppressing the grigeens' natural magic." He looked ready to be sick.

Nevaine shook her head. "What if they've found a way to use it? Long ago, there was a group of investors who wanted to get the grigeens to work with them on a project. I was a child so I didn't know the details, but my parents were so angry, they had the people escorted out of the kingdom by a group of guards."

"But how? Damn it, they're going out of sight. We have to find out where they're going." Sean grabbed her hand and dodged behind the group of vendors and customers to run alongside the shabby buildings. Once they were across from the alley the grigeens had gone through, he dropped to a walk and released her hand.

The urge to run after the guards and destroy everyone involved with hurting the grigeens was still hitting her, but her rational thoughts were slowly winning. Blasting their way in now might free some of them, but definitely not all. She wasn't leaving this place until she'd freed all of those grigeens—her Challenge could wait.

Sean waited near the entrance of the alley for a few moments, then casually strolled in. Nevaine waited a bit longer, waiting until she was certain no one was watching them, then followed.

The alley wasn't well used; probably no one except the grigeen chain gang and their keepers normally came down here. There were a few doors from the backs of businesses, but none of them looked like they'd opened in a long time and all had debris piling up around them. Sean dropped into a deeper doorway and pulled Nevaine with him. A moment later, the two whip and leather guards marched past them.

Nevaine held her breath as they left. All they had to do was turn to look back, and she and Sean would be spotted. But whatever the two were thinking, it wasn't about what was behind them.

She and Sean waited a full five minutes to see if anyone else would be coming. When no one else appeared, both of them went back to the alley.

"It has to be that building." Nevaine paused after they went farther down the alley. A large, dark, wooden building blocked most of the alley. There was a passage around one side of it, but it was narrow and didn't look used. The building was three stories high, with no windows aside from thin bands along the top just under the eaves. They would probably not let in much light, as they looked like they hadn't been cleaned since the place had been built. The door was double wide and blended in so well with the building that, at first, she didn't see it.

"No guards?" She kept her voice low.

"I doubt anyone would try to break in. Most likely there are plenty of guards inside."

"We need to get a layout of inside before we go back to report to the others. How are you at climbing buildings?" Nevaine looked up at the surrounding buildings. It would be tricky, but she'd climbed worse as a kid. Sometimes getting away to read took a lot of work.

Sean rubbed his hands together. "It's not one of my primary skill sets, but I can probably manage if you lead."

"Hope you can keep up." She flashed him a grin as she jumped up to grab the sloping edge of a half roof above them. She quickly pulled herself up and, keeping low, ran across to the next roof. Soft swearing and a few oofs behind her said Sean had made his way up as well. Being taller than her would help him with reach, but she had less bulk to haul up—so they were almost an even match.

She kept low although it was doubtful any one would be looking up, especially down an alley that no one was supposed to be in. Eventually she got them to a roof that was directly next to the dark building's windows. She waited until Sean caught up and was also crouched beneath the bank of windows.

"We shouldn't risk more than a few seconds looking." Nevaine kept her voice at a whisper. There might not be anyone below to hear them, but always better to assume the worst. She pointed to the left then to the right. "At three, I'll look left, you look right." At his nod, she held up one finger, then two, then three. Both of them popped up but kept low in the window.

Even though she had an idea of what was happening inside there, it still took all of her willpower not to shout or smash the windows. Grigeens, far more than just the ones they'd seen in the street, were chained to small devices. As she watched, the devices grew brighter and the grigeens looked weaker. A guard pulled an extremely bright metal disk off one of the rods it sat on. Then he replaced it with a dull one and walked into a room in the back with the bright one.

Then Nevaine and Sean both dropped down.

"Easy...you can't go after them yet." Sean took a hold of both of her hands.

"That's horrific. How are they...I don't know where to start."

"Where we're starting is going back to Clait and the rest, making a plan, and freeing *all* of them." Sean's eyes were intense as he peered into her own. "We can do it."

She leaned into him. "Thank you. When I think of what they're doing...magic isn't something grigeens do, like us. It's who they are. They are sucking the life out of them. I will refrain from going after the guards unless they try to stop us. If they do, I'm destroying them."

Sean laughed. "You know they will."

"Then I have no choice. I just hope the ones who marched them down the road are there when we attack." She wasn't a violent person, most of the time. But she was more cut-and-dry about situations like this than either of her sisters. There was only one outcome—the grigeens free and the guards dead. She'd like to destroy the higher-ups who made this happen, but she doubted they had the time to hunt them down.

"Let's get back. We don't want Clait charging in here." Sean squeezed her hands and let them go.

Nevaine's way down was shorter and more suited to her climbing ability than Sean's—she dropped and rolled as she hit the ground. He swore and went down another story, then also dropped. Far less gracefully than her, but he made it.

They had a brief moment of worry when a pair of drunks stumbled toward them as they came out of the ally, calling them odd names. Sean headed them both off, saying they had the wrong people, then came back with a frown. "Let's go." He wasn't running but moving quickly through the thinning crowd.

"What's wrong?"

"I'm not sure, but neither of those two gents were nearly as drunk as they were acting and both were sorcerers. Low level, but still."

Nevaine had just been congratulating herself on the fact they'd made it in and back without being noticed. A quick glance told her someone had noticed them—the two fake drunks were a few groups of people behind.

Neither looked drunk anymore and had their hands on the hilts of their swords.

Chapter Fifteen

Nevaine swore softly as she saw them.

"They're back there, right? I hate being right. We need to lose them and get out of town." Sean was looking everywhere, but barely moving his head.

"Are they with the grigeen chain gang?" Nevaine was already putting together some serious spells in her head. Her magical ability was balancing smaller spells into a new formation—she'd be creating something special for those people torturing the grigeens.

"I don't think so," Sean said. "They're more subtle than them. Clearly this entire town knows what's going on, and if anyone official was concerned with us, they'd be less stealthy." He grabbed her hand and darted down a side alley. "We need to confront them without confronting them."

Nevaine saw the two coming down the alley after them. She grabbed Sean's shoulder, spun him against the side of a building, and kissed him. Best thing she could come up with, but kissing him just brought back emotions she wasn't dealing with right now. She broke off the kiss and looked up as the two following them stopped. "Can we help you with something? My husband told you we're not whoever you think we are." She stepped back and took out her sword when she saw that both had their swords out. Sean was armed as well.

"You told the guards at the gate that you had a contract and were heading up into the Pantiar Mountains. The people we were waiting for were doing the same. We were working together, but they're late." The first man had been holding a drunken hunch but rose to his full height as he spoke.

"Shouldn't you know what your partners look like? We're not working with anyone, nor do we intend to. I'd move along if I were you." Sean didn't step forward but his sword was steady.

The second man had been watching Nevaine, or rather, her sword. In a flash, he lunged for her. She blocked him and spun for an attack of her own. She wanted to use a spell, but something in the back of her mind said not to. The second man quickly engaged Sean.

The fact that Sean had sensed they were sorcerers but neither of their opponents were using spells might be what was encouraging her not to. Sean didn't either and seemed to be not even working hard to keep his opponent at bay.

Nevaine pressed the man fighting her back down the alley. He was taller and had a much longer reach, but she was agile and used to sparing with her much taller sister, Piallen. She got a strike in, a long slash across the bicep of his sword arm. He dropped his weapon, then looked ready to cast a spell, but stopped. Instead, he took off running.

Sean was mostly playing with his opponent now. The man was flustered and uttered a spell; the fingers on his left hand flicked behind him. Sean wouldn't have seen the spell gesture but Nevaine did. A moment later, the man screamed and collapsed. His body twitched a few times, then froze—he was dead.

Sean looked up. "I didn't do anything."

Nevaine sheathed her sword and looked back down the alley. "He tried to use sorcery and it killed him; we need to run."

Sean took off down the alley, with her right behind him. They weren't going the way they came in, so she was trusting that he had an instinct of which way to run. He turned down two side alleys, then finally stopped. They weren't far from the gate they'd come in, but he kept looking behind him. "I know we have to get back, but that was a pjilan spell that took out that guy. We can't use magic or sorcery when we come back." He looked down the crossroad, then led them toward the gate. "That was fast and nasty."

Nevaine wanted to ask more; that spell term didn't even sound familiar. She had heard of anti-magic spells, but nothing that could cover a large area like an entire town. This wasn't the place to discuss spells, though.

There were new guards this time, and they didn't even look up as she and Sean left town. They picked up speed as they walked farther away.

"He was attacked for starting a spell? I saw his hand move for a sorcery spell, but he didn't finish it."

"No, he didn't. That's not good. A pjilan spell not only kills the victim, it takes their magic." He looked back, but there was no one behind them and the town was starting to get lost in the distance. "That spell must cover the entire town and yet was subtle enough that I didn't sense it until it killed that man." From the look on his face, it was the last part that was really upsetting him.

Nevaine wouldn't have even looked for a spell like that as she didn't know they existed. Another argument for learning sorcery alongside magic. "We're still freeing those grigeens." There was no way that she was leaving them to their fate. "Whatever someone is doing with this gathered magic, it can't be good. Did you notice that no one came after the man who died?" His scream had been painfully short, but it had been loud. Yet no one came to see what happened.

"We will get the grigeens out—I swear we will. And there are ways to get around a pjilan spell—we have to find a way to carry a spell or two with us, but it has to be self-contained. Once we're back in town, we can't use any magic. I really want to know what they're doing with the stolen grigeen magic, though."

"Fighting on the front? Or building up for something larger?" Stolen magic had extremely limited applications—or at least that's what she'd learned. But somehow the rulers of the Offialian Empire must have found a way around that.

Sean started moving at a jog. "I'd guess something larger. The people they're fighting against can't be much of a threat at this point."

Nevaine nodded and ran alongside him silently. They needed to free the grigeens, then get them somewhere safe. The place Zila ruled over might only work to keep them hidden against non-magic users. Neither she nor Sean had tried to use magic to try to see past the spell. For this group, they needed something no one could get through. Not to mention it had looked like there were a few hundred grigeens in that building.

They got back to the grigeens just as the sun was edging down.

"You made it." Clait looked at both of them, then scowled. "It's bad, isn't it?"

Nevaine quickly told them what was happening to the captured grigeens, as well as the pjilan spell and the result of it.

"I haven't heard of one of those spells being used in a long time." Clait lashed her tail. "An extremely long time. They're not stable spells. I'm surprised they extended one over an entire town."

Sean nodded. "I was concerned about that as well—it could be tied to the magic they are taking from the grigeens, but I'm not sure of the purpose. Both of those men were clearly sorcerers, yet it was only when the one started losing the fight that he tried a spell. If there are magic users in town, they have to be aware of it."

"Or it's how they're kept out," Nevaine said. "Once I was aware of it, that pjilan spell felt like it was crawling on my scalp. There's no way I'd stay there, even if accidentally using magic wouldn't have killed me."

"Agreed." Sean looked around their small band of grigeens. "Getting in and back out will be tricky with limited magic, but we'll need a place to take them once we get them out. I'm not sure that your little ruins are secure enough. A strong magic user can blast through those illusions."

None of the grigeens looked happy about his assessment, but they also didn't look like they disagreed. They'd been hiding for a long time, getting picked off from time to time as the humans trapped them.

Onlian stepped forward. "Once we free them, I think there is a safer place we can go. Old ruins that Zila has forbidden us to go to. But they have powerful spells on them."

A larger tabby grigeen shook its head. "Which is why he forbids us from going there. There has to be another option. Maybe we should wait."

Halui spun on the tabby grigeen. "No. We've lost too many already. Those in town are slowly being killed. How many have already died?" She glared at the rest of the group. "I will go save them myself if need be."

Clait and Onlian both stepped up behind her. "Not alone." One by one, all of the grigeens except the tabby came forward. "Stay here, or go back to Zila. But don't get in our way." Clait was so mad, her words were barely loud enough to hear. Aside from the tabby, who backed down. He didn't move beyond hunching down on himself.

"Do we have a plan?" Sean looked over, but both Clait and Nevaine shrugged.

"Get in, get them out, and escape," Nevaine said. "Now, what was that comment about a way to work around a pjilan spell?"

Sean ran his fingers through his hair. "It's not really a way to work around it, per se. We each create a single spell, one that can be used attached to something. Sort of shove the spell in a bottle and throw it. The spell hits and works, but it's not directly connected to the spell caster." He shrugged. "It's a battlemage spell, but usually only used in long sieges. That way, if a magic user gets too weak to cast a spell, they still have some ready to go."

"I've never tried anything like that, and if you'll note, we don't have any bottles." Nevaine didn't doubt him; she just wasn't sure that it would work.

He looked up at the setting sun. "We're not that far away, and we don't want to get there until it's completely dark. Let me sort out things in my head." He nodded to everyone and walked a little way off.

The grigeens were edgy. Now that they knew what was going on, they wanted to rescue their people immediately. Nevaine didn't blame them, but this was going to be risky even before finding out that there was a killer spell in place. She sat down and pulled out the spell book Gliandra had given her. The pages glowed lightly when she opened it, a handy trick since night was falling.

The first spells she read wouldn't work. If Sean could figure out how to pull this off, the spell needed to be one that would work well on impact. She doubted that any of her normal augmented balance spells would work. She needed a low-level, non-augmented magic spell, or something equally simple from the side of sorcery. Something preferably destructive.

Which would work better if she had a better idea of what they were going to do. Her original plan had been to blow up the doors, then she and Sean race in, blast the guards with spells, free the grigeens, and run.

Not the best plan she'd had, even before finding out that magic was off the table. She re-read the spell she'd been looking at and smiled. A stun spell. Not as violent as she'd hoped, but it could be handy. It was low level, and just slowed down the victims' movements to almost nothing beyond breathing.

For about ten minutes.

She frowned and looked through a few more spells. Not another spell that would work. As much as she wanted to blast the guards and that building apart, she knew getting the grigeens out was more important. There had been a lot of banks of grigeens, and she knew they couldn't let any of them be left behind.

"I have a spell in mind. Small explosions—they're more noise and smoke than actual firepower, but they'll work embedded in this." Sean grinned and held up a small rock. "I'd demonstrate, but I don't want to call unwanted attention to it. You can feel that it's here, though." He held out the stone.

Nevaine felt almost an echo of a spell in the cool rock. One thing they had around here were rocks. But he'd have to show her how to get her spell into them.

"I might have found something too." She held up the spell book. "Will this work in those rocks?"

He read through it and nodded. "I think so. That's an old spell and not one I'm familiar with, but we should be able to get it into the rocks." He turned to the grigeens. "We'll need all of you to stay completely silent. Once inside the building, Nevaine will throw some of her stun spells and I'll hit them with the smoke and noise. You'll have to get most of your people free. When we run out, Nevaine can throw the last of her spelled rocks to make sure we're not followed, but we have to go quickly. Even if we fall behind, keep going."

"Are you going to be able to find the other grigeens with the smoke?" She knew she and Sean could get the ones closest to the doors, but the rest would be farther back.

Onlian nodded. "Yes, we can sense our kind without need of sight."

Another group of grigeens, new ones from the look of it, led by the tabby, stepped forward.

"We would help as well. I was wrong before; we have to save them. These were already heading this way." He nodded as the new group approached. Twenty more grigeens might make the difference in getting the others out.

"Zila is wrong. My parents were taken when I was young—I won't let that happen to anyone else." This came from an old, almost white, grigeen. Who really looked like he wanted bloodshed.

Sean quickly went through the plans—and the words of caution—with the new group. Then he spelled a few dozen rocks.

Nevaine watched him but he did it so fast, she was lost. "Do we really think we can use that many before getting caught, and how did you do that?" She pointed to another massive pile of rocks. "Those are mine, I presume?"

"Never can have too many weapons or friends—my own personal rule. This is a variation of a spell your sister Lizeth published under an assumed name two years ago. It wasn't a well-hidden name, but it's a decent spell. In theory, it can pull the essence of a poison out of a body. Mostly used now in field healing. But I modified it. It now takes the essence of a spell and transfers it into an object." He picked up a rock, but looked up suddenly. "Don't tell your sister, okay?"

Nevaine laughed. "Deal, but show me." He held up the rock to her, had her repeat the modified essence spell, then cast her stun spell. She felt the spell in it, but it took too long. But by the time she got to the third rock, it was almost immediate. And unlike feeling as if she'd been casting the same spell a few dozen times, she hardly felt tired at all. She'd have to talk to Lizeth about this modification—it could come in handy for many purposes.

They hid the contents of their packs under bushes nearby, loaded up on spelled rocks, and then headed to town.

Grigeens had excellent night vision, so Clait and Halui took the lead. Nevaine also had much better than average night vision.

"What?" Sean said from alongside her. "You keep looking over here."

"I'm impressed at how well you see in the dark." She hoped he wasn't using a spell; they had no idea how far out that pjilan spell went around the town.

"It's a spell." He held up his hand. "It was placed on my eyes as a baby, before my family left. Many of their fighters are so *blessed*. It doesn't register as a spell anywhere." The dose of sarcasm in his voice at the word *blessed* pointed out what he thought of the spell—even if it did help him.

"They permanently spell infants?" She almost stopped walking in shock. There was a class of spells, deep ones, that could help a fighter when they grew up. They took a massive amount of magic and could end up not working right. A gift could become a curse when the spell was first applied and cripple or kill the child. They were banned in all civilized lands.

"Yes, it was the final reason that my parents left. The military did it to me without asking them."

Nevaine muttered a few swearwords as things connected. "Not only is that a horrifically barbaric thing to do, but I think we know what they are doing with the grigeen magic. They're funneling it into more soldiers. Those spells can be used in adults as well. We can't let them keep the magic they've stored." The risk to adults was even greater than to babies, and took more magic. But it was one way to increase the abilities of your army.

"You're probably right. If they were increasing what they were doing in terms of making more powerful soldiers, then magic from grigeens and whoever else they can steal it from would help," Sean said.

Nevaine walked faster and caught up to Clait. "They were storing the stolen magic in disks. Can that magic be restored to the grigeens it was taken from?" She had no idea how they'd do it, but if there was a chance, they needed to save those disks.

"No. Small bits will return to the original owners upon destruction of the containment spell, but the rest will be released back to the wilds. The freed grigeens should recover their magic as they recover. Destroy whatever they were using."

"Excellent plan. Please be careful," Nevaine said. Clait had been her childhood best friend—only friend aside from her sisters and her books. She couldn't lose her.

Clait stopped and ran to be picked up. She peered into Nevaine's eyes. "We will always be together—no matter what separates us. You are part of my pack."

Nevaine hugged her friend. "And you are mine. But run if you have to. Okay?"

Clait sighed. "Okay. You, too, though." She licked Nevaine's cheek then hopped down, and they continued toward the village.

The town was badly lit, which wasn't a surprise. Sean took the lead as they approached the outer wall. He pointed to the low brick wall, and Halui and the rest of the grigeens easily climbed up and over.

Nevaine brought up the rear to find him waiting down a familiar alley. "Good thinking. That wooden gate would have made too much noise."

"Yup, and it might have been set up as a trap. We'll need to make sure the grigeen go out over the wall and avoid gates."

"I'll pass it along," one of the grigeens closest to them said, and then started softly chittering to the rest of the grigeens. It was so quiet, even standing right there it was hard to notice anything was being said. But in less than a minute, all of the grigeens turned to Sean and silently nodded.

Sean nodded back and turned down the alley. They kept the main road in sight as they cut through different alleys. There were few streetlamps and only two guards on the main road—there was nothing in the alleys.

Nevaine held her breath when the guard on the side of the grigeen factory paused at the mouth of the alley. There was a flickering torch there, barely enough to see him. But he just pulled out a wineskin, finished it off, then moved on.

Sean waved the grigeens forward as he crossed the road. Nevaine stayed behind as they went. She held on to two of the stun rocks and had her pack turned for easy access to more if she needed. Even the lighter-colored grigeens were dark on this moonless night, but an undulating dark shape crossing the road might cause an alarm.

They made it through and, as earlier, there were no guards outside the door.

"That's it?" Clait asked. At Nevaine's nod, she raced up to the window before Nevaine could stop her.

Nevaine watched in silent annoyance.

Then Clait was back. Her face was a mixture of sorrow and fury. "They are still draining them. Five guards that I can see."

"Clait, I know you want those guards dead. Trust me, so do I. But we have to get the grigeens free."

Clait was silent at first. "I know. But if we can..."

"We will take care of them." Nevaine nodded and joined Sean near the doors.

Chapter Sixteen

Sean looked down at her when she came up; they were only a hand's width apart. "We will do this. I know we will. Regardless of what happens, I wouldn't change a thing." He bent down for a quick kiss, then leaned on the door.

Nevaine stayed silent but took the second door. The small non-magical explosives from Sean's pack blew up both doors. Nevaine and Sean hit first, both throwing their rocks around the entire building.

Then the swarm of grigeens came flooding in and started freeing the others.

Sean started for the back with a handful of rocks. "I'll get the magic disks."

Nevaine worked on getting the grigeens free. Some were so weak that she had no idea if they would make it very far. Looking around, she found an empty produce cart. She shoved it out the doors and flagged down Onlian. "Can the larger grigeens push this? Those ones are too weak to run." She pointed to the ones being helped out.

Onlian rose on his hind legs, and Halui climbed on his shoulders and took one side. Another pair took the other side. "We adapt quickly."

Nevaine ran back inside as Clait took over getting the weakest grigeens into the cart. She'd freed a row of grigeens, helped get them out, and was going to the final row when Sean came running out.

"There are some nasty things in there, and more magic holders than I can carry. We need to get out and set this place on fire." He grabbed the chains holding the last of the grigeens and broke them. The grigeens ran slowly, but they ran.

"We don't have a spell we can use for fire."

Sean grinned. "This should work." He ripped a piece of his shirt off, flung the end on the sputtering torch at the end of the alley, dropped three of his spell rocks in, and threw it at the blasted-open doorway. The timing was perfect: the flame got a boost from his spell rocks and quickly lit the building on fire.

The grigeens were already trotting down the alley and going back the way they'd come. But while the grigeens could handle the cart, they weren't fast and it had dropped far behind the rest. Sean took over and sent the four grigeens to help others.

He was faster than the four grigeens but not fast enough to lead. Nevaine took over leading them and got them back the way they came. She was almost to the outer wall, with the sounds of shouting about the blazing building starting to be heard, when a group of five guards appeared before her. She motioned for the grigeens to stay down the alley. Had she access to her magic, the guards wouldn't be a concern. But luckily, she still had her rocks.

The guard closest to her laughed as she pulled out five stones. "Rocks against swords? Not sure how or why you set that building on fire, but rocks won't save you."

Nevaine grinned—*never underestimate a person trained in knife throwing*—and rapidly threw all five in order. The guards each froze as the spelled rocks hit them and the spell was released. She probably could have taken them all with a single stone, but she didn't want to take that chance. She waved for the grigeens to go for the wall. "Keep running, no matter what," she said as they climbed over.

Then Sean and the cart showed up. "Help me get this over the wall." There were at least thirty weak grigeens in the cart, but there was no way they could lift the entire thing over the wall.

"We can't. We'll have to carry them." If they were strong enough to hang on, ten to fifteen grigeens each wouldn't be hard to carry. But many of them were barely conscious.

Sean leapt over the wall and started walking away from it with his head tilted. He dug into the dirt with his foot, then took a step back. "Can you throw them this far?"

"Yes, but…" Nevaine shrugged and started throwing grigeens to him. He must have marked out how far the pjilan spell hit as each one that came to him floated once it hit his arms. Not far, and they clumped around him. That was some impressive magic. She threw the last one and then climbed over the wall.

Sean's floating grigeens hovered about three feet off the ground and followed where he went. "This spell won't hold long; we need to run."

"Sounds good to me." The sounds of alarm from the town faded as they ran down the road.

They'd made it just into the forest when Sean slid to the ground and all of the injured grigeens slowly landed as well.

Nevaine was tired—that was really a long sprint—but Sean looked almost as bad as the grigeens around him.

Clait and the rest had obviously kept running. Hopefully the ruins Onlian mentioned would work and weren't far. Nevaine had no idea what to do with thirty immobile grigeens and a quickly fading battlemage.

"I'll be okay, just overextended."

"I thought the spell rocks didn't tap into your magic?"

"They shouldn't. I think it was catching those grigeens, then running." He rolled to his side. "I can get up."

"That would be a good idea, but move extremely slowly." The voice came from behind her, and she felt cold steel at her throat. "I'd hate to kill your lovely *wife*." It was the man who'd tried to ambush them in town—the survivor. There were no sounds of guards or anyone following them from the town—yet somehow, he'd managed to.

Nevaine held perfectly still, but was already pulling together a few spells to shock the man.

"Easy there. I told you, we're not the people you're looking for." Sean slowly got to his feet.

"Take your sword belt off slowly and kick it away from you."

Nevaine smiled to Sean. She felt the man's hand shake. Sean didn't look happy but he removed his sword belt and did as told.

Nevaine wasn't sure why the man hadn't tried using magic; they were far out of town and that spell couldn't reach them. And she'd injured his sword arm during the fight. Nevaine swore at herself for forgetting about that; he wasn't using his dominant hand to hold the sword at her throat. Sean held out his arms to show he didn't have a weapon, and she grabbed the man's left hand that held the sword. She sent a magical shock into his body that flung him away from her and dropped his sword at her feet.

Sean grabbed his own sword and held it against the back of the man where he landed in the dirt. "Stay there. Why did you come after us? And we know you're a sorcerer, so don't try anything."

"I'm not a sorcerer. Okay, not much of one. Hin had the spells. Told him not to use them. Idiot. He had the map on him, too, but by the time I came back, someone already took his body. He was sure you looked familiar. That's why we went after you. I went after you for the same reason. I saw you two free all those creatures. Building your own factory? Count me in."

Nevaine came up and kicked him. "They're grigeens, they aren't creatures, and those people were killing them. We set them free. You followed the wrong people."

Sean stepped closer to the man. "Sorry. As you can tell, she's not tolerant of jerks. But she might be if you tell us everything you know. About the empire, the town, grigeens, and magic. I'd talk fast if I were you. She's really good with knives." He smiled to Nevaine.

She didn't like the idea of hanging out here this close to the road, but they might get something useful from him. Not to mention, Sean was already looking more recovered and additional rest would help. They still needed to haul those injured grigeens farther into the forest and find the others.

"I...you want everything? Can I sit up? It's hard to talk with a mouth of dirt."

"Fine." Nevaine stepped back but dropped to the dirt in front of him. "Just remember I'm right here, and he's still got a sword at your back." She took out one of her knives and held a showy, but not very useful, spell in her other hand. She had plenty of useful ones she could grab but none of them looked impressive.

He sat up slowly, and his eyes widened as he saw her. His eyes might not be enhanced, but she was close enough that even in the dark he could see the knife and the spell.

"And don't you need to talk now?" Nevaine waved her knife in his direction.

The man's name was Jol. He was a former farmer in a distant town that Nevaine had never heard of but Sean nodded over his head about. All of the major towns and cities had decrees against anyone but the guards using magic within town limits. He and his partner had paired up with a pair of thieves to meet in Wath and go treasure hunting in the Pantiar Mountains. A secret store of gold and jewels was up there, and the dead man had the map. The two they were waiting on were currently three days late.

Nevaine leaned forward. "If you two had the map, then why were you waiting for these other two?"

"They said they had a way into the passage where the treasure is. The rumors of this secret stash have been around for hundreds of years, but a map was needed, as well as the exact spells to get inside. Neither Hin nor me are strong magic users—those two were."

"They're probably dead, or got the map from someone else. Not to mention, really? Hundreds of years and a map just pops up? Probably better off not to have the thing."

Jol shook his head. "We tested it. One of Hin's talents—okay, about his only real powerful one magically—was truth of documents. He cast his spell, and it showed true."

They went a few more rounds of questioning, but very little in useful information resulted.

Nevaine got up as Sean came around to the front. This man wasn't going to help them, but his friend's map might.

"Wait. So why come after us if you didn't get your friend's map back? You know there's no way we can go back to Wath. Just what were you planning?" She should have caught that earlier but it had been a long day.

Jol winced. "I was afraid you'd kill me if I told you I had it."

Nevaine dropped back closer to him. "Why would we agree to work with you, providing what you're looking for is what we're looking for, if you don't have the map? Not to mention there are hundreds of spells—how would we know which one was needed?"

"I know the spell needed, but neither Hin nor I were strong enough to do it. You're going to kill me now, aren't you?" He gave a defeated nod. "That's okay. This wound you gave me will most likely get infected, and I'd rather die a quick, clean death." He lifted his chin. "Just make sure you kill me on the first strike."

Nevaine looked up to Sean, and he stepped back. "Look, we don't want to kill you, unless we have to. And we are going to the Pantiar Mountains, for our own reasons." She didn't like how quickly his eyes brightened. "Maybe you can help us, we can help you, and no one kills anyone." She released the spell and held out her hand. "Let us see the map."

Sean narrowed his eyes and took a step back closer to Jol. "Move very slowly. My sword is at your back, but she's really the one you need to worry about."

"I can show it to her, but I have to be touching it. And I have to be alive. Spent a good coin on that spell. It'll go blank if I'm not touching it." Jol paused, then reached into his vest slowly. He pulled out a dark folded paper, then held it out to Nevaine.

Sean pressed his sword tip against Jol's back. "Slowly."

Nevaine took the map but sat close enough to Jol to feel his connection to it. A spell linked them, so there was no way to do this without him. He'd been right on that. Always better to test, though. "Release it."

He shrugged and removed his hand. The paper went blank immediately. He put his hand back and the map reappeared.

The map was extremely old, and the darker coloring of the paper came from age. But the lines were strong and clear. The starting point was just past Wath and led up into the mountains. Halfway up, it went through an extremely twisted route and ended up in a valley. Another winding path with scary notes at almost each turn brought them to what looked like a large box in a cave.

Which could be any treasure map. But over the box were what looked like a series of words in gibberish. She couldn't read most of the words, but she knew what language it was. Native grigeen.

Chapter Seventeen

Nevaine let out a breath and calmed herself. She'd know for sure once they caught up to Clait and had her translate it, but there was a chance this was where the golden grigeen was. Which was both good and bad. She could hardly read the smaller writing in the two twisty sections, but what she did read had a lots of words like *death*, *dismemberment*, and *more death*.

"I think we have a deal. But, no magic from you...or what happened to your friend will happen to you. Sean knows a spell very similar to the one on the town. And, you obey everything either of us, or the grigeen who will be with us, says." She lifted her chin to the weakly moving grigeens. "Also, you help us carry these into the forest and swear upon healing your wound to never tell anyone where we take them."

Jol nodded. "His name is Sean, eh. Nice name. Yours?"

"Neve. Now, do we have a deal? I can heal your injury but it will be dependent on you holding up your end of the bargain. Fail us and your arm will lead to your death." She actually had no way of creating a spell like that, but he didn't need to know that.

"I will uphold them. We split the treasure? Three ways?"

Nevaine looked to Sean, and he nodded. "Four ways. My grigeen companion will also get a cut." They weren't planning on keeping anything except the golden grigeen if it was there—but it would look odd if they left it all to him.

"That's acceptable." He looked at his right arm, where she'd sliced him. He had it wrapped tightly but wasn't moving it much. "I could carry more of those wee grigeens if I had both arms."

Nevaine put down her knife. She'd been hoping to hold the healing over him longer, but he did have a point. She had him remove his coat and shirt. His bandaging had been both inside his shirt over the injury and outside. Odd, but the odor coming from the injury had been blocked by his double wrapping. She'd just injured him a few hours ago, yet infection was already starting.

"How did it get like this so quickly?"

"Ah, not been in Wath long, eh? New thing the folks in charge started. Unsanctioned fighting will lead to infected injuries. It does cut down on the brawling."

"Why did you draw swords on us then? Seriously, this is like a few days' old infection...you would be dead soon." Nevaine started focusing her spells for healing. She was better at healing than her sisters but it still wasn't an automatic spell. Sean looked ready to step in, but he also still looked overdrawn.

"Didn't think you two could fight so well. It was Hin's idea. Bad one, as it turned out." He winced as the night air hit his injury.

"This is going to hurt; I'm not going to lie." Before he could respond, she released the delicately balanced spells she held. None of them were extremely powerful, but together they would clear the infection and repair tissue.

Jol didn't cry out but his lip was bloody from biting it, and he had tears running down his face when she finally finished. The skin now had a deep red line where she'd cut him, but it was healing.

He opened his eyes and looked at the wound. "Damn fine work." He got to his feet and started to go for his sword. Then paused and looked to both of them. "It's okay if I pick it up, right? Won't use it against you or yours."

Sean was the one holding a sword, yet Nevaine was the one he was staring at.

Nevaine nodded; he was smarter than he acted. He must know enough about magic that he knew how tricky the healing spell had been—and how much power she must have. "Go ahead. If you betray us in any way, your infection comes back and kills you."

He watched her for a few moments, then got his sword and quickly sheathed it. Sean did the same, and they all walked over to the grigeens. They were stirring a little, but not enough to walk on their own. They were just sorting out carrying them when Clait, Halui, and fifteen other grigeens came through the woods.

"Did you get lost?" Clait snarled when she saw Jol and the grigeens he was already carrying. "Who is that?"

Nevaine stepped in front of her. "It's okay. He's working with us for a bit. Looking for some treasure up in the Pantiar Mountains."

Clait sniffed his shoes, then peered up at his face. "You are carrying some precious people—be careful or you'll wish it was these two who killed you."

He nodded, but kept quiet.

"We can help bring these back. Onlian did find a place and it has a different type of magic." She dropped her voice. "And don't use the name of that object around these grigeens—they pass out completely."

"Good to know."

Nevaine and Sean reclaimed their belongings and stuffed them back in their packs. Then they got all of the injured grigeens picked up. Jol was actually great at carrying them gently, and everyone followed Clait. It was the middle of the night and extremely dark, but the trip was shorter than it felt. Unlike the other ruins, these looked like nothing but piles of stone. The tabby grigeen stood guard and nodded as they approached. Rustling all around them pointed out that he hadn't been alone.

An odd feeling slid along her skin as they crossed through two tall piles of stone. Suddenly, a new world opened and there were grigeens everywhere. She didn't see Zila, but clearly more grigeens from that pack had joined them.

There were piles of food and water, and the stronger freed grigeens were helping feed the rest. Even though grigeens had excellent night vision, low magical glows were placed around the space, more in the back where the injured were. The grigeens that she, Sean, and Jol carried in were gently taken from them and placed on small piles of hay in the back.

Freed of his load, Sean looked around the space. "This is impressive." He walked around in awe, then went to the closest pile of rocks. "This spell survived the destruction of the actual building. And for a long time, too—the building was destroyed hundreds of years ago."

There appeared to be fresh water and shelter from the elements, not to mention that odd feeling on her skin when she came in felt protective. It seemed for a moment to know who she was. Had she come in with ill intent, she doubted she'd get back out alive.

"I don't get it. If Zila, and presumably whoever ruled before him, knew about this, why didn't they stay here? The spell over the other place is illusion only. This one has some teeth to it."

Clait came over. "The most I can get is that Zila forbade it. No one else seems to recall another leader doing so, but Zila is one of the elders in the pack. And he has always forbidden it."

Halui was nearby and looked up with a snarl. "He also forbid us from rescuing our own. We saved four hundred and twenty-three grigeens tonight. Over four hundred of our people he left to be tortured and die." Her fur was hard to see even with the glowing lights, but she looked far poofier than normal. She was less than half Zila's size, but if he had been here, Nevaine knew who would win that fight.

"I don't agree with what he did, but he must have had his reasons." Clait looked around the large space. "However, I don't sense anything wrong with this place. Do you?"

Nevaine was shocked at Clait giving the benefit of a doubt to Zila, but she sent her magical sensing spell out. She'd checked when they came in, especially after that spell had investigated her, but not deeply. She did so now and started to shake her head, when a spark in a far corner caught her spell's attention. It wasn't a spark she could see with her eyes, but it was clear in her mind. "There is something. I don't think it's bad...just powerful." She pointed to where it would be. "I don't see anything, but I feel something over there."

Sean had been walking around the ruins, touching broken stone, but looked up at her words. He walked to where she pointed and closed his eyes. "This is old, very old. More so than the ruins or the spell that protects it. There's an artifact buried in there."

His eyes when he opened them had the same hope Nevaine felt at his words. The golden grigeen might be right under their noses. They had no idea what the artifact did, but grigeens in nature were protective, so an artifact of them might be as well. Getting it without all of the traps shown on Jol's map would be wonderful—and far less likely to end in death or injury.

"Can we get to it?" Nevaine looked at the injured grigeens. She couldn't focus on her situation until they were safe. If that was the golden grigeen buried there, removing it could risk their lives. "Later. Once things are safe."

Sean looked around and nodded. "It's not going anywhere. And it could be what's feeding the spell on this place."

Clait went where he stood and sniffed. "There is something familiar, but I'm not sure what. What are the plans for defense? Those humans behind the factory will follow."

Nevaine felt her energy fading. Adrenaline could only keep someone moving for so long. "Do we think this spell of protection will keep everyone safe for a while? We won't be any good, nor will any of them, if we're exhausted." She nodded toward Jol, who gave a few huge yawns as he helped settle some of the grigeens into hay pile beds.

Sean looked at the bricks and rubble around them. "I think so, but I'd still like to set a spell out from the perimeter. It's sort of like the one on the other hideout, but with a stronger point of dissuading anyone from coming closer."

"A battlemage spell, I assume?" Nevaine shook her head. He was back to barely standing. "You don't have the strength for something like that. Not alone, anyway. How hard would it be for me to assist?" It was extremely difficult for most magic users to function together on a spell. Nevaine's talent of layering spells made it easier for her to work with others, but she'd never tried with anyone other than her sisters.

Sean started to shake his head, then shrugged instead. "Normally, I'd say too hard to even think about. But in this case, and since it's you and your odd balancing magic, it's worth a try. Not to mention that I don't want to be dragged back by my heels if I collapse out there. Mostly what you'll do is mirror me, follow my spell, but you'll be giving it more strength." He walked toward the front.

Jol looked up. "Are we leaving?"

"Nope, just going to reinforce things. Stay here." Sean was good at projecting not being exhausted, but Nevaine could tell.

They nodded to the tabby guard and then walked out into the forest. Sean was counting under his breath as he walked and stopped at fifty paces.

"I'd prefer this was out farther, but you're tired too. A shorter perimeter is easier to keep up." He gave her a grin. "Let's see how good you are."

Nevaine opened her mind to what he was doing magically. Battle magic was different than either regular magic or sorcery, but it had a simplistic manner to it, in a way. It was more direct than many spells. Following him wasn't hard once she figured out what he was doing.

The spell twisted around them; then, with her boost, it went out in a circle with the ruins in the middle. Even being on the casting end of it, she could feel the edges of it. There was a powerful yet subtle feeling encouraging her to go the other way. Had she been in the woods, she would have avoided it completely.

She also felt a tug. "You added a grigeen feeling leading away from here?"

Sean smiled as he took her hand and they went back to the ruins. "Just a slight one. It's a rabbit, a spell used to lead people astray. Works great if you know what they're looking for." His steps were getting slower as they reached the ruins.

"And your casting...it was too much. You are an incredibly stubborn man." Nevaine all but dragged him through the passageway to the ruins.

He staggered inside, then collapsed against a pile of rocks. "Same could be said of you. I think I'll rest now." He shut his eyes, but the rise and fall of his chest indicated he'd just fallen asleep.

Nevaine was tired, but not like him. She pulled their packs over to his rock pile and covered him with a blanket. Then set up a bedroll next to him and looked around for Clait.

She found her not far away, conferring with another grigeen. Clait jogged over.

"Sean and I set a persuasion spell around the outside of this place, but he's already asleep and I want to be. Is everything okay right now?" Many of the grigeens were also asleep, but the ones who were up seemed to be on guard or helping some of the very sick ones.

"Worked together on a spell, eh?" Clait gave a broad grin, but it dropped as she looked around. "Things are okay now, but they can't stay here forever. I'm worried what will happen when we leave."

"Me too. But we'll think of some way to protect them." Nevaine hated the thought that they might have freed these grigeens, only to have them all captured again. But she also was about to fall asleep standing up.

"Go rest. I'll wake you if you're needed. Oh, your friend was actually quite helpful. He's asleep over in the corner." She pointed where Jol had fallen asleep sitting up.

Nevaine smiled—hopefully the grigeens would at least have an ally when she, Sean, and Clait left. Then she yawned again and went to curl up near Sean.

And woke up hours later with a well-muscled arm flung across her torso. At least Sean had slept well. He was still dead to the world as she crawled out from under his arm.

The grigeens were bustling about as if this was a well-kept hospital and recovery ward. And there were more than before. Nevaine found Clait scowling at a pile of old bricks in a corner.

"More from the original pack joined us, I take it? And what did those bricks ever do to you?" Clait was in the wrong place to be in the spot they thought might be the golden grigeen. Nevaine didn't feel anything magical here—well, nothing more than what all of the bricks emanated anyway.

"The ruins are hiding secrets. I don't believe that they were destroyed—I think they destroyed themselves." She didn't take her eyes off the pile. "And yes, it is believed that fewer than ten grigeens, including Zila, remain at their old place. Onlian and Halui have taken over running this location and they went to convince Zila to join them—there's a real fear that when the humans come out this way, they could find the old enclave. But Zila wouldn't budge." She gave a shrug.

Clait was a strong proponent of helping people as long as they were willing to help themselves. She'd now given up on Zila.

"Ha! I saw you!" She pointed a paw at a brick. "You moved."

Nevaine narrowed her eyes, but they all looked unchanged. Like an ancient pile of rubble. "How did it move? And how long—" She cut herself off as a part of a brick twitched. "I saw it too. Are we in danger here?" They were still far too close to Wath and that factory. Even with the spell she and Sean put up, being out in the forest wouldn't be a good idea. But she'd hoped this could at least be a safe place for the grigeens until the sick and injured recovered. That might not be the case, depending on just what was making those bricks move.

"I'm not sure, but I don't sense any maleficence here. Just…curiosity?" Clait turned to Nevaine. "How long can human spells hang around? Especially ones that might have minds of their own?"

Nevaine mentally reached out toward the brick that had moved. Clait was right; there was an intelligence there. "I have no idea on either. I've never heard of sentient spells, and therefore have no idea how long one could hang around." She stepped closer to the bricks and crafted a searching spell. Just a little one, and added on a translation spell. That was harder; it would attempt to translate the spell they were facing. It rarely worked, but she figured it was worth a try. Something was in those bricks. And she trusted Clait about what she'd sensed.

At first, she thought neither spell worked. Then three of the bricks in front of her stacked on top of each other. None of them had been intact, but they reformed out of the dust around them. She felt a soothing sensation, followed by the passage of far more years than she could guess at. Then a warmth toward the grigeens.

"Wow. Thank you, but I still don't understand. Can you help protect them?" She didn't care if anyone thought she was crazy for speaking to a pile of bricks. She knew there was something in them.

Two more bricks shifted and she got more images. These ruins had been hidden for hundreds of years. Made long ago, by a wizard long dead. This land was not part of the Offialian Empire.

Nevaine knew the Offialian Empire was always expanding and, depending how far out they were from the center, it could be they were seeing the ruins of a fallen land. But the tone she'd felt was that this land wasn't part of the empire *now*.

That was interesting and scary at the same time. She wasn't sure how such a spell could be made, let alone that it embedded sentience to the building that lasted hundreds of years after the caster had died. For the most part, the communication with the bricks was more images and feelings, but *wizard* had been a distinct term. And not one used by anyone she knew. Wizards were a unique class of magic users and had supposedly all died hundreds of years ago.

"Communicating with rubble now?" Sean came up behind her. "How'd you find some intact over here? I've only seen pieces and dust in most areas."

"They're sentient," Clait said. "Nevaine and Sean, meet the building. Building, meet Nevaine and Sean." She looked past them. "I don't know that we want to tell the others just yet."

Sean's look of disbelief fled as soon as he dropped down to the dirt next to the stacked bricks. He closed his eyes, reached out, and pulled back in shock. "They *are* sentient."

Chapter Eighteen

Sean turned back to the bricks. "You have been through much, haven't you?"

Nevaine couldn't feel the communication from the bricks, but obviously Sean could. He laughed and whispered to the bricks.

"Nice to know you're a brick speaker. Do you know of any spells that could do this? They mentioned it had been a *wizard*, and they weren't part of the empire." Nevaine could sense part of the discussion between him and the bricks, but it was like just hearing something on the edge of comprehension.

"A wizard?" He said a few quiet words to the bricks. "There is more power here than it appears. Let me check something." He leaned even closer to the bricks, still whispering to them. Then he pulled back, looking thoughtful. "I asked if that artifact over there is what we're looking for. They said no, but it's one connected to them. They are close with the earth, like the grigeens, and feel the presence of the object we're looking for in the mountains. Right where we feared it might be. They will also protect the grigeens, no matter what."

"That's good to know." But she wasn't sure how far the protection could go. The grigeens couldn't spend their entire life inside this safe space. "They have any shortcuts for getting the item?" Since it made Clait uncomfortable and apparently knocked out the rest of the grigeens, she was not going to utter the name until they were away from the pack.

"Not directly. But they said we can take some of their dust to help connect to it. Both of us should carry a little in our packs, but aside that it will help, they really can't or won't say more about it. However, they are relieved that someone is going to rescue it."

"Rescue? That's an interesting term for a relic." Clait kept sniffing the bricks but still seemed unsure of them.

"That's what they used and like *wizard*, it felt like a deliberately selected word." Sean took a large pinch of dust and tucked it into a pocket on his tunic, then handed some to Nevaine.

She shrugged and put it away as well. Not sure how it was going to help, but she was pretty sure it wouldn't hurt. One of her mottos was "Never say something couldn't hurt—the Universe might set out to prove you wrong."

Clait moved closer to a large pile of dust, stomped in it a bit, then rolled in it. She shook herself when she got up.

"Didn't you just shake it all off?" Nevaine asked.

"But the essence of them is with me." Clait nodded like the wise old grigeen she wasn't. "It won't work with humans, but the wizard magic was extremely earth based. Therefore, he imbued his building with that. And the essence of that speaks to my people." She tilted her head. "I think I feel a gentle tug. Won't find it for us, but this dust should hopefully keep us from making too many mistakes."

"And hopefully not dying." Nevaine looked to where Jol was helping move some injured grigeens about. "Should he get some?" She put a lot of weight on Clait's intuitions about people; she could be picky but was a good judge of character. She liked Jol. But he was still someone who tried to kill her. Twice.

Clait and Sean both looked over at him. "No." They echoed each other, then laughed.

Sean went first. "I don't think he'll go against us again. You really scared him with your threats. And, in theory, he needs us for the magic portion. But I don't want to share this trick with him."

Clait watched him for a bit, then turned back. "Agreed. He has been a big help, but his heart is mixed. Better to keep him in the dark about some things. Not to mention, who knows what he'll do once we're back home."

Nevaine nodded and got to her feet. Good points, and they reflected her own thoughts. "So, do we leave now? How long do we wait to see if there's a threat coming this way? And how long will that spell of ours around this place stand after we're not here?" Obviously, some spells lasted an extremely long time after the spell caster was gone. But most faded away quickly without being reinforced regularly by the mage or sorcerer behind it.

Sean rose and dusted himself off. "I think the sooner, the better. I can add another rabbit spell as we go and have it lead off in another direction. The spell we did should last a few weeks. I tied it to the rubble outside this place. Hopefully, by then a better solution will be found."

Nevaine turned to Clait. "It would be better coming from you. Could you tell the grigeens that, as much as possible, they need to stay inside while we're gone? Explain to them about the spells here." She wasn't sure if telling them they were surrounded by sentient brick and rubble would soothe them or make them flee. Right now, they didn't have the time to test things.

Clait nodded and headed off to Onlian and Halui.

Jol came over. "Still good with our plan, right?" He kept his head down.

"We are. Is something wrong?" Sean asked.

"Nah, just thinking it's kind of nice here with these wee grigeens and all. I still am game for it, but do you think they'd let me come back and stay for a while once we're done?"

Nevaine would have figured that he'd be off to the cities with his riches, once he got them. But he did seem to fit in here. She'd say he could stay now, if they let him, except she needed his map. And his hand on said map. "You could ask them. I'd start with Onlian and Halui. They're getting things rolling. We'll leave in a half hour."

He nodded, then wandered his way to Onlian and Halui. Nevaine shook her head. He didn't seem to face any conflict head-on, but got there eventually. Probably why he ended up working with someone like Hin.

"Thanks for getting me a blanket last night." Sean smiled as he folded his blanket and shoved it in his pack. He looked like he was going to say more, then shut his mouth tightly instead.

"What?" Nevaine got her things put away quickly. "You were going to say something else."

"I...I'm still not sure how you feel about me." He held up his hand. "And yes, I agree being in the middle of trying not to get killed is not the time to deal with it."

"I don't know either. The Sean I knew doesn't seem to have been the real Sean. But I'm not trying to make things difficult." This Sean was different than the one she'd been dating for a few months. She didn't know if it was a change she could deal with or not, and if there were more things she didn't know about him.

He took her shoulders, looked down into her eyes, then leaned forward, and planted a kiss on the top of her head and quickly stepped back. "Understood." He gave a nod and went to speak to the two grigeens closest to the entrance.

"I know that look." Clait came over. "You need to be less set in your ways. Sometimes people aren't who we thought, but they end up being who we need." She gave a nod, as if that ended the issue.

Nevaine ignored her.

"There haven't been any sightings of anyone from town, by the way." Sean adjusted his pack as he came back. "Beyond that they originally turned down this way after leaving town, then immediately went the other direction."

Jol coughed. "That might be me. I didn't want anyone to follow you since I had my own bad reasons, so I left a weevil spell. It should have only distracted them, though."

Sean narrowed his eyes. "Well, it did more than that. They still aren't coming this way. Still, I think we should get out of the area before they come near here. This place can hide and protect itself, but us being nearby could draw unwanted attention."

"I can get us to the safest place to get on the Pantiar Mountains trail." Jol was still second-guessing things, from the look of doubt on his face.

"That would be wonderful." Nevaine patted him on the back.

Sean nodded. "Might save us some time. I'll set a rabbit spell, or weevil, once we're a bit farther out."

Jol took the lead but seemed to want one of them up with him. Sean kept him company.

"As long as no one ever starts calling them grigeen spells. Poor rabbits and weevils." Clait lashed the tip of her tail as she marched between them.

"I doubt the rabbits or weevils would care," Nevaine said as they walked through the forest.

"True. But still."

"Are you okay? I mean, being around these new grigeens, what they've been going through...it has to be hard," Nevaine asked.

"It's just so...we always wondered what it would be like when we found more of our people. That they are here...is going to be interesting. My people will want to get them out of the empire."

"Astarious has no agreements with the Offialian Empire."

Clait winced. "Which is where the problem is. My people will try to change that, one way or another."

As Clait's friend, Nevaine understood. As a princess of Astarious, that didn't sound good. She'd need to speak with her parents the moment she got back. If they got back. Maybe something could be done to bring the grigeens over without starting a fight between the two lands.

"Let me see what I can do."

Clait dropped back. "I trust you like you were my own kit, and there is no ill blood between my pack and the royal family. But please move quickly. This will change everything for my people."

"I know." She looked up and saw that Sean and Jol had gotten ahead of them. "Let's keep up and focus on not dying."

Clait started jogging. "Excellent plans. I approve of both."

Sean released his rabbit spell, this one taking off in a different direction from them or the grigeens completely. Jol confirmed that there was nothing but wilderness in that direction for a dozen miles or so. Then he and Sean dropped into a spell discussion. The sorcery training given to military had a few similarities with battlemages. Including that spell.

Nevaine took out her blue spell book and worked on practicing sorcery in her head as they walked.

"How can she read and walk at the same time?"

Jol must have turned back and seen her.

"It's one of her strongest gifts. Never get between a woman and her reading material." Sean had raised his voice a bit, but then dropped back to a lower conversation.

Nevaine went back to focusing on her spells until they stopped.

At the side of a looming mountain.

"Is that snow?" Nevaine spotted white stuff at the top. Astarious wasn't flat but only had one large mountain range that was far east of the capital.

"Yes, but we don't have to go that far up." Jol gave a weak smile as he patted the pocket with the map.

"That is a much steeper incline than I expected." Sean saw the trailhead before she did. It was hidden among some low trees.

Clait trotted under the trees, then came back. "Indeed. Since I will be the least likely of all of us to have difficulty on this trail, I propose that I stay with Jol. You two cover our flank." She started up the trail. Jol shrugged and followed.

"She's not subtle, is she?" Sean asked as they followed. It was steep and narrow, but at least there was a trail. And one mostly covered by trees so if anyone had followed them, they'd be harder to spot.

"Not at all. I'm sorry if she's making things more difficult." If Nevaine could set him free or accept who he really was, knowing that he'd misled her, she would. But she was extremely torn.

Sean stopped and put his hands on either side of her face. "I won't draw this out, but..." He gave her a simmering kiss that reached deep into her soul and muddled her mind. "I know how I feel about you. I'll wait until you figure out how you feel about me." He stepped back and followed Clait and Jol. "Come on, we don't want to give Clait things to worry about."

Nevaine blinked a few times and tried to focus on what they were doing. That had been a seriously impressive kiss.

They were still a few feet behind the other two when three dirt-covered thugs jumped in-between them. All had short jagged swords and looked slightly crazed.

Chapter Nineteen

"Give us everything or die where you stand." The one closest to Sean and Nevaine waved his sword.

"We've got a coward and a 'geen up here. I get to keep the 'geen." That was from a tall, skinny one closer to Jol.

"I don't think so."

Sean spoke as he drew his sword, and Nevaine went for two of her knives. She was grateful for the oracles giving her a sword, but sometimes small blades were better.

"No one is taking anything. Back down before you start leaking." Nevaine took her fighter crouch, another way she made up for a shorter reach.

"We just want your things. We're out of supplies." This was the third attacker. He looked calmer than the other two and appeared in better condition. But his hands shook.

All three looked like they'd been trapped in the wilds for months.

"Why don't you go back down? Wath isn't far." Nevaine kept watching all three. "I really don't want to hurt you."

The first one started laughing hysterically until the second one hit him. Then he shook it off. "Can't leave the mountain. We've almost found it. If we leave, it'll be gone forever."

"How long have you been up here?" Sean didn't even ask what they were looking for. He probably figured it out, like Nevaine.

"Don't know." The third one looked up into the sky. "What day is it?"

"Markius fifteenth," Jol answered quickly.

It was good he did, as neither she nor Sean would probably have had a clue. Different lands had different calendars. Not to mention months. On the other side of the ocean, this was the seventeenth of Julai.

"That can't be." The middle one looked around, as if seeing his surroundings for the first time. "Six months? We've been here *six months*?" His voice rose at the end of his sentence and he rocked back and forth. "No. You told us a week. Then two weeks." He lunged for the third man but was off-balance enough that he missed and ran into Nevaine. She managed to not stab him but kicked him away from her.

The first man ran toward them with his sword raised, and it wasn't clear who he was planning on using it against.

Sean stepped forward and blocked his sword. Nevaine resumed her lowered knife fighting stance. Yes, magic might resolve this situation, but something in the back of her mind said to hold off on that. Considering that Sean hadn't gone for magic either, and as a battlemage that should have been his immediate go-to in a fight, maybe that odd warning was speaking to all of them.

Clait had been holding back, but was watching all three attackers carefully. "The mountain has destroyed them." Her voice was just loud enough to carry and held a lot of sadness. "They weren't always like this." She scampered out of reach, atop a boulder, as the first attacker lunged for her. "Stop that."

"That is truly the date." Jol sounded sad also. He turned to Sean and Nevaine. "This is why they don't come back. No one ever comes back."

"You knew this happened?" Nevaine stayed in her crouch but the one who had attacked her threw his sword, dropped to the trail, and started wailing and sobbing.

Jol shrugged. "We knew something happened. But figured we'd avoid it."

The third man looked at his companion, then to them. "We will have your belongings, if you're lucky. If not, then your lives." As he lunged for Sean, the first one turned and came at Nevaine. Jol stepped back near Clait's rock but kept his sword ready.

The one who attacked her was shorter than the others but still taller than Nevaine. But he moved oddly, as if he was fighting his own body to get a swing in at her. She easily deflected his sword with her knives; there was little strength behind his swing. "Look, we can give you some food. Just stop this. You won't win."

"We need it all. All. Now." He lunged forward faster than expected but still missed her.

She sliced his arm as his strike overshot. It wasn't even a disabling swing on her part, not like she'd used on Jol in their first encounter. But the man dropped to his knees, sobbing.

A few moments later, Sean had disarmed the third man. He didn't drop, but his head went down.

"Kill us. We've been infected. We have to have it all, all the treasure, all the food—

everything. I saw a group of women fighters when we first came in. Hardened adventurers. They were like us now. They ran off a cliff not far from here. I didn't heed the warning." He moved faster than Nevaine expected and lunged for Sean's throat with his hands extended.

Sean's reaction was automatic, and his sword went through the man's chest. "Damn it, why did you do that? We can help you!" He pulled his blade free and held the man up.

Blood burbled from his lips. "I'm free now. Thank you." Then his head rolled back and his body went limp.

The other two rolled to their feet and ran into the bush next to them, yelling—neither took their sword.

"That was horrible." Jol looked ready to be sick and couldn't look at the dead man.

Sean wiped off the blood on his sword and put it away. "He goaded me to kill him. All they had to do was go down the trail for a few hours."

"They couldn't." Clait climbed down from her boulder. "This place protects what it guards by driving people insane. Short-term, it shouldn't hurt us, but the mountain will try to delay us long enough for us to become like them. I'd say the one you killed was the lucky one."

"It's an intention spell." Nevaine tried to recall where she'd seen it. It wasn't in the book she'd been working on, so it was probably something Hisu had brought up. "It latches on to the intent of the victim, then warps it and makes it feed on itself. Treasure hunters want to obtain something—this spell makes them so obsessed that they need everything. It also keeps them from leaving."

"That doesn't sound like something a mountain should be able to do." Jol looked around the rocks and trees in worry, then dropped his voice. "Can it hear us?"

"No, and I don't think it's from the mountain." Clait's tail twitched as she wandered around, sniffing the area. "It doesn't feel of that. But it does feel like wizard magic."

Jol looked from Sean to Nevaine. "There haven't been wizards in a thousand years. Or so said my da in the old stories he'd tell."

"There appears to have been a strong one here, and he might have something to do with the ruins the grigeens are in." Nevaine wasn't sure what more to say to him, but she really was hoping that if it was the same wizard, having some of the sentient brick dust that he created would keep them safe. Or at least get them in and off this mountain before the intention spell hit them.

She really hoped that it wasn't the case that there had been two wizards in this area and they didn't get along. If that were the case, and one spelled the ruins and one the mountain, having that dust on them could make them targets. In the books she'd read, wizards didn't like others of their kind. Which was one of the reasons there weren't any of them left.

Sean tilted his head and closed his eyes. Then he opened them and shook his head. "I don't think we can presume anything, aside from the need to get there and get back off this mountain as soon as possible."

Nevaine nodded. "After you, Jol."

He pulled out his map, looked at it briefly, then started up. "Looks like we go this way for a few more hours, mostly up. Then it gets tricky."

Clait stayed up with him, but Sean and Nevaine were closer to them this time. There was no way to know if there were others who'd been up here too long awaiting them, but if there were, being together was better.

Especially since Jol wasn't much of a fighter.

They walked in silence, and Nevaine didn't bring out Gliandra's book. She had a feeling that she didn't want to be caught reading if there were more lost souls roaming around.

The mountainside seemed peaceful enough. A gentle breeze wandered through the trees, and she heard a distant waterfall. Of course, if part of the intention spell was to encourage relic hunters to stay until they went mad, making things seem pleasant would work in the spell's favor.

"Not reading?" Sean asked next to her.

"Shocking, I know." Nevaine laughed. She'd grown up with others mocking her for the love of reading, but it didn't bother her.

"Actually, it's one of the first things that attracted me to you. You were wandering the market, reading as you shopped. Well, the second thing." He winked. "I like to read, but I don't read as much as you, nor do I know anyone who does. Even my brother who is a university instructor doesn't read as much as you."

"You have a brother who *teaches*?" She smiled. "Is he handsome?"

"Pah. Trying to get me riled up." He narrowed his eyes, then laughed. "No, he's as ugly as an old stump."

"Unrelated question, but did you feel like you shouldn't use a spell when we were attacked back there? It wasn't that I couldn't, just that I shouldn't. It was odd."

"I did. But I didn't notice it at first. It felt like someone was holding me back. I hope that's not going to be a problem when we find what we're looking for. According to his map, we're going to need magic and sorcery to get in once we find the place."

"I was thinking the same. Maybe it's part of the intention spell. Wizard spells are different than sorcery or magic, and anything could be added to it."

"Which brings up the question, why did the ruins tell us to come up here if they are related to the spell on this mountain?"

"No idea."

They continued in silence until Jol came to a stop. "We have a problem." He was facing a three-way split in the trail. The center one went sharply up. The one on the right also went up, but seemed to be heading more east than up. The left one almost looked like it was heading down. "The map isn't helping." He held up the map for both to see. It showed the areas around them but had gone fainter on all three trails.

"This is why people end up wandering around this place until they die." Sean ran his hand through his hair as he looked around.

Clait paused, then sniffed each trail. Her fur went up at the first two but when she sniffed the third, the one to the left that appeared to go back down, her fur went back to normal. "This way." She turned and pointedly looked to Sean and Nevaine. "You should be able to feel it too." She smiled to Jol. "It's part of the magic they have."

Nevaine put her hand over the pocket with the dust. At first nothing happened, then a gentle tug pulled her toward the left. "This is the one I'd be least likely to believe was correct, but I think Clait is right." The trail's steep curve down didn't seem right, but the dust in her pocket tingled when she faced that way. It ignored the other two.

Sean paused at each trailhead a bit longer than she had, but he eventually nodded. "Agreed." He looked to Jol's still doubting face. "I have a feeling that once a path is chosen, the map will continue."

Nevaine lifted an eyebrow. He was making a big assumption there. It could be that once a trail was picked, the map kept going, regardless of whether it was the right path or not. But she was willing to trust the brick dust.

Jol shrugged and kept his map held high as he and Clait took the downhill path.

Nevaine was watching it over his head and saw the faint trail markings deepen on this direction and fade completely on the other two as if they no longer existed. A shiver went up her back. That would be a nasty spell if, even with a map, phantom trails could appear.

The downhill path was even steeper than it looked, and she was beginning to doubt the brick dust, when it slowly started back up again. The trees changed as they went higher and the snow seemed to be getting too close for her comfort. They had light jackets but nothing that could handle tromping through the snow.

There were two more multiple path options. Both times, Clait checked first, then Sean and Nevaine confirmed. Jol just watched silently after the first time.

It was extremely easy to see why people would get lost, what with confusing paths and a spell that trapped them.

"One thing, though—why does the spell want to trap them? Wouldn't chasing them away be better for the mountain?" Nevaine broke the silence. She usually worked out these issues in her head, but knowing the reason might be important.

"Maybe the spell is feeding off of them," Sean said.

Nevaine frowned, but didn't say anything. That was possible, but if this spell was connected to the one in the ruins, it shouldn't need to take lives to keep running.

"Maybe it's to keep them from coming back," Jol added. "If they can leave when its starts getting bad, and they recover once they get off the mountain, then they can try again."

Nevaine nodded. "And they'd have the information they got from prior trips. This is a tricky spell."

"And if it is from a wizard, they were incredibly powerful. Two spells still running strong after perhaps a thousand years?" Sean sighed as he looked up the trail. "That's serious power."

They sat down to rest for a bit at a flat outcropping. Nevaine and Sean shared their pack food, but Jol was more impressed with the dried fish.

"This is wonderful. Glad Hin said we needed to follow you. Didn't work out for him, though." He munched on fish and travel bread, looking like he hadn't eaten in months.

"Did he really think we were the people you were supposed to be working with?" Nevaine wasn't clear on why Hin led the attack against them if he actually thought they were companions.

"I don't know. He first said you were, but then changed his mind and said you could help us anyway." He looked around. "Is there any more bread? I need more."

Nevaine pulled back at his emphasis on the word *need*. His eyes were starting to get glassy. "I think we may have a problem."

"Just a few more pieces."

"I didn't think it would hit this fast. I'm not feeling anything. Are you?" Sean turned to Nevaine. At the shake of her head, he added, "I'll give him some of my dust; that must be protecting us." He started to pull some out but Nevaine beat him to it.

"Here, Jol. It sounds odd, but you need to keep this in your pocket. Then you can have more food." She dropped the dust into his hand and watched as his eyes cleared.

He shrugged and tucked the dust away. "Ooh. I'm so full now. Thank you, folks, for sharing." Whatever had been starting to happen earlier was gone now.

Nevaine and Sean shared a look. They'd only been up here for a few hours and that spell had already gotten into Jol. That dust from the bricks was more important than they thought.

They finished their rest in silence, all four looking out over the valley floor before them. Sean hadn't looked happy when Nevaine had handed Jol the dust, but aside from shooting sideways glances her way, hadn't done anything.

Jol and Clait started back up the trail, but Sean held Nevaine back.

"You shouldn't have split your dust. We've no idea if that will change the way it works."

"And yet, you were going to do the same. I realized the risk when I gave it to him. But he was already showing signs, and I'm a better risk than you."

"How so?" He dropped his voice. "You are a princess, and I think the kingdom would be happier about getting you back than me."

"And you're a stronger mage and fighter. I'm good, but you stand a better chance of getting us through this." *Always protect your strongest piece so they can protect everyone else.* Her mother was good at such sayings and concepts—and they stuck. Princess or not, she was less important for the success of this journey than he was. Even though it was her Challenge. There was something inside her that thought this golden grigeen was more important than whether she got to be an official heir or not.

"Coming? There looks like a good place to stop for the night not far from here, per Jol," Clait called from a few feet up the trail.

"On our way." Nevaine gave Sean a smile. "Thank you for thinking of protecting me, but this is the better way to do it." She followed Clait and Jol, with a silent Sean coming up behind.

They stayed on the path for another few hours as the trail went higher, close enough to get a better look at the snow way up the peak, then turned right. There was a valley on their left and the trail narrowed further, but still had room enough to walk single file.

Nevaine kept one hand on her sword and one on her larger dagger. This would be a place to ambush a group if one was desperate enough.

"According to the map, this area will be the last flat, protected area for a while." Jol held his map higher as he turned off the trail they were on and down an even smaller one.

Sean stayed on the trail a bit after they'd turned off. He stood still with his eyes closed and seemed to be searching for something when Nevaine looked back. He finally opened his eyes and followed them. "Nice of the map to show camping options."

"It does show places along the trail, but only when we're closer to them." Jol kept walking but the trail faded to almost nothing and they walked through clumps of encroaching grass.

Clait had been running through the tall grass that was along the edge of the trail, but hissed and tore back to Nevaine. "We don't want to go that way." Her tail lashed.

Jol stopped and held up his map. "There's not a lot of options, according to this thing. Not sure about you folks, but I don't want to be on that cliff trail when darkness falls."

"There are animals that way." Clait was breathing through her open mouth, trying to identify the scent she'd found. "Big ones."

"What are some dangerous animals in this area?" Nevaine turned to Jol. "We're not from around here."

He nodded. "I picked that up. Up here we'd have cine cats, but while they're nasty, they're only a bit larger than Clait here." His eyes went wide, and he looked around. "Skri bears. This would be a perfect place for them, and they'd be looking for food now."

"Skri bears," Sean said. "I've heard of them. I thought they lived farther up the mountains."

Nevaine hadn't even heard of them but kept watching for any animals.

Clait wrinkled her nose. "It's hard to tell, but they are that way." She pointed toward the direction they'd been going. Then slowly turned behind them. "And now, that direction, too."

Chapter Twenty

"So, what do we do?" Jol kept his voice steady, but he didn't look calm at all.

"We fight? Or we run?" Nevaine had enough education to know that there were times for both—but she didn't have the practical experience for dealing with wild animals.

"Or we stay here for a bit." Clait sat down. "There's something off around here. Listen." She tilted her head.

"The birds are back," Sean said. "They stopped as we came down this path, but if they're back, there probably aren't any predators around here beyond us. There could be an illusion spell making us think there are dangerous animals nearby."

"Someone planted scents around here to make us avoid the area? But what if we didn't recognize the scent? Hard to be scared off if you don't know what you're supposed to be scared of." As she spoke, a light breeze went across the grass. She smelled something now. A musky smell. She might not have known what it was, or what it was supposed to be, but she did smell something.

"I think we should keep going." Sean held up his hand. "Full darkness will fall in less than a half hour. The scent is coming from around us, so any direction we pick could be wrong. The way behind us is the more dangerous option."

"I agree." Clait started down the path. "But you all might want to have some spells handy. If there are bears ahead, your swords and knives won't do much."

They walked slowly, with Jol gladly stepping back to let Nevaine, then Sean, go ahead of him. Clait continued to lead, but also stayed walking in the long grass. With her head and tail down, she would be hard to see.

Nevaine kept a balanced stun spell ready. The odd feeling of not using magic hadn't appeared, which could be good or bad, depending on what had tried to stop them from using it before.

Clait's tail poofed, and she moved closer to the trail. "Something is definitely there, but I don't think it is animal. It wants us to think it is."

"So, human?" There weren't a lot of options if it wasn't an animal.

"Or? Not sure."

Nevaine glanced back. Sean nodded that he'd heard, but from the look on his face, he didn't know what Clait was alluding to either.

The area that had been on Jol's map was now visible: a rock formation with a small clearing in front of it. The rocks were massive and didn't look to be easily climbed—hopefully giving protection on one side.

Nevaine was about to move closer when a chill went through her and stopped her. It wasn't just the wind. There was the sense of a person.

"Did you just feel..." She wasn't sure how to describe it, but as kids, she and her sisters were fond of ghost stories. This felt like what a ghost would. Or a weird spirit. Or something else that didn't have a body.

"Yes," both Sean and Clait said quickly.

"Feel what? The breeze? It's a bit cold." Jol hadn't moved forward but a quick glance back showed that he didn't have the same wide-eyed look Sean and Clait did.

The wind came back from the opposite direction. If the sense of the person that went through her the first time hadn't been enough, this second pass would have been. The wind wasn't moving naturally, and the feeling of someone around her was worse.

"Who's there? We don't mean you harm. Show yourself." Part of her was calm because it simply refused to believe in ghosts—stories or not. The other part was curious and the idea of a real ghost was squishing out any fear she'd held. There were absolutely no scientific books pertaining to spirits being real.

Sean held a nasty-looking spell—at least from what she could sense—but didn't say anything.

Nevaine stepped closer to the clearing; the wind went around them again and was stronger this time. "We won't hurt you; we just need a place to stay for the night."

Just as she was about to decide that she was imagining things, a light-gray image appeared before them. It was tall and looked to be a man, an older man, in an ancient-looking robe. Clait scurried up next to her and hissed at him, with Sean taking her other side.

A look behind them showed that Jol had passed out and was sprawled across the grass.

"You shouldn't be here. Fear my wrath!" The ghost raised his arms and gave a moaning sound.

"What are you going to do to us? You're on the wrong side of the life-death barrier." Nevaine tilted her head and stepped closer. "Did you get stuck? I had a theory that spirits could get stuck and that most of the time no one on the life side could sense them but some-times—"

"How can you see me? And if you can, why aren't you running? Any of you?" The ghost put his hands on his hips. "A grigeen? You did survive then!" He came forward and dropped in front of Clait. "But you're not from here...although, you have the scent of my cas-tle." He looked back toward Nevaine and Sean. "You all do. Is it still standing? Are the wars still going on? I'd hoped to protect the grigeens until they were over."

Sean stepped forward. "You're *the* wizard? The one who spelled the bricks? And this mountain?"

"What? The *bricks*? Well, I'd guess that would be an interesting way to put it. Oh. The castle is gone, isn't it? Are the grigeens safe?" He shook his head. "No, I knew the castle was gone. That was long ago. But saving the grigeens had been...after I died." He dropped to a rock and managed to not go through it. "It's difficult...time doesn't stay the same here. In answer to your question, yes, I believe I am trapped. My name is Pantiar. I am, was, a wizard of great renown long ago. I sense magical abilities in you all." He looked past them to Jol. "Is that one going to be okay?"

"I think he just passed out. Not every day we see ghosts." Clait nodded. "I'm Clait, and yes, my grigeen pack is far from here."

Nevaine and Sean introduced themselves as wandering adventurers; Pantiar narrowed his eyes but didn't question it.

Jol groaned, and Nevaine went to him. "Get up slowly. It's okay. Yes, there's a ghost. No, it won't..." She stopped as Jol collapsed again. "This is Jol. He's a bit skittish."

The ghost drifted over and looked down. "He is from here. You three are not. Are you a new wave of invaders?"

"No. We're just looking for a relic." Nevaine waved toward the darkening sky. "Do you mind if we set up here for the night? I assume there aren't really any bears?"

Pantiar laughed. "Glad to know the spell still works. I have a feeling I've been here a long time. By all means, camp here. Do they still call the forest and mountain by my name?"

"Not sure about the forest." Sean dropped his pack and started gathering wood. "But this mountain range is named after you. It's almost a curse word, though. People come up searching for riches and never return. Your work, I presume?"

"Good to know about the mountain. And about thieves getting their comeuppance. Trying to steal my things...of course I would have put safeguards on them. That's not nice." He paused. "I don't recall setting curses up against people in these mountains, though. Yet I fear I've forgotten a fair amount."

"Why guard things if you're dead? Can you use them?" Nevaine watched as he varied in appearance, fading in and out without any direct reason she could tell.

"They're my things. They need to be guarded." He faded a bit as he folded his arms.

"Why?" Nevaine was wealthy; being a princess, that came with the territory. But she'd never understood wealth for wealth's sake. And it made even less sense if you couldn't enjoy the things you were hanging on to.

"Because...they're my things." He scowled and faded more. "Ah, and they are dangerous." He grew less transparent. "That was why. I knew that. The items I protect are too dangerous for anyone to have. That's why I'm still here." He smiled.

"Couldn't you have destroyed them?" Sean finished building his fire and went to check on Jol. He was still out, so Sean grabbed him by his shoulders and dragged him closer to their little camp.

"I...I could have. I had a distant hope that someone strong enough to use them would come. Another wizard. But I feel in my soul that there are none left."

"As far as my research goes, the wizards have been gone for an extremely long time." Nevaine stepped closer to the ghost and dropped her voice. She thought Jol was really unconscious but there was a slim chance he was faking it until he was ready to come to terms with a ghost, so she needed to watch what she said. "Did you have a golden grigeen statue in your collection?"

Pantiar faded a bit, then slowly nodded. "I did. It was to protect the grigeens. How did you know?"

This was going to be complicated; she still didn't want anyone here knowing who she was—her value as a ransom would be the least of her worries. But she needed to tell him something. "We were sent to find it, to release it back into the world, from what I gathered. Most of the grigeens in the world vanished after a battle a few hundred years ago. We have a small pack near us, and it appears this kingdom has them but they are being drained of their magic." That was as close as she was getting to telling him what was really going on and it wasn't far from the truth.

"Someone is draining them?" Pantiar almost looked alive now, aside from still being gray. "I will rend them from limb to limb! They will know my wrath!" He stomped in a circle, flinging his hands around.

"Can you leave this mountain?" Sean asked.

"I can...not. And my presence is fading here. The golden grigeen was to save them. But if someone who wanted to hurt them got it, or any of the other relics, they could destroy not only the grigeens but anyone they wished."

"I'm thinking you should have destroyed them." Clait had been silent but was quietly swishing her tail as she watched the wizard. "You left an arsenal of dangerous relics around, and eventually your spirit won't be around to protect them."

Pantiar stopped his stomping and looked down. "I should have. I had too much pride. I made all of them, you know."

"And you can lead us there? But I need to warn you, we only want the grigeen statue, but our friend is a treasure hunter."

He nodded. "I can help, but it's been a long time since I was there. I might not recall the exact way."

"We have a map, of sorts." Sean nodded toward Jol. "It's his, and his hand has to be on it to show anything. But if you could come along, that would help."

"I've been in this spot for a long time; it was comforting to me. But it is time I move on. I will help you get the grigeen statue, then destroy the rest. Maybe it's time to finally leave this world and go onto the next."

Jol started groaning and slowly sat up. Pantiar vanished as Nevaine and Sean went to Jol's sides.

"How are you feeling?" Sean asked as he helped him sit up.

"You're not going to believe this. I thought I saw a spirit from the afterlife coming to take me." He rubbed his head and gave a weak laugh. "It was silly, but I was terrified."

Nevaine smiled. "Actually, you did see one. A spirit, that is. But he's on our side. He's not taking anyone anywhere. We're safe."

Jol's eyes went wide as he looked between Sean and Nevaine. "They aren't real. Just children's stories."

"Pantiar? You might as well show yourself." Nevaine wasn't always the most patient person, and she didn't want to have a debate all night on whether Pantiar was real or not.

She kept watching Jol, but the widening of his eyes told her when Pantiar appeared.

"Hello, lad. I'm not even sure if *I* can cross to the next world now...I'm certainly not sending anyone else through."

Jol didn't pass out this time, but he didn't look reassured either. "Pantiar? Like the mountain?"

"One and the same. I feel a bit of my magic on you, as well as your friends. How is that possible?"

"The brick dust from your shelter in the ruins. We rescued local grigeens and they are hiding there." Clait stayed near the fire, looking pleased with herself.

Pantiar laughed. "That would do it. Are we ready to go now? Now that I'm committed, I'd like to start."

"The cliff trail isn't one to try at night—at least not for the living. We'll leave in the daylight." Nevaine got up and went back to the fire.

Pantiar followed her as Sean helped Jol to his feet. "You are a magic user, yet also have used spells of sorcery?"

She wasn't sure where he was going with it, but she nodded. "Sean is better trained than me but yes, I'm finding sorcery to be interesting."

"In my time, both practices were just coming into their own. They both were offshoots of wizardry; did you know that? Is it true that the wizards are all gone?"

"In the land I'm from, yes, and have been for over a thousand years. Here? I'd ask Jol, but I'd think if there had been, they would have come for your collection, don't you?"

"Excellent point." He leaned forward, as if reading something deep in her eyes. "You will protect them when I'm gone, yes? The grigeens?"

"Of course. But as I said, Sean and I don't live in this land." The grigeens in Astarious were protected, but they were too far away to help out the ones here once they went home. *If* they made it home. She really hoped that if she did die on this quest, she didn't come back as a spirit.

He smiled and leaned back. "Oh, you will find a way. I have no fear."

Jol was still looking spooked as he, Sean, and Clait came over to the fire. He sat as far away from Pantiar as he could while still staying in the warmth. Darkness was falling and the temperature had dropped dramatically.

They got everyone food, which Pantiar was most interested in. "I haven't smelled food in longer than I can recall. And dried fish? Ah, a favorite of mine."

"Haven't other people been up here with food?" Jol was enjoying his, but not in the obsessed way he'd been at lunch.

"Yes, but while they could never see me, as you four can, they could feel me. So, getting close enough to smell food wasn't an option."

"How'd you become a ghost? If you don't mind me asking?" Like Nevaine, Sean seemed more fascinated by Pantiar than concerned.

Clait had been holding back until the talk of protecting the grigeens. She was now curled near his ghostly feet, eating and looking up at him adoringly.

"Ask away. It is nice to speak to people again." He shrugged. "I was overconfident. I'd reached the limits of wizard powers, but wanted more. One day when I was visiting my storage hut—because of other wizards not being all that far away, I kept my most important relics and spell books up here—I was chased by a group of relic hunters. Unbeknownst to me, my reputation had grown, and people were now coming to find me and my things. I thought at first that they needed my help as one of their companions had been run through with a sword. They had a spell blocker, a good one, and once I was focused on healing their friend, they attacked me and fatally wounded me. I destroyed them, even with their spell breaker, and made it back to my cave, but it was too late. I died." He shrugged. After a thousand years, he seemed used to it. "I woke up in this form years later. Still here, but I think I'm ready to leave."

"You have spell books?" Sean was trying not to sound excited but it was in his face. Sorcerers were more likely to use books than magic users, although they still used them.

"Aye. Not sure if even the likes of you could read them, though. Unlike that wee one your friend is carrying, these bite back if used wrong." The look on his face indicated there was more he was going to say, then thought better of it.

Nevaine automatically patted where her book was stashed. "How'd you know?"

"I see a lot of things, even now. But keep your book safe—you might need it. Sorcery seems to have a better time up here in my mountains than magic. Could be that in some ways it's closer to wizardry."

They all fell into silence at that point.

Jol finished eating, said his good nights, and set up his bedroll. Clait was already curled up and didn't seem to be planning on moving.

Sean got to his feet and turned to Nevaine. "I can keep first watch, unless you want to."

Pantiar had been staring into the fire, but looked up. "You don't need to keep a watch. I know we just met, and I am deceased; however, I can still run a spell of protection. I don't sleep either, so I'll keep watch. You are saving the grigeens—for that, I will protect you with my ghostly existence."

Sean and Nevaine nodded their thanks, then set up their own bedrolls and went to sleep.

Nevaine wasn't sure whether she was awake or asleep—or somewhere in-between—and the oracles were reaching out. Then she heard her sisters arguing and knew she wasn't awake.

Chapter Twenty-One

Nevaine twitched as their voices sounded like they were right next to her, but she couldn't see anything, even in her dream.

"This isn't the way. That deer took off and left us." Lizeth, but her voice sounded much younger.

"I'm the better tracker, and I say it's this way." Piallen also sounded like a child.

Nevaine searched her memories, but this exchange didn't seem familiar.

"And getting lost made Nevaine slip and hit her head. I'm the eldest. We need to get help." Lizeth was in full imperious princess mode.

Ah. Nevaine recalled the situation now but obviously not exactly what she was hearing—as she was unconscious because of misjudging a tree branch. She was probably about ten, Lizeth would have been twelve, and Piallen was eight.

So how was Nevaine hearing something from the past, that she hadn't heard the first time, and why?

"Can't you sing heal her?" Piallen was close by.

"Boan told me not to try until he said I was ready. Healing songs are tricky. You stay here and I'll—"

Nevaine wished she could see what cut Lizeth off but whatever this was—a dream, vision, memory—she could only hear.

"What's that?" Piallen sounded her full eight years old now. A scared eight years old.

"It looks like...stay down!" Lizeth must have pulled her sister to the ground as Nevaine heard a thump. "Grigeens. Thousands of them. Are we going mad?"

"I don't think so, but we have to follow them!" Piallen sounded like she had gotten to her feet.

"We can't leave Nevaine. Not to mention, they've vanished. They were spirits." Lizeth's tone changed to one of fear. "I have to tell Scruff."

Piallen sounded like she was scrambling around, looking for them. "How did they vanish like that? I can tell Tobias, but he won't believe me."

"We need to calm down. Maybe not tell anyone, even Scruff and Tobias. I'll go get help. You stay here."

"I'm faster than you."

Which was true. Piallen was shorter than Lizeth at that age, but still faster than both of her older sisters.

"Fine. Get help and stay on the trail."

Nevaine heard footsteps running away, then a cold touch on her shoulder. She jerked awake to see Pantiar shaking her.

"I'm sorry, my child, but you seemed distressed."

Nevaine rubbed her eyes; it was still dark, so she couldn't have been asleep for long. "I was having an odd...dream." She didn't think that was what it was, but the middle of the night was not the time to be sorting it out. It felt extremely real.

He nodded. "Always listen to those. They often have hidden secrets. Go back to sleep. I believe tomorrow will be a long day for you flesh-and-blood people." He brushed her lightly on the forehead, and she dropped back to sleep. It wasn't a sleeping spell per se, mostly a strong suggestion to sleep. One that her body agreed with.

"YOU PLANNING ON SLEEPING the entire morning away?" Clait's voice was too close and when Nevaine opened her eyes, she realized she *was* too close. Her furry, big-eared face filled Nevaine's entire view.

And she'd already had breakfast of dried fish, which didn't make having her face that close any better.

Nevaine rolled away. "I just went to sleep." The light-blue sky and chorus of birds greeting the day proved her wrong. "Okay, okay, I'm up." She sat up and looked around. She felt good, but wasn't sure about Pantiar spelling her back to sleep like that. The odd dream she'd had lingered with her, but she didn't know if she should bring it up right now. The grigeens had their own spiritual beliefs, so she wanted to speak to Clait privately about what she heard before sharing it with the others.

And ask her sisters about it, if she made it home. She'd never heard of ghost grigeens.

Jol bustled around the camp, fixing plates of food and heating water for tea. He looked over as she sat up in her bedroll. "Tea or food first?"

"Tea, please. It's a lot colder up here than in the forest." She pulled her bedroll and extra blanket tighter around her.

He smiled as he brought her a mug of steaming tea.

"Is this youlan tea? I haven't had it in ages." She felt her muscles relax as she sipped the strong tea blend. It was rare in her country, but a stash had been obtained when she was fifteen. She'd become obsessed until they ran out.

"Yup. I can give you some when we get off the mountain. Hin and I found a bunch in an abandoned warehouse in Stoilsburg, but it's not that uncommon. Around here." There wasn't a threat in his voice, just curious observation. He already knew they weren't local, but his smile said he wouldn't push things.

Nevaine returned his smile and took another sip. Even though he was turning out far different from the man who'd held a sword to her throat, she still didn't think he needed to know where they were from.

Sean was up and came back with more branches for the fire. He also looked a little damp and had changed clothes.

"There's a stream nearby?" Most likely terribly cold, but Nevaine really would like to be clean. They had soap, small cloths, and towels in their packs, but those weren't helpful if there was nowhere to use them.

"Yup." Sean looked at her tea mug as he took one from Jol. "Drink another one of those before you try it, though."

Pantiar had been lost in thought as he stared into the fire, but looked up at Sean's words. "It wouldn't be much but I could make the water a little warmer. Just tell me when you're ready, but bathe fast—the spell won't hold for long."

Sean and Jol both stared at him.

"You didn't tell us you could do that." Sean gulped down a mug of tea.

"Well, she's a lady. You should always offer to help ladies. Not that they need it, mind you, but it's the right thing to do." He shrugged. "Plus, I didn't think of it until now."

Nevaine was more than willing to take the help. She finished her tea, rolled out of her blankets and grabbed fresh clothes, soap, and towels.

Sean pointed behind the rock. "Right back there, a nice, sheltered, and extremely cold, pool."

Pantiar shrugged. "It's ready for you, but as I said, move fast."

Nevaine took his words to heart and took an extremely quick bath. The water had definitely been chilly, but she didn't want to think what it would have been without wizardly assistance. She was stepping out just as she felt the temperature of it drop.

Clean and dry, and only a little chilled, she joined the others and got some more tea and food.

"We're all sticking together to find this?" Jol still wasn't that close to Pantiar, but looked less disturbed by him.

"Yes, we discussed it when you were...out." Sean smiled. "Pantiar doesn't recall a lot, but he can help."

"I can indeed. Those are *my* relics you're looking for, by the way." Pantiar was doing his looming, scary ghost appearance right now.

"I understand." Jol took two steps back.

Nevaine watched him. Might as well deal with Jol now. "You're okay with hunting this place down, knowing none of it can come with us?"

"He might be able to have one. One I choose, though." Pantiar dropped his scary look.

"Thank you. Mostly, at this point I just want to get this done. It's like I feel I have to follow through, you know? Can't explain it." Jol shrugged and put away the food.

Clait had been mostly hanging around Pantiar, but Nevaine thought she should tell her about the weird dream before they started on their way. She waved to Clait to follow her as she stepped a bit farther from the others.

"Secrets?" Clait looked far too excited about that. She'd almost been disappointed when Nevaine grew up to not be the type to keep secrets or gossip.

"Sort of." Nevaine watched the others as she told Clait her weird dream.

Clait's eyes went round. "I recall that. Piallen came, and all of us grigeens ran with the healers to get you. Luckily, your head is very hard, so no permanent damage was done." She scowled. "But neither of them mentioned ghost grigeens."

Pantiar had appeared to be watching the remains of the fire after Sean put it out, but looked up at those words. "Ghost grigeens?"

That got Sean's and even Jol's attention.

Nevaine sighed. "Just a weird dream. But, *are* there ghost grigeens?" She looked between Clait and Pantiar. She didn't want to explain the entire event; the fact that some of it coincided with Clait's memory was enough for her to guess it wasn't just a dream.

Clait started to shake her head, then scowled as Pantiar nodded.

"There could be. I exist, don't I? Grigeens don't have wizard-level magic, but their magic is exceptionally nature based. I wouldn't be surprised if they wanted to come back as ghosts. But I don't think that's what you saw. I'm not sure what it was, but I don't believe the grigeens are dead." He put his hand over his heart. "Such a massive loss, I would feel here."

Clait shrugged. "We don't have stories of any ghosts, but the world is an odd thing."

Jol looked around, then also shrugged. "I've never heard of any, myself."

That ended the question for now, and everyone loaded their packs on.

They'd started to leave the clearing, when Pantiar froze as if he'd hit a wall. He moved to either side, but couldn't go forward.

"We might have an issue." He glared at the space in front of him, but couldn't go past it.

Clait walked around him slowly. "How long has it been since you left this clearing?"

"I don't know." He scowled. "Maybe three or four hundred years. My spells took care of other things, and I really liked this spot."

"You're stuck," Clait said. "That could be why you've lasted so long, but it also means that you're tied here."

"I can't leave? That is not acceptable." Pantiar's eyes grew stormy.

Sean bent down and picked up a smooth rock that fit easily in his hand. "I think we can get you mobile. Or perhaps Neve would do the honors. Her sister did invent the spell." He grinned and held out the stone to her.

Nevaine narrowed her eyes, but took the stone. "I think I get what you're talking about. But he's a ghost, not a spell." Sean's modified version of Lizeth's spell could move a spell into an object, but she had a feeling that ghosts were different.

"Actually, all ghosts are, in our own way, spells." Pantiar looked at the rock in her hand. "Can't say I know any trick with a rock, though."

"She'll cast a spell to tether your essence to the rock, then carry the rock with us. I'd guess that you'd have the same range around her and the rock as you had here." Sean was far too pleased with himself.

Which he should be. If it worked.

Pantiar shrugged. "Otherwise, I'm stuck here, and I find I don't like that. Spell me, young lady." He closed his eyes.

Nevaine looked to Sean, then pulled up the transference spell. She treated Pantiar as a spell, and felt a tug on the rock. He still stood before her, though.

Jol looked around. "He's still there. Did it work?"

"One way to find out." Nevaine held onto the rock and walked to where the trail resumed.

Pantiar paused, but followed. "Excellent! Good thinking, my boy, and whatever you do, please don't lose that rock, lovely lady."

They all went down to the main trail, with Jol taking the lead with his map.

Pantiar drifted right behind him, peering at the map. "That's interesting. Not one of mine. I kept mine up here." He tapped the side of his head. "Looks like one of the other wizards, though. And it's old. Where'd you get it? It's keyed to you only?"

Jol nodded. "Hin got it a year or so ago. It wouldn't key to him, but we were friends, so he checked with me and it bonded. He wasn't sure why."

Pantiar drifted a bit closer to Jol, then drifted back. "I can't speak for your friend, but you have a sense of sorcery about you. More like wizardry than magic."

"Neither Hin nor I were strong, but yeah, he was a magic user. One of the reasons we went on jobs together—we balanced each other out."

"So, how come the map didn't work for me?" Sean brought up the rear but obviously had been listening. They had to go single file but were still sticking close together.

Aside from Pantiar, who drifted about. "Ah, it has to be reset. It will stay linked to Jol until he dies. But, the only one who could claim it would be another sorcerer or wizard who hadn't killed him. It's a standard hidden map spell."

Nevaine smiled. Standard for him was far beyond anything she'd even heard of. If she could, she'd hang on to him and learn everything she could. He was like a walking book. There was a chance that he wouldn't go to the afterlife immediately after destroying the relics and maybe she, Sean, and Clait could stay in the mountains for a bit before they went home.

If they figured out how to get home.

The return from a Challenge was supposed to be automatic, yet Lizeth, Finnian, and Scruff didn't reappear for over four weeks after the start of her Challenge and looked extremely ragged as they'd climbed out of the ravine. There was no guarantee on their return. Not to mention taking things back from the Challenge wasn't an approved thing, and she had a feeling that golden grigeen needed to go back. Getting it might not be the only part of her Challenge—getting it, surviving, and getting it home might be more like it.

"Lost in thought again." Clait had drifted back to walk a step ahead of Nevaine. "Did you know that Scruff traveled almost exclusively on Lizeth's pack during their adventure?" She twitched her tail. "But he is older than me, so I won't push the issue."

Nevaine laughed. "Do you want to ride on my pack?"

"Do you think I'm ancient? Pah." She strutted ahead, with just the tip of her tail flicking as she went.

Clait had an ability to draw Nevaine out of dark thoughts when she'd been younger, and it looked like she'd just done it again. Scruff was by no means old, not for the long-lived grigeens, but he was older than Clait and Piallen's grigeen, Tobias. But he really wasn't the outdoorsy type. She wasn't surprised to hear that he'd ridden when he could.

An hour later, a low-level debate started between Jol and Pantiar, which eventually resulted in the group stopping. The trail had moved away from the cliff, which was good, but the route was heavily overgrown, which was not good. And now they were at a fork in the trail and apparently neither trail was right.

Sean and Nevaine looked over Jol's shoulder to the map.

"Neither of them?" Sean looked around, but it really only looked like there were two options.

"As I was telling our young friend, there is a third." Pantiar shook his head and pointed to the trails. "That one is death; the other also death. Just different." He scowled at them. "Wish I could recall why I did that. A bit odd, if you ask me."

"There must be a way to find it, even if this map isn't working." Sean looked around. "Or it is but we're not close enough to the right way to find it. Maybe if all of us get closer, the dust will lead us." He had his hand over the pocket with the brick dust in it and motioned Nevaine, Clait, and Jol to step closer to him.

Pantiar looked on. "Might work. There's a lot of power in those bricks."

Sean kept moving the four of them together until they were touching, then slowly started walking them in a circle.

"Or it could just be entertaining," Pantiar said.

Nevaine ignored the laughing ghost and focused on the dust. A slight tug came from a massive rockslide. "I think it's that way."

Sean steered the group back and paused. Then he nodded, followed by Clait and Jol. The rockslide was huge and unstable-looking, yet it appeared that was the way they had to go.

Pantiar scratched his head. Oddly, his hand didn't go through any part of himself, just other things or people. "I can't imagine why I would have sent it that way."

"How are we going to get up there?" Jol didn't look happy as he stared up.

Clait bounded from rock to rock. "Won't be a problem for me, but I know how unstable two feet can be."

Sean walked around the base of the slide. "This doesn't look old. There's nothing growing on these rocks yet." He held out his hand and tilted his head. "I'd say less than two weeks ago, and it was triggered by a spell. We have someone ahead of us."

Chapter Twenty-Two

Pantiar sniffed the rockslide. "Excellent observation, young man. Yes, I'd say eight or nine days ago, a group went through here, with at least one powerful sorcerer." He slapped Sean on the back and somehow made it so his hand didn't pass through him. "You might have a nice challenge facing you. Sadly, I won't be able to help fight, but I shall cheer you on."

Sean didn't look worried at Pantiar's words, but he wasn't happy. He slowly walked around the rockslide and finally picked up a thin trail. "For those of us not on four extremely stable legs or floating around, this will be the best way up. We need to be careful, though; I feel some stronger magic waiting. Whoever did this most likely set some traps." He gave the hillside a scowl, as if that would keep it from flinging spells.

Nevaine didn't sense anything about the path but she'd admit that Sean's battle magic was more suited to the situation. He also had more sorcery than she did, and she wasn't going to stop and see if there was something she could use in her book right now. That was something her father had taught her: when in a group, always make sure people are doing what they do best. Common sense, but it was amazing how many times she saw leaders not do that and either try to take over everything, or force the wrong person into the wrong job. Ego had no place in trying to reach a goal.

Sean led this time, although Jol was right behind him. As soon as they started up the hill, his map came to life and pointed to a winding trail under the rubble. They walked alongside the rocks and downed trees as much as possible, although Clait ran on top of the debris, sniffing with interest at various parts.

Pantiar drifted along, sometimes up ahead, other times behind. She noticed that he gauged how far away from her, and the stone of his she carried, he was at all times. He seemed to be working something out but Nevaine didn't want to interrupt him. For someone who probably hadn't interacted with people in almost a thousand years, he was doing well. But it made sense that he might need to retreat into his own thoughts from time to time.

Even she didn't think this would be a time for trying to read a book, so she studied the things around them. Piallen was the most outdoorsy of the sisters, with Lizeth being the least. Nevaine liked the outdoors, but mostly just as a chance to escape the often annoying people in the palace. And read, of course. She knew that if she managed to survive, complete this Challenge, and be named second heir to the throne, she'd have to deal with more annoyances in the way of the courtiers and nobles of the kingdom. And waving a knife to get them to back off was extremely frowned upon.

That was one thing she was really not looking forward to, and when she had been younger, she had seriously considered abdicating her right to the throne to avoid it. She had very little in the way of diplomatic skills and that most likely wasn't going to change suddenly. She knew how diplomacy worked; she just didn't like a lot of people who were involved in it. But out here, diplomacy wasn't an issue.

Maybe she could see about moving to the wild northern forests of Astarious and be a queen there. Once all three sisters were confirmed, they could spread out within the kingdom.

"What's that?" In her musing, she'd been paying more attention to the debris in the rockslide. "Is that a hand?" Seeing dead bodies wasn't shocking, but nor was it common.

Sean stopped and looked across, but it was Clait who nimbly ran over to it. She sniffed from a few inches away, then rose on her back feet with her mouth partially open.

"It is. But what's odd is that no animals have been after it." She dropped to all four feet and stepped back. "Note that it's intact. And has been sitting here for over a week?" She tilted her head and stared, as if the hand would give her answers. "Scavengers both on the ground and air are all around here, yet none of them came by. That is odd and disturbing." Her tail lashed and she bounded farther up the slide. "Another one here, and I see at least four more." She looked back down. "All intact, no bite marks." She looked ready to go up farther.

"Can you come back down?" Nevaine called as a chill hit her. "I don't want you getting lost, and there is something seriously wrong here." She hadn't felt anything from the rockslide when they started, but she did now. Evil. She couldn't have said what evil felt like until right now. It was as if every dark, horrifying, and nausea-inducing feeling in the world combined into one mass. It was taking everything she had in her not to race down the hill and keep running until she got off the mountain.

Clait twitched her tail and looked ready to keep going up, but came back down.

Sean hadn't stepped closer, but he did hold out his right hand toward the rockslide. That his left hand clearly held a spell of some kind wasn't lost on Nevaine. "Whoever did this hid it well. The sorcerer who caused the rockslide had a group with them. And they're all buried in there."

"That's not good." Pantiar drifted over the slide. "Nor is the fact that the animals have left them be. Nothing can hurt me, but I think the four of you want to run."

He kept his voice so calm, at first Nevaine didn't register what he said.

She wasn't the only one, as everyone stood still for a few moments, then Jol started running back down.

Sean grabbed him. "We have to go up. Besides, it's actually shorter."

Nevaine was in agreement with Jol; up felt worse and the distances were close enough to each other for her.

"The spell wants you to go down. We need to go up." Sean swore as the first hand they'd seen started moving. "Now!" He all but dragged Jol and Nevaine with him as he moved as far away from the rockslide as he could but still went up the hillside. Clait easily kept ahead of them.

"Are they alive? Or like those former guards?" Nevaine didn't slow down, but had to ask. There was no way that anyone should be able to have survived a fall like that, not to mention, it happened over a week ago.

"Not alive, but they're spelled differently than those guards were. I can't tell with what, but I'm thinking it's not good for any of us." Once Sean had gotten Jol and Nevaine following, he raced ahead to find paths. There weren't many here, the one destroyed by the rock slide was probably the main way up, but he kept them moving upward.

A rumbling came from the rockslide, and Nevaine looked over. Four pairs of arms were now forcing their way out of the rocks. That most of them were bent in unnatural conditions answered the how-could-they-be-alive part—they weren't.

"Cozins! It's the end of times!" Jol ran past Nevaine and Sean, yelling.

Clait took off after him. "I'll stop him, but don't dawdle!"

Pantiar drifted above one of the pairs of arms. "Oh dear, this one lost its head. I don't think they're cozins, those being creatures of myth, but I do believe the one who killed them, and caused this mess, also put a reanimate spell on them. Extremely not good. And rude, really." He seemed more annoyed at the spell user in general than the fact that five dead bodies were now crawling out of the rocks. More rocks were moving, indicating there were more completely buried.

Nevaine kept going with the rest, but watched as best she could as the undead corpses shambled free. The one without a head was definitely at a disadvantage. That he'd gotten himself almost completely free of the rocks before tumbling off the far edge of the slide said a lot for the spell that was moving him.

Whoever did this still deserved to die, but it gave her a better understanding of how strong they were. Cozins were the reanimated dead and supposedly brought forth the end of times in some religions. Nevaine had read about them but never thought she'd see them. Or some version of them.

The first one picked up speed as it finally crawled free of the rockslide.

"Shouldn't we do something? I know we're moving faster than it," she looked back; a second one was now free of the rockslide, "them. But I don't think they should be running around." She searched her memory for appropriate spells, but de-animating the dead hadn't been in any of the spells she had studied with her magic tutor.

"I can't stop them." Pantiar drifted over to float alongside them. Seeing him passing through the trees was a bit disturbing, but not as bad as the undead following them. "There's a unique signature on them that is blocking me. I know my wizard spells aren't what they used to be, but this feels aimed at me."

Jol had kept his lead, with Clait slowing him down a little, but not much. Sean stayed as close to Nevaine as the trees allowed, and both of them kept looking back at the slow-moving undead.

"Are they picking up speed?" Nevaine wasn't stopping to check, and looking back while running through a dense forest wasn't a good idea. But they looked closer than she'd thought. And there were now four of them on the trail.

"I believe they are," Pantiar said. "You go ahead. I'm going to see if I can shut them down." He spun around and went back.

Jol and Clait had kept running to the top, but both were standing still with their backs to them when she and Sean made it up there.

"We need to keep going." Sean climbed to the top. "There's—" His voice dropped as he froze, just as the other two had.

Nevaine felt a cackle of electricity in the air, and she kept her head down. The others were frozen because of a spell, and Pantiar was busy dealing with the undead. She was stuck in-between.

First, she calmed her mind. Someone who could freeze a battlemage like Sean wasn't to be messed with. Possibly the same person who caused the slide. But if they had been a week ahead of them, why come back? Had they been waiting for someone to come by all that time? She shook off those thoughts—why they were there wasn't important; what they were doing was. There were a number of spells that could freeze people for a period of time. As far as she knew, none would hold more than an hour and they were extremely difficult to create.

Unfortunately, those undead would be upon them in less time than that. Whatever Pantiar was trying to do wasn't slowing them enough. They were trudging up the slope slowly, but they were still coming. Even if she knew a spell to stop them, it might mean that she wouldn't have enough magic for whatever had frozen her friends.

A shield spell would help let her see what she was facing. Whoever was up there hadn't called out, but possibly knew how many people had been coming up. Sean was frozen the moment he got to the top and from their positions, so were Jol and Clait.

She formed a floating shield spell, one that became stronger as force was thrown against it. It was a low-level magic spell, which helped in case the spell user up top could sense spells—they'd notice this one only once they fired at it and not before. She also wanted an aggressive spell ready. There had been a lightning strike sorcery spell in Gliandra's blue book that had worked well in practice. Unlike most sorcery, it didn't need words, nor finger gestures, which was good; she'd be balancing a magic blocking spell as well as a sorcery lightning one—there wasn't room for anything else. A glance back showed that Pantiar was still trying unsuccessfully to slow the undead and that there were now six. They looked to have uniforms of some kind on, but no weapons.

Whoever was up top was silent. They might have known someone else was down here, but not sure where she was.

Nevaine checked her spells one more time and crept closer to the top. She was exceedingly good at jumping after years of dealing with two sisters who were taller than her. Taking a deep breath, she kept low as she ran the last few feet, then jumped in the air.

There was a cloaked person about fifteen feet in front of her, moving their fingers in a spell. Her shield flared as they flung a spell at her, most likely the same one that had frozen her friends. She immediately called up the lightning spell and hit the cloaked person in the chest.

Her opponent rocked back but didn't fall, and another attack caused her shields to flare.

"Pantiar! I need you!" She hadn't called before to keep where she was a secret. That was over now and clearly he wasn't able to get the undead to stop. "Now!"

The ghost appeared suddenly but kept looking back down the hill. "I've almost got them. What's wrong?"

"Clait, Sean, and Jol are spelled." She grunted as the sorcerer facing her flung a stronger spell against her shields and pushed her backward half a step. "And that thing is probably the one behind those undead, too."

Chapter Twenty-Three

Pantiar moved quickly toward the cloaked person, but was shoved back and off the hill by a massive wind.

Nevaine reinforced her shields and reclaimed her lost step. She couldn't tell much about the person, aside from them being tall, powerful, and having a thing for cloaks. She added a tricky bit to her lightning spell—literal stickiness—it would keep it attached to the person longer. She couldn't increase the spell's power, but she could make it stick.

She flung the spell at the head of the person, figuring that even if it didn't hurt them much, it would be an annoyance. At the same time, she sent a spell breaker at Sean since he was closer than the other two. Running three spells wasn't easy, but it helped that she was extremely good at balancing.

The spell breaker hit Sean but dissolved around him. Yet, she thought she saw his fingers move slightly. The lightning spell hovered around the head of the attacker and while they were still trying to send spells at Nevaine, they were having to focus more on fighting the lightning.

Nevaine sent two more spell breaker spells at Sean, then pulled out two of her knives and threw them at the cloaked mage.

The mage was flinging their hands, trying to get her lightning spell to dislodge, and one of the blades went right into the palm of their hand. The other hit their shoulder. They stumbled at the impact, but it didn't hurt them enough to make them drop their spells.

Sean fell forward as the spell holding him finally shattered. He rolled and bounced to his feet, firing massive strike spells on the cloaked attacker. Jol and Clait were still frozen, but Nevaine needed to keep focus on her lightning spell. Adding the sticky component also allowed her to keep building into it. It hadn't stopped the cloaked mage, but it was seriously slowing them down.

While Sean slowly advanced on the other mage, Nevaine moved to stand in front of Clait and Jol. Pantiar still hadn't reappeared but hopefully he could take care of himself. The mage fired a spell at Sean, but he avoided it. However, it slammed into Nevaine's shields and took them down. Her left arm tingled as the destabilized spell touched her. She shook her arm but the tingle remained. It also felt weaker than before.

Nevaine fed more power into the lightning spell, then sent a spell breaker at Clait and Jol. There was a chance she couldn't protect them. Getting her shields back up now would be problematic at best. The spell that hit her was doing more than tingling; it was also slowing her and her magic down.

She heard rustling behind her, and Clait ran forward, her tail huge. Jol stepped up alongside her and from what she could see, looked terrified. He didn't run away, though.

"Jol, can you see those undead? Or Pantiar?" Without her shields, looking away from the cloaked mage and Sean could prove fatal. Sean was advancing slowly; a spell slowed his movements, but the other mage couldn't freeze him this time.

"I don't see him, or those cozins. Wait...two of the cozins are coming up still." Jol didn't sound as terrified as earlier, but the fact he was still calling them cozins meant he was still freaked. Seeing harbingers of the end of times couldn't be a good thing.

"Keep an eye on them. I'll cover you." Nevaine still hadn't been able to get her full shields up but she did get some little shield blocks she and her sisters used to play with. They were simple, or non-augmented magic, which meant they took less energy. However, she knew they wouldn't last long with the power that the cloaked mage had. Her lightning spell and Sean's measured advancement was slowing the cloaked mage down, but she knew it wouldn't last.

And the tingling in her left arm was getting worse. She couldn't lift it more than a few inches from her side now.

"The cozins are almost upon us!" Now Jol did sound frightened.

Clait stopped marching toward the cloaked mage and turned to Nevaine. "Are you okay here?"

Nevaine nodded, even though she wasn't certain she was actually okay at this point. Her shield blocks had taken hits from the cloaked mage's attack on Sean and only two remained. They could move to block an attack, but two wouldn't be that helpful if the mage decided to go directly after her.

Clait ran to Jol, and Nevaine heard the two of them racing down the hill. Nevaine hoped that Pantiar came back from wherever he was sent. Neither Clait nor Jol had much magic.

Sean reached the mage and waved his hands as if pulling in a powerful sorcery spell, the air crackling around him. Then he punched the mage in the face. Twice.

The cloaked mage stumbled and the pressure against Nevaine's spell blocks dropped. Sean slammed the cloaked mage with a spell that dropped them like a stone.

Yells from behind her indicated that the undead were still coming, and Jol and Clait hadn't stopped them. And still no Pantiar.

Nevaine turned around and raised her right hand, as her left was hanging uselessly now. She threw a spell, one intended to freeze the undead in their tracks. Unfortunately, the numbness in her left arm messed up her balance and the spell went wildly off to the side. Not to mention freezing their feet might just make the things crawl after them.

Taking a deep breath to steady herself, she went for a simpler spell. On living beings it wouldn't work, but there could be a chance with nonliving ones. It was her take-apart spell. A modification of a few non-augmented spells, it literally took things apart. Nothing huge; mostly she'd used it on toy castles when she was young.

Jol and Clait joined her and once both of the undead were close enough, she let the spell go.

Bones flew through the air as they ripped through the tattered uniforms.

"A bit gruesome, but affective," Clait said. "What's wrong with your arm?"

Nevaine tried to move it, but it just hung there. "I got partially hit by a spell. Let's get to Sean."

Clait narrowed her eyes but followed as Jol and Nevaine went where Sean was dealing with the mage.

"Nice move on the punching." Nevaine had never seen that technique before, but it was effective. It distracted the mage enough to allow Sean's spell to knock him out. Sean had shoved back the mage's hood. It hadn't been clear with the hood if the mage had been male or female. It was now. Thick black brows took over the top of his lined face. "He's still alive?"

Sean was patting him down. "Yes. I wanted to find out what he was doing. As for my punching, got that idea from someone who threw two knives in the middle of a magic battle." He smiled and nodded to a rock near him, where her two knives sat. "I wiped them off for you, by the way."

Nevaine had plenty of knives, but losing weapons was never a good idea.

"My magic was limited, and it seemed like a good idea at the time." Nevaine picked up the first knife and got it put away before her left side buckled and she fell.

"Nevaine!" Sean yelled and ran to her as Clait did, too.

"I got nicked by one of the spells our friend was throwing. Numbness in the arm now spreading." Words were getting harder as more of her left side, including her vocal cords, went numb. "Must have been freezing spell, just working slowly."

Sean looked her over, his brow lowering as he studied the spell she'd been hit with. "This one is worse. The freezing one couldn't have killed us. Of course, if we couldn't move, those undead would have taken care of that. The spell you got hit with was meant to kill."

Clait ran to Nevaine's side. "Look at me...just me. Take deep breaths."

When Nevaine was young, she would sometimes have panic attacks. No reason; they just snuck up on her. Clait had always been able to calm her out of them. Nevaine wasn't having a panic attack, but keeping her calm was a great idea right now.

"Can you stop the spell?" She continued to focus on Clait. Spells of this level could act like poison—the more stressed the victim became, the faster they worked. Knowing that and staying calm about it were two different things, though.

"I'm working on it." Sean definitely sounded stressed. "Healing for battlemages is mostly just to keep parts together and functioning until the battle is over."

"Try a jolin spell." Pantiar's voice was so faint, Nevaine thought she imagined it. A dim version of him drifted behind Sean. "I can't help. My wizardry is gone for the moment. But I still know things."

Nevaine wasn't sure about the "at the moment" aspect. From the tone of Pantiar's voice, he wasn't either. She pushed that thought aside and went back to staying as calm and relaxed as she could. "Is it getting colder?" Nevaine shook as a chill overtook her.

Clait climbed halfway on her. "Jol, get blankets!"

Nevaine felt the blankets on her, but they didn't help against the cold. Staying calm was getting harder. She'd heard of people lost in snowdrifts who just wanted to curl up and sleep. Unless found quickly, they died that way. Nevaine felt herself wanting to do the same. It would be so much easier just to sleep.

"That mage is vile. He's added so many spells to this thing, I'm having a hard time breaking them down." Sean was fighting the spell creation, but it hung on.

"Seriously, try the jolin spell. It's simplistic but should buy you time." The faded-looking Pantiar looked around. "I think we need to leave soon."

"I'll try but it won't remove what's attacking her." Sean muttered some words and his fingers flicked. Whatever spell he was trying, it was one based in sorcery.

Nevaine felt warmed and a new type of tingling on her left side. The kind after falling asleep on an arm as the blood rushed back in. Hopefully that was a good thing.

"I can pull this spell out, but it's got to go somewhere." Sean looked back toward the still unconscious mage. "I'd wanted to find out who he was and if he'd come with others."

Nevaine felt more warmth flood her body; now it was becoming uncomfortable. "It's fighting back." She was able to grab Sean's arm with her left hand, which was good, but her body feeling like it was burning up wasn't.

"Hang on. We just have to get through this part. Clait, keep her calm." Sean's face was a mix of fear and determination as he kept the spell going.

Nevaine gritted her teeth and focused on keeping her breath steady. Easier to say than do as fire raced through her body.

It felt like hours later that Sean rocked back and her body started feeling normal.

"I'd say I wasn't sure if the cure was worse than the attack, but at least I'm not dead." She didn't sit up but looked over to the cloaked mage. "It's in him now?"

"Yup." Sean sounded exhausted. "I added a trap spell to it when I sent it over. It should keep him trapped."

Clait watched Nevaine closely, then nodded. "You'll be all right now." She got off Nevaine and marched to the attacker. "He got what he deserves. Did you find anything of interest on him?"

"No. Which makes me think he might have been left here to slow us down, just as those undead were." Sean grinned down at Nevaine. "Good job on those, by the way."

Nevaine slowly sat up with his help. "I only got rid of the last two."

Pantiar bobbed closer. "I was able to get rid of the other four before I was hit." He still looked incredibly faint; the trees and rocks behind him made it difficult to see him well. But he sounded better.

"So, there's someone ahead who's worse than cozins and a killer sorcerer?" Jol paled. "I felt his power when he froze me. It was strong, and he was going to take joy in seeing me destroyed."

Nevaine watched him carefully. They needed him and his map to get to the location and the golden grigeen. Whether it was her Challenge or not, she felt it in her stomach—the grigeens needed this thing to be found. Right now, Jol looked like running down the mountain screaming was a possibility.

Sean and Clait clearly picked up on it as well, as they both moved closer to him.

Pantiar was scowling down at the sorcerer, but picked up on the fear and turned to Jol. "I see the fear in you. And it's rightfully there. But know this: I can't directly lead anyone to the place where these relics are stored; I can only help. And thanks to this man, I am fading faster than before. They need you and your map to get them there." His voice was kind, yet trying to make sure Jol realized how serious things were. "Most of the items that are stored would cause untold pain and suffering if anyone in the Offialian Empire gained access to them. I will be gone soon, I believe. And without my presence, all of my protection spells will fade. Those relics will be free for any who want them."

Jol looked between Pantiar, Sean, and Nevaine. Then he turned to Clait. "And somehow, something in there can help the grigeens? Free them?"

Pantiar gave a small smile. "I believe so. There is a relic, the one your friends are after, that might change everything for the grigeens."

Jol nodded. "I'll stay with you then. But know that I don't have much magic."

"You have a sword, though." Nevaine put her second knife away. Everything was stiff, but she could move again.

"Not very good at that either." He shrugged. "But I'll try." He held up his map, waved it around, then glared at it. "It doesn't seem to be working."

Everyone crowded in closer, but the page was blank.

Pantiar narrowed his eyes and drifted over to the spelled mage. "He did it. He didn't kill you, but the spell that froze you broke the tie to the map. We've found the reason for the attack. I'd say someone, or someones, knew you had that map and had been waiting for you."

"I thought you said the person who killed, or in this case, disconnected, the map holder, couldn't claim it?" Nevaine asked.

"They can't. Which indicates there are more ahead of us," Pantiar said.

Chapter Twenty-Four

"How far can you go again?" Sean asked Pantiar.

Pantiar winced. "Far shorter than before. Probably only a few feet. That limitation was what snapped me back when that mage shoved me off the cliff." He turned to Nevaine. "Guard that stone well. I fear that without it, I would vanish completely."

Nevaine patted the stone in her pocket. "I will."

Sean shrugged. "Then we connect someone else to that map, and go slowly. I presume it can't be the same person who held it before?"

Pantiar's head shake sent him off to the left. "Alas, no. It also wouldn't connect with Clait. It has to be one of you two."

"Me," Nevaine said, a moment before Sean could get his words out. "It makes sense. You are stronger than me, and if we need defending, you can focus on that, while I'll focus on the map." She held out her hand, and Jol gave it to her. He didn't look crushed at no longer being in charge of it.

"I can do it; we don't know what effect it will have." Sean looked over to Jol. "No offense, but you took a huge risk linking to it."

Jol stayed silent, but he paled a bit. That probably hadn't been made clear to him.

"No, we don't, but again, it makes sense that it's not you. You're the best one to fix things if they go horribly wrong. Now, how do we do this? If this man was with others, they might be coming back once they think that we're dead." She wasn't sure why they hadn't been attacked already.

Sean looked ready to argue but Clait walked over to him. "I don't like it either, but she's making good points. It's sort of her thing. She's also the best debater I've ever seen. She *will* win. It's easier to surrender."

Sean let out a sigh and quickly explained how she could claim the map. The claimant had to have a little bit of magic at least, as it stayed connected to them by that. Once the spell was set, she held up the map and it slowly came to life.

"That way." She took the lead but Clait ran alongside. Jol followed and Sean stalked behind, looking annoyed and waiting for someone to dare to attack them. Pantiar drifted nearby.

Nevaine's mind wandered to the Sean situation as the trail was empty. If that mage had others with him, they were hiding or following them so stealthily that neither Sean nor Clait noticed. Which would be almost impossible to pull off.

She'd felt Sean's terror at losing her when he was fighting against the spell that had been trying to kill her. He was handsome, funny, smart, and brave. Then why was she still holding off on her feelings for him? She admitted that she'd been falling for him pretty hard before the issue of him supposedly running away.

His kidnapping of her, while based on real fears she would die, was one sticking point. The Challenge was important to her, and his need to protect her could have cost her everything. That, plus his lying about not only having magic, and sorcery, but being a battlemage. Lying for any reason infuriated her, and being over-protective was something even her parents learned not to do around her. She was the smallest of her sisters and had been sick as a baby. But by the time she was five, she fought to be allowed to do things on her own.

Now she had a better grasp as to why she was holding back about him, but sadly, she didn't have a solution. Of course, they both could still die on this trip. Pessimistic, but it would resolve things.

"And that sigh was for what?" Clait kept watching everything around them, her white tail low.

"Nothing." But Nevaine glanced back to Sean as he scowled at bushes as they passed.

"Ah. That one is a quandary. He does care about you. Strongly. I felt it when he was healing you." She looked up. "But I know that's not the issue."

"No, it's not. But this also isn't the time." Nevaine froze as a shadow moved ahead of them. Pantiar was still floating along off to her left, so it wasn't him. Before she could say anything, another shadow darted. "Attack!" she yelled, and then put the map back in her tunic and drew her sword and one of her knives. Her magic felt odd after the spell connecting her to the map, so she stuck with mundane weapons.

Sean and Jol ran up to her with their swords out. Sean was also flicking his fingers in a sorcery spell. Pantiar came closer, then darted ahead. Nevaine knew he couldn't go far away from her and his rock, but didn't know what would happen if he tried.

The shadows hadn't continued, nor was there any sign of people—but something was there. She felt it crawling along her skin. Magic—or rather, sorcery—and not a good spell. "Do you all feel that too?" She kept her voice low.

All three whispered agreements.

"There's something unnatural out there," Sean added. "Worse than those undead."

"Worse?" Jol clamped his left hand over his mouth as the word came out too loud.

"Slouts." Clait managed to both hiss the word and make it sound like a swearword. "They were eradicated from our lands long ago. Obviously, not here."

Nevaine took a moment to match the word with anything she'd read. Nothing. "And they are?"

"They are tree guardians gone wrong. Sprites whose only intention is to kill. The result of a bad wizard spell." Clait glared at where Pantiar had gone.

"How do we fight them?" Jol managed to keep his voice lower.

"You don't. I do. Stay here." Clait raced into the trees before anyone could move.

"Damn it. I'm going after her," Sean said.

Nevaine grabbed his arm. "Don't. I trust her with my life, and if she needs us to stay back, it's for our protection. Grigeen magic isn't like ours." There was a lot more to it than that, but this wasn't the time to argue. When Nevaine had been twelve, there had been a creature of some sort, she was never told what, hunting just outside the grigeen area. She'd wanted to see and followed Clait and a few other grigeens. And had almost been swallowed by the earth when the grigeens worked their magic. She'd stayed clear when Clait told her to ever since.

Sean clenched his sword, and looked ready to go anyway.

"Please. For me, don't go after her." Nevaine gripped his arm harder. She physically couldn't stop him from following, but hopefully she could get it through his handsome, yet thick, head that sometimes protecting people wasn't the best option.

"Fine." He looked exceedingly unhappy about it, and increased his spell, but he stayed still.

"That little thing is going to kill a bunch of monsters?" Jol sounded like he was revisiting that running away option.

"Kill might be a bit much, but she's capable of it. She will make sure they are no longer a threat. Pantiar's out there too, so he might be able to guide her." Nevaine shifted her grip on her sword as she waited.

There was nothing. No sounds of fighting, chittering, yelling, or rustles in the trees and shrubs—nothing. Which was actually harder to wait through than hearing a fight. A part of her wanted to run in and protect Clait, even though she knew that could endanger the grigeen.

After what seemed like hours, a dirty, but proudly strutting, Clait came back to them. "We can continue now, but those things were set on us by someone. We need to be wary."

Pantiar followed her. "That was impressive. I always knew that grigeens were the best of the best. I'd like to find that wizard who changed those slouts. Give him or her a what-what." He shook his almost transparent fist, then shrugged. "Maybe I'll find them in the afterlife."

"Are you sure you're okay?" Nevaine didn't see any injuries, but it was sometimes difficult to see with Clait's thick fur.

"Just dirty." Clait scowled at the offending dirt. "I shall deal with it later." She turned and started back down the trail. "You might want to get that map out again."

Nevaine shook her head and took out the map. She'd been around grigeens her entire life but it seemed she was still learning about them. "Stay on this trail. It will only show one section at a time, so I can't tell how long we stay on it."

"Aye, the ones who spelled me with it, said it would do that." Jol nodded as he stayed close behind her while they walked.

"I don't understand why someone who had this thing, and knew what it was supposed to be, let you buy it?" Nevaine held the map at eye level so if any sudden changes popped up, she'd catch them.

"I thought it was weird too. But Hin made a deal with them and for some reason the lady who sold it to us couldn't use it."

"Maybe not a sorcerer." Sean was back to scowling at the woods around them but was keeping closer now. "It won't work without sorcerous ability."

"I can't really use a lot of sorcery just yet, but good to know it just needed the ability. But wouldn't someone who had the map, and knew how to get in, want to follow the person they sold the map to? I'm guessing they weren't the most upstanding people?"

Sean nodded. "I've been keeping watch as we switched back and forth on the trail. No one is following us. But that's probably who's ahead of us. Their timing was off because of Hin and Jol waiting for their magic users, then being with us. Following Jol would have been noticeable in the plains but if they had a general idea where we'd be heading, they could get ahead and wait."

"They could have been at this game for a while. But if that mage back there had been working with them, he could have been spelled to the map." There was plenty of speculation in her comments, but there was also a lot of weirdness about this entire situation.

Pantiar turned to say something, then vanished.

"Pantiar? Where are you?" Nevaine knew the attack by the mage had left the ghost weak, but they needed him to hang on until they found the place where he'd hidden his relics. The map worked to get them to the spot, but not inside. They needed him for that.

They waited for a few minutes, but when he didn't reappear, Nevaine kept following the map. "He can't go far, since I've got the stone. We need to find this place soon." She shoved aside the thought that he might be gone for good.

They kept walking for a while, the trail splitting twice, when Pantiar popped in just as if they'd been talking. "That's probably because that one had already been connected to it. I felt it when he was unconscious." Pantiar looked around. "How did we get here?"

"You vanished almost an hour ago." Nevaine found it hard to talk to someone she could barely see, but aimed her gaze at where his head appeared to be.

"What? That's impossible." He drifted about. The trees here were getting thinner as they were climbing higher. "We were just talking about the map and that mage."

"And then you vanished." Sean had drifted a bit more to the back.

"This is not good. Were you attacked while I was gone? Can you walk faster?" He moved ahead of Nevaine and Clait.

"No, we weren't attacked while you were gone, and not sure on the moving faster." They were already moving at a brisk pace, but the altitude was getting to her. And to Sean and Jol as well, apparently. Nevaine was from an area that was close to sea-level. The town Sean was from was a bit higher, but not by much. Judging from the harsh breathing from Jol, he was from someplace lower as well.

Grigeens apparently simply didn't have issues with breathing and altitude no matter where they lived, as Clait seemed to be free of problems.

"Oh, yes. Forgot about the thinner air. Okay, just come along, I'll dart ahead." He took off ahead of them before she could remind him about the tie to his rock. He slammed back toward her almost immediately.

"What was that? Did you spell me?" He glared around.

"The rock I carry? The one from your clearing that you can't move too far away from? Remember?"

He continued glaring, then eased off. "Ah, yes. Forgot about that for a bit. Carry on." His voice was light and cheerful, but from what Nevaine could see of his face, he didn't feel that way. He was worried, and so was she.

The trail went on for another half hour, then stopped. Nevaine walked around the area slowly, holding out the map, but nothing. It didn't respond, and there wasn't a trail she could see.

"There's someone here." Sean kept his voice low, and Clait's tail poofed out.

Nevaine wasn't sure if she sensed anything, but there was a stillness around them. And they'd been waiting for whoever was working with that mage to show themselves. Since the map had only been showing small sections at a time, she had no idea how close they were to the cave with the relics.

Chapter Twenty-Five

Pantiar drifted a few feet into the bush, but at this point his capacity to move away from Nevaine and the rock was so limited that his ability to spy was useless.

"There's a spell over the ground and trees." Clait kept close, but was sniffing furiously. "It's an old one, not old like our ghost, but at least a year or so. And it's been regularly updated." Her tail lashed. "It is another immobilization spell, but it hasn't been triggered yet."

"Aye, a year ago. That's when the rumors of the map started. They claimed to have found it in an old ruin." Jol stayed a bit behind the others.

"The map is old. It's been fiddled with for sure, but the basic part was made by a wizard." Pantiar drifted to the edges of his range, then back. "I would like to know which wizard did it. But whoever it was, they weren't the ones behind this spell around you. I could try to displace it...but not sure how much ability I have left."

"No," Sean and Nevaine said at the same time. Sean nodded to her to continue. "We might need your remaining wizardry later. One of us can deal with the spell. It also could be why the map isn't showing a direction."

"And since you have the map, I get this." Sean smiled at Nevaine. "I'll need to get a bit farther ahead of everyone to break down the spell."

Jol stepped closer to Nevaine. "I'll stay here. Make sure the map stays safe." From his twitchiness, he was more worried about him being safe.

Sean stalked off into the woods, and Nevaine focused on spells. Oddly, while her magic abilities felt strained and peculiar since her connection to the map, her sorcerous abilities felt stronger. She mentally reviewed what she'd read in Gliandra's blue book.

If the attack was broad, having a wide spell would be a better idea than something tightly focused like her lightning spell. Unfortunately, she hadn't read very far in that book, and now was not the time to try to catch up. One of the spells came to mind, though. A defensive one, it would deflect an attack from force or magic. She preferred the more aggressive spells in her studies, but this might be a case where defense was better. Not to mention, this was the only wide sorcery spell she had read so far. The finger movements were simple, just a sign repeated by the left hand. The words were as well, although they weren't ones she understood; the translation and word emphasis had been in the book. She traded the map for a knife, and set the spell. It took two tries as the finger movement had been trickier than it seemed. But she finally felt the spell flow from her.

Clait was a few feet ahead of her, but turned to nod when she felt Nevaine's spell moving over her. Jol stepped even closer. But if he sensed the spell, he didn't react.

Pantiar had been drifting to the left, but came back. "They're coming. I don't sense Sean, though."

Nevaine paused, but she couldn't stop her spell now. Regardless of what she and Sean might end up as, she couldn't think of him injured. Or worse. Taking a deep breath to push worry aside, she focused on the spell.

Unlike the spell that appeared to be invisibly masking everything, hers crackled with light-green and blue arcs. Made sense—one of the best defenses was to make your opponent think twice before attacking. And this spell should make them think twice. Any force against it was slammed back into the user. She wondered how that worked with physical weapons.

"Shouldn't you have your sword?" Jol whispered at her side.

She shook her head, but turned it enough that he could see she was repeating a spell under her breath. Experienced sorcerers could drop the words on some spells—she didn't have that skill yet. And explaining that her knives were better weapons for her than her sword wouldn't make a difference.

Three opponents came from the front and both sides. If there were any behind her, they were making a lot less noise than these three.

Her guess would be that the first one, the one ahead of her, was the sorcerer casting the spell: a tall woman, with dark hair pulled back, and a nasty snarl as she stalked forward. She was coming from the direction Sean had gone, but there was no way to know what had happened to him.

Either the sorceress didn't sense the spell Nevaine cast, or she believed the crackling arcs were for show. The woman shook her head and fired off a disable spell.

It hit Nevaine's spell, but instead of making it weaker, it seemed to fuel it. The spell slammed back at the woman, and she barely dodged out of the way. She wasn't looking so smug now.

The two people on the sides, a man and a woman, charged forward with swords raised. She threw her knife and quickly grabbed a second one.

The man took the knife in his shoulder but it wasn't enough to stop him. He'd just reached the perimeter of her spell when the crackling arcs grabbed his sword and flung it—and him, since he wouldn't or couldn't let go—far off into the trees.

Jol fought with the second woman until they got close to Nevaine's spell. This time, the spell shoved the opponent back a few feet.

"Get back within the spell," Nevaine called out. She wasn't sure why there was a change in reaction to force from her spell, but it wasn't good.

"Aw, a scared new sorceress. Whoever taught you should have pointed out that going against a strong sorcerer is a bad idea. That spell will just slow me, not stop me." The sorceress flashed her shields and started moving forward.

Nevaine wasn't sure if the spell the woman was using could get through to them or not. The woman guard Jol had fought was back to creeping forward outside of the perimeters, but the one who'd gone flying hadn't returned.

Still no sign of Sean.

"Oh, if you're waiting to be saved by your friend, I'm afraid he's gone." The sorceress took a few more slow steps. She was on the edge of Nevaine's spell, but it wasn't pushing her back.

Nevaine ignored her fear about Sean. Obviously, if this woman had seen them all together, she'd noticed that he was missing and was trying to use that to mess with Nevaine's head. Instead, she focused on strengthening her spell. She'd confirmed where the concealment spell was coming from. The spell the woman was casting was low enough, and she was strong enough that she was only slightly impacted by Nevaine's spell.

Increasing the power to the spell did slow the sorceress down more, but she was still coming for Nevaine.

Jol yelled and ran for the sorceress in a massive move of heroic stupidity—but one Nevaine might be able to use. As he raised his sword to strike her, the sorceress raised her hand to probably spell him into something nasty.

Nevaine took a chance, charged her knife with her lightning spell, and threw it just to the left of the sorceress. The woman saw her movement and turned to block it. The knife struck her in the upper chest, but the kicker was the fireball that hit the woman from behind.

The pressure of the concealment spell vanished as a beat up, but still very much alive, Sean came up behind the sorceress. The sorceress was fighting back from his fire spell, but then Nevaine dropped her own spell and pulled her destabilizing spell together. This one required a lot of balancing, and Nevaine still hadn't made it work right. And it was drawn from magic, not sorcery. Her magic still felt weird but she unleashed the spell as the sorceress was extinguishing Sean's fireball.

Nevaine's spell flung the sorceress in the air, spinning her madly, then dropped her to the ground. If it worked, she'd be too disoriented to walk, let alone cast spells, for at least an hour.

"What did you do?" The sorceress collapsed and couldn't lift her head.

"More importantly, what were you trying to do?" Nevaine asked as she and Sean moved toward her.

Sean sneered down at the sorceress. "She and her friends—they're dead now, by the way—had a racket going to rob relic hunters. They even had a torin stone. Those suck out magic and allow the owner to claim the magic for their own. I've only seen one once in a museum, and it had been disabled. Nasty things." Sean rubbed his face where a long slash bled, then leaned into the sorceress's face. "I destroyed that too."

"You lie." She tried to get up, but fell back. "No one would turn that down. You took the stored magic, didn't you? You're going to betray these people in the end, take their powers and all the relics for yourself."

As she spoke, a dark feeling came over Nevaine. Sean *was* a battlemage, and power was the most important thing to them. How did she know he wouldn't do just what the sorceress said?

Then Nevaine shook her head. "Damn sneaky little spell there, my friend. But that just makes mine work harder to block you. I'd drop yours immediately." Nevaine's spell was working as she'd designed it. It would keep the opponent down and unable to use most magic or sorcery. If they surrendered to it and did nothing, they'd be free in an hour. If they fought, they'd never get free.

However, Jol was starting to stalk Sean.

Sean was watching Nevaine, though. "I wouldn't do that. The stone is destroyed. I can show you where the remains are. The pieces will still have residue of the magic she stole."

"I believe you. She cast a trust spell to get us to believe her." Nevaine looked where the sorceress still struggled against the spell trapping her. "And she's still not releasing it. You're going to die if you don't let go."

Jol paused as the spell faded, and he shook his head. "Why was I going after Sean?" He quickly lowered his sword and stepped back.

"She was getting in your head," Clait said as she sniffed the sorceress. "You're lucky it was her who went after you and not me." She bared her teeth, turned, and flung her back feet.

"Sean, do you need healing?" Nevaine looked him over. He had clearly been in a serious fight, but it didn't look like anything was broken.

He shook his head tightly. "I'm fine."

Pantiar had faded out at some point at the start of the fight, but he seemed more aware of what had taken place while he was gone. "Troxilan sorcery. Pah. Cheap charlatans. Now, I believe we should get moving. And if they really had a torin stone, we need to grab those pieces." He looked at his transparent hands. "Well, you do. Preferably the one who destroyed the stone."

Nevaine took out her map. "Yup, the stretch is shorter than before, but it's working again. Where did you destroy the stone?"

"You don't think I did it." It wasn't a question, nor was it an accusation. But his eyes were filled with sorrow more than pain from his injuries.

"Of course I think you destroyed it." Nevaine kept walking to get away from the sorceress. "It was her spell that messed with us."

"But a tiny part of you isn't completely sure." He kept pace alongside her but didn't look over.

"I am sure." She dropped it as they came across a group of bodies. Signs of heavy magic showed on all of them.

"Wow. Glad you never went after me with magic." Jol stayed as far away from the bodies as possible.

"We trust you, Sean. Just take us where you left the stone. I agree with Pantiar that the pieces shouldn't be left behind. Those things are dangerous until they are ground to dust—and not by any power we have here." Nevaine had heard of them, in more than one of her books. However, she'd almost relegated them to myth as no one writing the books had reported having actually seen one.

Sean nodded and led them off to the right, where a large boulder sat. He reached behind it and pulled out what looked like a handful of rocks that glimmered in the light through the trees. "What's the best way to carry these?" He turned to Pantiar, who floated over them, scowling.

"They won't do any damage as long as they don't get magically put back together. Put some in your pack and scatter the rest on your person. You'll be safe."

Sean dropped some in his pack, then scattered the rest in his pockets.

"Couldn't we divide them? Is it dangerous for him to have them all?" Nevaine wasn't worried about Sean grabbing the magic for himself at this point. But powerful items, even if broken, often had nasty side effects.

Sean looked up, but Pantiar spoke first.

"I wouldn't recommend it. The threat to Sean isn't a big one, but dividing them could affect all of you."

Nevaine got it; Sean would take any magic hits by carrying all of the pieces, but hopefully she and the others could help him if something went wrong. She hated it, but she understood it. "Fine. Let's get going." She paused as she passed Sean. "Are you sure you don't need any healing? You won the fight, but you look rough. We've no idea what we'll come up against."

"I'll be fine." He shrugged but was keeping some distance between them. "And not knowing what we'll face is a good reason not to heal minor wounds. You might need that power later on." He didn't sound angry, but he did look like he was still dealing with her lack of trust in him.

Something they'd have to deal with later—like maybe when they got home. The sorceress had tapped into Nevaine's nagging concerns with her spell.

The trail here was almost treeless, with just a few hardy stragglers. The map continued to add bits of the path as they went, but much slower and in smaller sections. Everyone was lost in thought as they approached another trail split.

Nevaine took a step toward the lower trail, then another to the upper one. "And we're stuck again. I'm not feeling a pull from either the brick dust or the map on either direction." She stepped back to let the others try. She couldn't hand over the map, but the brick dust had helped them before.

All three tried and stepped back with shrugs. Pantiar drifted about, looking at an odd plant.

"Pantiar? Do you remember any of this?"

He looked up with a start. "What? Hrm. Actually, I recall this *plant*." He beamed at the spiky shrub with bright orange and yellow flowers. "They are hynerian roses. Almost impossible to grow in this environment—too cold for them; they like swamps." His grin grew larger as he looked around at their faces. "Unless they were spelled to grow here. By someone who loved them and was setting up a hiding spot."

Nevaine didn't see anything that looked to be a cave or something that could hold a bunch of relics. "Where?"

"Ah. Here." Pantiar couldn't anchor himself well, but moved to the exact spot between the two trails and drifted above it.

"I only see dirt. Has he gone mad?" Jol kept his voice low and didn't look over to Pantiar.

"Not mad, my boy—giddy. Taking care of this will set me free. I'm sure of it. And it's right here!" Pantiar made a triumphant gesture with arms in the air, then scowled. "It is here, I know it. Just can't seem to trigger the spell." He muttered a few spell-sounding words, and did the move with his arms again—and still nothing.

Nevaine went to him. "It has been hundreds of years. Maybe the location is somewhere else?"

"No. The roses were how I marked it. They could never grow here without the spell I left on them. I just need more magic."

Clait came closer to him. "What about the brick dust? Mine is embedded in my coat, but those three have some loose."

Nevaine pulled out her dust, followed by Sean and Jol. There would be no way to get all of it, since it had been shoved in her pocket, but she got the majority of it. "And what should we do with it, oh wise one?"

Clait grinned. "I'd suggest sprinkling it over Pantiar, give him a boost."

"But it'll just go right through him, won't it?" Jol still wasn't looking at Pantiar.

"Actually, that might work. The essence is what would stick with me, sort of like Clait still having it on her, even though it's passed through her fur." He looked around, then drifted a foot or two closer to them. "Probably have all of you do it at once, but move back to the trail after you release it. I might be a foot or two off on where it is."

Sean and Jol looked doubtful, but all three stepped up together and dropped their dust on Pantiar and quickly went back to the trail. It looked like it was just passing through him, but then the dust started sparkling and falling slower.

Pantiar smiled and opened his mouth to yell, but no words came out. Then he and the dust vanished, and the mountain began to shake.

Chapter Twenty-Six

Nevaine and the others dropped low as the shaking continued and the few trees swayed back and forth. The shaking lasted at least a minute, then stopped. Pantiar was still missing, but a faint shadow, much larger than him, was forming where he'd stood.

Sean was the first to his feet, with a spell held in his fist. Nevaine and Jol followed, although Jol only held his sword. Clait stalked toward the image slowly, like she was hunting prey.

"What is it?" Jol didn't move.

"No idea, but maybe you should stay here, just in case something goes after us." Sean gave Jol a smile and followed Clait, with Nevaine on his heels.

A chill flowed through Nevaine as they moved closer. "It's turning into something solid. We might need to wait. That goes for you too, Clait." The image was becoming less transparent and had developed a bit more shape, but it was still difficult to see what it was becoming.

"Is Pantiar inside that?" Jol had taken a step closer, probably out of curiosity.

"No idea." Sean was still in the front, but had stopped at Nevaine's suggestion.

The coldness grew worse, but eventually a cave appeared. In the middle of nowhere, with nothing around it. Just a random cave.

Clait took off running and dodged inside as soon as it was solid.

Nevaine yelled, but Clait was gone, so she started to run after her.

Sean grabbed her arm. "We need to find out how safe it is first."

She removed his hand from her arm. "I'm following her. Come with us, or not." She raced after Clait. The coldness intensified as she was swallowed in darkness. She felt Sean run in after her, but couldn't see anything.

Then Sean called up a torch spell and held it high. They were inside a cave, but it was just them. No Clait, no Pantiar, and no dangerous relics.

"This wasn't what I was expecting." Nevaine kept her voice down as she and Sean surveyed the area.

"Nevaine? Walk through the back wall." It was Clait's voice, but she sounded extremely far away.

Sean looked to Nevaine and motioned for her to go. She smiled; he was learning that protecting her wasn't always needed. The back wall looked solid, even with Sean and his torch spell moving closer to it.

"Okay. Let's go through together." Nevaine grabbed his free hand and they stepped into the wall. That was possibly one of the weirdest feelings she'd ever had. It was like walking through a few feet of tree sap. But they came out into a brightly lit room with a tail-lashing Clait and a solid-looking Pantiar.

"My friends! You made it!" Pantiar rushed forward and shook both of their hands. He was not only solid now, he looked younger than he had. Much younger.

"How are you like this?" Nevaine looked around. This was more as she expected. Far more relics than she could immediately count filled shelves and wooden boxes. None of them had any dust and all looked new.

"It's the magic I left here. The dust you all gave me helped me open the passage, but it wasn't until I got inside that the rest of the transformation occurred. It's a good thing you found me. That map of yours wouldn't have gotten you in."

"Why didn't you tell us?" Sean had dropped his torch spell but was now making a slow walk around the room—carefully not touching anything.

"I forgot." Pantiar shrugged. "Being dead can do that to a person."

"So, you're no longer dead?" Nevaine knew wizardry was vastly different than magic or sorcery, but she had a hard time believing that it could bring someone back to life after almost a thousand years of being dead.

He shook his head cheerfully. "Still dead, can't change that. But this is a repository of my wizardry and powers. It is tied to me, and I to it."

"Then when it is destroyed, you'll be gone?" Nevaine had gotten used to the odd ghost, and even though he was dead, she was going to miss him.

"I am afraid so, but it's not a sad thing. I do believe my spirit stayed here because of these and the damage they could cause if they were released into the world. Even the one you want, the golden grigeen, could cause untold mayhem in the wrong hands." He tilted his head, then turned to Clait. "Please go get your friend. There are more armed people coming this way. I can hide this, but he will be exposed."

Clait darted through the wall immediately.

Nevaine looked where she'd vanished. "Maybe we should get him. Jol isn't sure about strange magics."

Pantiar frowned. "No, I feel that you two will have to fight when you leave this place. You should both only leave when we are certain you will survive the battle." He tilted his head and looked up to the ceiling. "Or battles. Could be more than one...I can't see that for certain. Clait can go back and forth."

Nevaine tried to look at the relics, but she stayed near the wall they'd come through. No matter what Pantiar said, if Clait wasn't back soon, she was going after her.

"She'll be fine." Sean had come next to her without her noticing. "Don't you get annoyed at someone trying to rescue you?"

"There's a difference between being overly protective and helping someone if they're under attack." Nevaine knew the difference was thin, but they were different things. "I wouldn't try to stop Clait from something she needed to do."

The rest of their conversation was cut off by Jol's whimpering as he came through the rock. Clait preceded him, looking annoyed.

"He is stubborn." She shook her fur and stood back as Jol entered the room. His face was pale and he had his sword raised in shaking hands.

"This is real?" He pointed to the rock wall behind him. "I went through rock. Real rock?" He started twitching.

"Yup. Looks like our friend here has reconnected to his power. Glad you listened to Clait and came in." Sean removed Jol's sword from his hands.

Probably a good idea.

"It wasn't me. Those people Pantiar mentioned were making enough noise to raise the dead." Clait turned to the ghost. "No offense."

Pantiar grinned. "None taken. Now let's see what we can do to sort these. Jol can keep one; I will select some to choose from that won't cause problems. And you will take the golden grigeen, once I find it, but the rest must be sorted and destroyed."

"Why do we have to sort them?" Sean asked. "Just find the ones we're keeping and blast the rest."

Nevaine laughed as Pantiar shook his head. "Because they're all different magics, I take it?"

"Smart girl." Pantiar waggled his finger at Sean. "I had hopes for you, my boy, but you *do* have to think beyond that battlemage training. That's what's wrong with this country—too much focus on fighting. I know you're not from here—well, you were, but not now—and those two with you definitely aren't, but even *your* kingdom should focus on logic and spell craft."

Jol had still been recovering, but he caught Pantiar's words. "I thought you folks were just from another part of the empire?"

Nevaine and Sean shared a look, and she shrugged to let him respond.

Sean nodded. "We're from another land completely, and it's safer if we don't tell you where or how and why we're here."

Jol opened his mouth to ask questions, then shook his head. "Okay, then. I'd rather not know, to be honest." He turned to Pantiar. "So how do we sort these? And are you certain those folks outside can't get here? There sounded to be a lot. And all heavily armed."

Pantiar walked to the closest pile of relics. "Until we finish this task, they can't even see, nor feel, should they walk over, this place. But I need to reiterate, once we've destroyed these, and I can be free, this place will vanish and you four will be standing in the middle of where it stood. You must be prepared to run."

"I thought you said we had to fight?" Sean still wasn't touching any relics but he'd followed Pantiar over to the side.

"Yes, but that would only be if you have to. The best choice is to run." He gave a sideways look to Sean. "You will find allies once you get off my mountain. And then that battle training will come into play."

Nevaine wasn't certain about the logic of that. The trail down to the plains was long, and there would be a lot of places to be ambushed along the way. "Four of us against an untold group of armored fighters?"

Pantiar waved his hands dismissively. "I'll explain more once we've grouped these things together. But it is doable." His smile seemed forced, though.

Nevaine knew what he was thinking—their odds of surviving once this place vanished weren't great. But she felt the power coming from the piles of relics around them. If this many high-powered items fell into the hands of any kingdom, even her own beloved

Astarious, the repercussions would be horrific. It was worth risking themselves to keep these things out of the hands of others.

"Where do we start?" She followed Pantiar and Sean. Clait did as well. Although she could easily pick up things with her paws, her assistance would be limited to smaller items.

Jol stood in the middle, looking unsure. "I can help, I guess. My sorcery isn't strong, though."

Pantiar turned, put his hands on his hips, and looked Jol up and down. "Never underestimate your gifts, my boy. Why don't you start on this section here, along with Clait. Lesser magics in these but they still need to be handled carefully." He pointed to a table that contained much smaller relics. "When you touch one, it will let you know what its core is. There are four main groups: Qul, Wai, Hau, and Lu'um—the four powers of wizardry."

Those words didn't mean anything to Nevaine, and Sean narrowed his eyes as he picked up a large bowl.

"It's hot." Not enough for him to drop it, but he kept moving his fingers.

"Aye, that's Qul—fire." Pantiar looked pleased, as if he'd just invented fire himself. "Put those there." He motioned to a spot along the wall. "I want you to feel all of them so you know what to expect. Each of you take the one closest to you."

Nevaine reached for what looked like an engraved rock. Although it was clean, her hands felt like they'd just dug into one of the gardens back home. "Dirt?"

"Close enough. Earth. That's Lu'um. Put those over there." Pantiar pointed to another section along the wall.

Clait picked up a golden pendent. "Ah, if my old magic languages hold true, this is Wai, water. Feels like a cool stream flowing over my paws."

"It is." Pantiar's grin grew wider as he pointed to a third section.

Jol cautiously picked up a small brooch. Then scowled. "I don't feel anything."

Pantiar stepped over to him. "Nothing? Are you certain?"

Jol focused on the brooch. "A slight breeze?"

"Aye, that would be Hau, air. Please place it in that far corner. Those pieces need more room than the others."

Once she knew what she was looking for, it was easy to feel which element was at the core of each relic. Jol was slower, but the others got through them quickly.

Nevaine paused as they got through the pile and a golden statue sat in front of her. It looked like Clait and was sitting with its tail wrapped serenely around its legs. It was also about the size of Clait. "Found this, but I've got a feeling it's going to be heavy." She picked it up, not surprised when she felt invisible dirt flow over her hands. Lu'um. It was lighter than she expected but still larger than she had hoped.

"Put that in Sean's pack, if you would." Pantiar continued sorting.

"What do we do with it?" Finding it was great, but she still wasn't sure what it did or how it would help the grigeens. And part of Nevaine also wanted to keep it with her; it tugged at her heart and made her feel restored. But Sean was physically stronger, and while not as heavy as it looked, it would weigh her down when they were running.

"Oh. That will be clear when the time is right. Yes, very clear." Pantiar quickly turned back to the few relics that hadn't been sorted.

"You don't know, do you?" Sean asked.

"I did...once. I know it is important. I was hoping that turning back into my corporeal self, even briefly, would bring back the memories. But it hasn't. However, powers beyond us wanted Nevaine to get it, and I see in her face that it is calling to her. You will figure it out."

Pantiar had been building a small collection of relics off to the side of his table. "Now, Jol, for your turn of heart, and helping the grigeens, you may keep one of these. Take your time, and pick them all up. The right one will call to you."

"What do they do?" Jol went over to them.

Nevaine had noticed that while the relics would give off their core element, none of them indicated what they did.

"I've got a blocking spell on all of them, or none of you could safely touch them. The right one will call to you, never fear." Pantiar hovered over Jol as he studied them.

Jol still looked doubtful, but he slowly picked up each piece. Finally, he settled on an almost completely round sphere. One side was flat, so it didn't roll away, and it fit in his hand. "This one gives me comfort. It's earth, or Lu'um. But it makes me feel like I'm home." He smiled as he held it. "Not the home I had, but one I'd like. Hard to explain."

Pantiar smiled and touched the relic. "Excellent choice. Your heart is true and this will help you create a place of joy and comfort for you and others. It is keyed to you, and you alone now. Wait until you are someplace safe to use it."

Jol grinned and tucked it into his pack. "Thank you. I'd like to create a place of safety for the grigeens."

Clait came over to him and rubbed his legs. "Thank *you*. As pointed out, we're not from here, and I did wonder how they would remain safe once we left. Those ruins they are in will protect them for a while, but they're too close to towns. There needs to be a safe place farther out."

"My thoughts as well. Plus, hopefully, I can find a way to free more."

Pantiar's eyes lit up. "I have just the place. It was land held by me long ago and is still unspoiled because of the spells I left." He touched

Jol on his temples and whispered a few words. "This will lead you there. The spells will fade, but they will help you as they can."

The last items were sorted, and Sean adjusted the golden grigeen in his pack for the eighth time.

"My friends, now comes the time of my taking leave of you. I do wish I'd met you all when I was still alive, but knowing you now brings me great joy. Jol, I ask you to stay in the middle of the room as you will keep us balanced. Clait, if you would take the Lu'um pile, I will give you the spells once we're all in place. Nevaine, please take Wai. Sean, you are strongly connected to Qul, so fire will be yours. I shall take Hau, as I have been drifting in air for a thousand years."

They quickly said their goodbyes, and Nevaine shocked the old wizard by giving him a hug. "I will miss you."

"You will be a strong leader." The smile that twitched on his lips showed that he'd almost said queen.

Right now, Nevaine would simply be happy for everyone to survive and the grigeens to be restored.

They all put on their packs. None of them had their swords out, or even Nevaine's knives, but they were ready. Yes, running away might be the better option in this case, but none of them were counting on it.

A whisper went through the room. To Nevaine, it told her the spell to use to destroy the water relics. They were based in the water element, and this spell dried them out. She nodded as she held it in her mind.

Pantiar waited until Sean and Clait also nodded. "Now. Farewell!"

All four cast their spells at the same time, with Jol watching wide-eyed behind them.

The cave shook, all of the relics vanished, and then Pantiar and the cave disappeared as well.

All four of them were left standing on a patch of dirt, with armored fighters coming at them.

Chapter Twenty-Seven

The people in armor didn't appear to be knights, unless knights here all wore cast-off armor. But there were at least twenty men and women charging them, and all armed with swords or pikes.

"What's this?" Clait grabbed two small objects in the dirt near their feet: a thin fabric and jeweled collar, and a stickpin.

"For you and Sean…they will protect and guide you." Pantiar's voice was so thin that it was hard to make out, but Clait buckled on the collar and threw the pin to Sean, who pocketed it. "Now, run!" His voice faded to nothing on the last word.

Jol was closest to the trail down and didn't need more encouragement. Plus, the people after them were in every direction except the downward trail.

The lowering sun indicated they'd been in the cave far longer than it had felt, so the ones looking for them must have gone up the trail to look for them. But they were still close enough to see them.

Jol took the lead, with Clait bounding right behind, while Nevaine and Sean stayed toward the rear.

"Do I have to remind you that I'm a stronger fighter and magic user?" Sean said as he easily paced her. "I should be in the back."

"No, but thank you. I think that having two of us might be a good idea if they catch up. Besides, Pantiar said there would be battles." She now had one knife in her hand and a spell at the ready. One she discarded as they ran. Even though the map should be dead now, and her connection to it as well, her magic still felt odd. She'd rather not use it unless needed, and wasn't certain she trusted her sorcery.

Sean gave up arguing and stayed where he was. Good idea, since if he dropped back, she would have as well. Getting off this mountain wasn't going to be easy, even if the twenty people chasing them were their only problem.

She had a feeling they weren't.

"Do they think we have the relics?" Nevaine kept her voice low but pitched so only Sean could hear.

"I'd think so, especially if they saw us appear out of thin air. It looks like a few of them dropped back, probably to see if they can find a way into the stash. Someone figured out our packs weren't large enough for all the supposed relics." Sean started muttering under his breath as they careened past the rockslide.

That neither of the supposedly trapped sorcerers had been where they'd left them could be either good or bad. They were both either dead, and their bodies carried off by someone, or they somehow escaped.

Jol yelped and almost ran into a tree. "Sorry, thought I saw an arm."

They had just made it past the rockslide when arrows started coming at them.

"I didn't see that any of them had bows. Who's firing at us?" Clait wasn't out of breath, and Nevaine knew she was keeping a slower pace because of Jol.

"Second group, to the left. Damn it, they're going to block us," Sean said.

The arrows were being shot from far enough away that they were easy to avoid, but the location of the archers was moving.

Nevaine's sister Piallen could run and shoot a long bow with unheard-of accuracy, but most archers stopped to fire. These archers were good and heading to block their descent.

"I've got an idea. Go ahead of me." Nevaine grinned as she balanced the sorcery in her mind. Her sorcery was limited, but there was no reason that she couldn't balance sorcery just like she did magic.

"Nevaine—"

"Nope." She cut him off. "We are all in danger and we'll all take risks. I have a plan. Go."

He watched her as they ran, then finally gave a tight nod. "Just don't die." He picked up speed as she dropped back.

Nevaine smiled. Pantiar was right; there might be hope for Sean after all.

The timing of what she planned was crucial. *When there were more opponents than could be handled, set them against each other.* Something her mother was fond of saying.

This was a tricky sorcery. Creating illusions, making them solid for a brief time, and not getting caught wasn't easy, even with magic. Once she had it set, she slowed down even more. The people chasing them were still back there. Running downhill in armor wasn't easy, but they were close enough to make the spell work.

She took a deep breath, said the words, and moved all of her fingers on both hands into the necessary intricate movements. A massive flight of spell-arrows flew toward the armored attackers. At the same time, pikes flew at the apparent location of the archers. The believability of pikes flying that far was nonexistent, but she doubted that the archers cared when they thought the pikes were coming for them.

Both sides stopped, and she raced down the mountain.

The others had kept going after the slide and ambush, but not gotten far. From Sean's shrug, the slower pace wasn't because of him.

"I stalled both groups, nothing more." The odds of those pikes and arrows actually hitting anyone was slim, and they would vanish in minutes. "They are still behind us. We should run." She passed everyone and kept going. They were all right behind her.

The greater number of trees would help keep those arrows off them, as well as slowing down the people in armor even further. But they shouldn't get overconfident.

They were quickly at the section of trail that ran along the cliff. Nevaine slowed down; this wouldn't be a good place for speed.

"Now it's my turn to stay back and guard," Sean said. "We can't make it through this part quickly, and I have some sneaky spells to slow our friends down."

Nevaine nodded. "Deal." She could share the risk-taking. Then she started along the cliff trail. She forced herself to focus on the path ahead of her and not listen for sounds of fighting behind her.

"He will be fine." Clait jogged between Nevaine and Jol. "You want him to trust you—you need to trust him."

"I do trust him. But—"

"No buts. Trust goes both ways. Now, if you don't mind, my fancy collar and I will be taking the lead." Clait jogged past her. The collar really was lovely, if odd. It had narrow green gems embedded in light-gold and white fabric. Nevaine hadn't seen it in the cave, but there had been so many relics that if it wasn't part of the water group, she might not have seen it.

Clait kept a good pace along the trail, finding the best places to pick up speed.

Still no sound of Sean behind them, though.

There was no place for Nevaine to switch with Jol behind her—not any that would be safe at the pace they were moving, anyway. But not knowing if Sean was okay, injured, or dying was eating at her.

The laugh in her head sounded suspiciously like Clait. And her parents, sisters, Sean, and anyone else who'd worried about her in the past. She took a deep breath and focused on the trail.

Jol yelped behind her, and Nevaine turned back.

"Sorry, didn't mean to scare you." Sean was running behind Jol and looking extremely pleased with himself. "I know we're stuck on this part for a few more minutes, but I might recommend running as fast as we all can once the trail is away from this cliff. There are some really angry people chasing us."

The smug tone in his voice made Nevaine want to turn and find out what he did. She muttered about cocky battlemages under her breath and picked up speed to stay with Clait. The trail finally moved away from the cliff, and Clait took off at full speed.

Grigeens were far faster than humans, so she was quickly out of sight. Jol was keeping up, but his breathing was becoming labored. Sean, like Clait, seemed to be fine.

"You said run...why aren't you going faster?" Nevaine turned to Sean. They were running, but she knew it wasn't his fastest speed. And whatever he'd done to the people following them hadn't slowed him down.

"Same reason you aren't, and Clait is around the next bend. We all go together."

Clait *was* behind the corner as they ran by and joined them. "I scouted down to the drop for the plains. No one in front of us, but the trail of dust behind us says our friends haven't given up." She grinned. Grigeens were fast, but even so, it had taken an hour on the way up. She'd gone down and back in a few minutes. "This collar seems to enhance my natural abilities. A wonderful gift, indeed."

Clait continued in the lead, but stayed in sight. Nevaine kept Jol in front of her. He was their slowest and most vulnerable piece. She and Sean switched as to which one was in the back.

Not that it mattered, at this point; if they were attacked, everyone would have to fight.

It didn't take the same time down as it had up, but they were nowhere as fast as Clait had been. Nevaine would have to investigate that collar once they got home. If the grigeen council didn't get to it first.

She was curious about Sean's stickpin. But that would have to wait.

The dust behind them showed that their pursuers were picking up speed. Most likely the archers were first, but no arrows had been seen yet.

"I think we're going to make it!" Jol's voice didn't have much *oomph* left, and Nevaine didn't want to point out that there was nothing stopping their pursuers from following them on the plain. Pantiar had said help would come, and they had to hope he was right.

They were in the final switchback, one that unfortunately was almost completely exposed, when the arrows started again. Sean got one in his pack but kept running. The arrows dropped off. Running and firing was tricky enough, but racing down a switchback and firing through trees was too difficult.

Sean leaned forward, but kept running. "I'm hit. Let me stay back and slow them down. I don't see anyone down there to help us."

Nevaine got closer and realized that the long arrow had gone through the top of his pack and struck Sean's left shoulder. There was only a trickle of blood, but that would change once the arrow came out. Already his left arm was hanging low.

"No, we stick together. Can you use your left hand at all?" Nevaine had more than a few books on physiology, and where that arrow hit wasn't good. It was most likely embedded in a major collection of important muscles.

He lifted it a few inches, then let it fall. "Not really. It'll mean I can't do spells and fight with a sword at the same time." He didn't slow down, but he looked like he really wanted to.

Nevaine hit the plains a few moments after Clait did, and already had a knife and a spell ready. If the fighting got up close, she'd switch to her sword, but she had more than a few throwable knives at the ready.

Clait raced ahead and dove into a clump of shrubs. Nevaine and the others kept running, with Nevaine covering Sean's left side. She'd never seen Clait hide when challenged and was about to call to her when Clait jumped out of the shrubs with thirty or so grigeens behind her. There were more racing out of anything they had found to hide in. Some even had dug into the dirt.

And there were hundreds of them. Far more than just the group they had left in the ruins.

The grigeens all charged past them and raced up the trail, with Clait's white tail waving like a flag.

Nevaine, Sean, and Jol turned and started to run after them. Grigeens were fierce, and while she'd heard of great battles they'd won against amazing odds, no one other than grigeens had seen them, so there was little to support their claims. They were facing armored fighters and archers with nothing but teeth, claws, and earth magic.

Clait stopped and sat on her back feet. A shield glimmered in front of her and the rest of the grigeens; then it raced forward and surrounded the approaching archers and fighters. They were slowed down to a fifth of normal speed. The grigeens charged. Even when they ran into the area covered by the shield, they weren't slowed.

Nevaine held her arm up when Sean tried to follow. "No. This is their battle and we'd only get in the way." She wasn't sure how she knew that, but she did. "Besides, you're injured. Maybe pull out that pin Pantiar gave you?" He'd said it would protect Sean, which wasn't a bad idea right now. Even if sitting out of a fight was against some sort of battlemage code.

"It's in my upper left pocket. I'm not putting down this sword yet." He clearly wasn't happy, but wasn't moving forward and was smart enough to admit he couldn't grab the pin.

Nevaine took it out and immediately recognized it as Qul—fire. It looked like a simple stickpin with a small red stone at the top, however.

"You'll have to touch it; it would have been triggered to you."

Sean moved the fingers on his left hand. They didn't move a lot but he could do it. She carefully put the pin in his hand and held it there until she felt him grab hold.

"It's a very tricky relic." Sean grinned as some of the fighters made it past the grigeen block. Although they were fighting them, and appeared to be winning, fighting armored people was harder than the archers. Who could no longer be seen.

Sean's left arm rose with a spell in his hand. Whether the spell was his or from the pin, Nevaine couldn't be sure. But it glowed red, then went up his entire arm. The arrow was still in his shoulder, but somehow the pin was allowing the arm to function.

Three armored fighters got past the grigeens and charged forward. Nevaine readied a knife. Hitting the few places that weren't covered by full armor was tricky in practice—and this wasn't practice. Her shots would need to count.

But Sean stepped in front of her and Jol, his left arm crackling with a magical dark-red flame. He aimed his arm toward them, then said, "Sut yItlhutlh." The flame running along his arm leapt to the three attackers, engulfing them completely. Then it vanished, and the bodies dropped to the ground.

Chapter Twenty-Eight

Nevaine was stunned, but not as much as Jol. He turned and ran away. She'd seen his face as he fled, and he looked more frightened of Sean than of the people who had been after them.

"Wait!" She turned but he was already slowing down.

There were more people running toward them from that direction.

"Clait! Sean!" Nevaine ran to Jol and shook his arm. His eyes were wide and he'd clearly reached the end of his ability to cope.

Sean's arm was back by his side and the flames were gone as he ran to them. Clait was a bit behind and the grigeen army was following in an extremely orderly manner.

"We need to get back to the ruins." Clait was a bit dirtier than before, but not injured.

"Those can't protect us if they follow us." The main reason the spell on the ruins worked was because it was based on misdirection. It wasn't strong enough to handle a full attack. A group this large running into an empty area and vanishing would be noticeable.

"Trust me." Clait winked and darted toward the forest.

"I say trust her." Sean waved his hand in front of Jol's face. "He's going into shock; we might have to drag him."

Nevaine looked at Sean's arm. "You lead and keep your sword ready; I can pull him with one hand." She tugged, and Jol followed. He wasn't in shock, but something shut him mostly down. As long as his legs and feet moved, she'd be happy. He stumbled along but walked. She kept her hand on him, though.

The grigeens swarmed around them, escorting them after Clait. They also seemed to somehow be helping Jol along.

The new group of people chasing them weren't wearing armor, nor did they appear to be archers. They looked like townsfolk. Many had swords; some had pitchforks. She couldn't see their faces, but the yelling was clear. They were pissed. Most likely about the liberated grigeens.

Clait got them to the ruins but the townsfolk had already entered the forest. There was no way they wouldn't see where they went. Then Clait and five large grigeens pulled away from the rest.

"Get him inside, and you two come with me." She ran toward Sean and Nevaine, then took off toward the group following them.

Nevaine got Jol into the ruins, then she and Sean raced back to Clait.

Nevaine took hold of Sean's good arm. "You shouldn't be here. That arrow..."

Sean shook his head. "I can't feel it right now, probably thanks to the pin. I know I'll pay for it later, but I have an idea what Clait is doing."

Nevaine bit her tongue as they ran toward the grigeens. She wasn't sure what she expected, but all of them standing on their back legs humming certainly wasn't it.

Clait raised her paws to her collar. The shield she'd generated before was back but larger and more imposing. Nevaine was pretty sure that Clait was causing it, with help from Pantiar's collar, but they were making it look like all six of the grigeens were doing it.

Sean caught on before she did and held his left arm toward the shield. His arm crackled with fire, then the flames roared along Clait's shield, making the humans facing it back away.

Nevaine grinned and let loose her lightning spell, also set to appear as if it was coming from the shield.

"The grigeens will be free. All of them! Your homes will be swallowed and burned, your lives forfeit, if one more grigeen is harmed or captured." It was Clait but she was somehow making her voice loud-er—far louder—than normal.

The people on the other side of the shield weren't professional killers; up close, they looked like merchants and farmers. There were a few hardened-looking fighters, but not many.

They slowly moved back.

"We need our livelihood back!"

Nevaine stalked forward. "Your livelihood was gained from mur-dering innocent beings? People with voices, lives, and hearts of their own? How can you stand yourselves? I'm embarrassed to be the same as you." Two bolts of lightning, larger than the others, crackled over the villagers' heads. Two of the men who looked like they knew how to fight snuck around the edge of the shield. She sent knives into both, knowing few could see the blades until they hit.

There was something augmenting her spells and knife throwing. She was beginning to feel invincible. She glanced at Clait and Sean, and realized that they felt it too. Relics often had a cost and they were seeing this one. The problem with feeling invincible was that usually it wasn't true.

Clait was expanding the range of the shield, but Nevaine slowed it down and ran next to her friend. "Trap them, knock them out, do something, but this needs to drop." She didn't think Pantiar would have meant to cause problems with his gifts, but something was wrong. Both Sean and Clait looked ready to charge the town itself.

"No. We can destroy them all."

"This isn't you. Send them back, make them never come here again, but you aren't a killer. None of your people are."

Clait blinked and took her paws off the collar. The shield stayed but started moving in instead of out.

"Let me run a spell through it, then close it around them and knock them out." Nevaine looked to Sean. "You have to drop your spell as well."

"But..." He shook his head and nodded. The flames vanished and his left arm fell to his side.

The townspeople and guards were still trying to figure out what was happening. Nevaine had a plan, but it was going to be hard. She balanced a sorcery spell for forgetting and one for sleep. She let it go, gasping at how much it took out of her. The spell hit the shield, then bounced to everyone within it.

They all dropped to the ground, and Clait banished her shield.

A few closer grigeens ran forward, checking the bodies. "Not dead."

"Good. They won't recall anything of this, aside from the fact that grigeens should be left alone at all costs." She'd added that to the forgetting spell. "But we need to get back to the ruins before they wake up." She stumbled as she turned. The spell combination had worked, but the world was blurry.

Sean ran to her side, catching her with his good hand.

"I'm okay." But she didn't have the energy to push him away.

"You have one arm and an arrow sticking out of you." Clait shook her head at Sean as she marched over. "Let us carry her."

"I'm fine." Nevaine took another step, and Sean's hand was the only thing keeping her from landing on her face.

He looked ready to argue, then nodded.

Grigeens came out of the forest and surrounded her. And tiny paws, dozens of them, carried her.

Even slightly delirious from the backlash of her spell, this had to be one of the oddest ways of travel ever. She forced her eyes to stay open and watched as they passed under the trees and through the arch of the ruins. A flash of cold hit her as they went under the arch, but then the temperature went back to normal. Her grigeen escorts gently took her to a soft pile of straw and laid her down.

Clait and Sean came to her and peered down.

"How do you feel?" Clait asked.

"How do you two feel? I'm not sure what Pantiar was thinking with those relics, but you two looked ready to take on the empress herself." She was feeling much better now that she was lying down, but things spun when she tried to sit up.

Sean turned red. "Yeah, felt that after the fact. This pin is handy, but needs to be examined more."

"Same with my collar." Clait grimaced.

"We need to get that arrow out of you." Nevaine knew the best person to heal Sean was Sean. This would be a time that having another battlemage would come in handy.

"There are healers here." Clait proudly nodded to a trio of grigeens waiting nearby. "He refused treatment until you were healed."

"I'm just suffering from overextending my magic—I'll be fine." Sean had leaned against a pile of hay. "He isn't." She forced herself to sit up, but Jol ran forward and grabbed Sean before he could fall.

"I'm fine." But his face was already getting pale. He gave a yelp as the grigeens and Jol put him facedown on the hay. Then, at a chittering from the grigeens, Jol stepped back. Nevaine had no idea what they said, but he obviously did.

"He'll be fine. It's not a deep injury." Clait nodded. "The healers already studied him. Now, you rest. We haven't been transferred back home, so there must be something else for you to do." She pointedly looked toward Sean's pack and the golden grigeen hidden inside.

Nevaine watched as one of the grigeens placed their paws on Sean's head, and he stopped twitching. In fact, he snored a bit. Whatever the grigeens were doing, there wasn't any blood as they removed the pack and the arrow gently. There was some conversation between them, but then all three stepped back and bowed.

"They have healed the wound but the arm will take awhile to recover." Clait bowed back.

Jol looked around, then stepped forward with his gift from Pantiar. "I know what I need to do now." He held up a matching stone that was covered in brick dust. "This was in that corner, hidden. When I bring them together, we will all be transferred to Pantiar's hidden valley. It's not just a building, but a valley that will be protected for hundreds of years." He grinned.

Nevaine was able to sit up and looked to where Sean was sleeping. "All of us?" She wasn't sure what she needed to do with the golden grigeen, nor if the hidden valley would block the oracles from sending them back.

"Yes, if you want."

Nevaine nodded and swung her legs off the pile of hay, then slowly walked to Sean's pack. "Let me check something first."

Jol nodded as he and the healer grigeens moved away.

Nevaine pulled the golden grigeen out of the pack. It was cool to the touch and lovely, but she still had no idea what to do with it.

Pantiar's stone in her pocket turned warm, so she took it out.

He was gone, so this rock shouldn't be connected to him. But somehow it was. She felt his essence coming from it.

Sean stirred and sat up. "Pantiar?" His left arm didn't move but he looked better. Still pale, but better.

"It's his rock. I was trying to figure out what to do with the statue when his rock acted up."

Before Sean could respond, yells and screams came from outside the ruins. A pair of grigeen guards came running in. "A new group has found us. They attacked the old enclave." As he spoke, Zila and half a dozen other grigeens straggled in.

Jol came running up. "I have to do this. Come with us."

Clait looked around and shook her head. "I fear we can't. But we will guard your escape."

"With our lives, if needed." Nevaine and Sean almost echoed each other, and she took his good hand.

"I have one more thing to do here, and I think I know what it is," Nevaine said as Pantiar's stone continued to warm her hand and a soft, wordless feeling flowed over her. "Go, get the grigeens safe. And take care." She gave him a quick hug, then Jol and the grigeens ran off. A moment later, there was a brief flash of light, and Jol and his grigeen wards vanished.

Nevaine nodded, then turned back to Sean and Clait. "We need the power of these ruins to destroy the statue." Neither Sean nor Clait looked surprised.

"And, if you destroy it as these people attack, they will think everyone was destroyed." Sean smiled. "I hope Pantiar is right about destroying it, though."

"It was his." Nevaine had a little energy for magic left; hopefully it would be enough.

Sean struggled to his feet, but waved her off. "I'll be fine."

All three stood close together. Nevaine held the rock over the statue and forced what little magic she had left into the rock and through it, into the golden statue. It glowed from the inside and cracks of red appeared.

The villagers charged in. The golden grigeen exploded.

A portal of clear stone whirled Nevaine, Sean, and Clait away as everything went blindingly white.

Chapter Twenty-Nine

The world spun, and Nevaine heard oracles whispering around them. At least, hopefully, that meant destroying the statue was the right thing and they weren't all dead.

Small, dark shapes ran past them as they tumbled inside the portal. Then everyone dropped to the forest floor.

Nevaine yelped as hundreds of grigeens raced past them, many brushing against her and Sean. At first, she thought it was the ones from the Offialian Empire but there were far more than that. All seemingly coming through the portal that she, Sean, and Clait had run through.

Even Clait seemed stunned as the grigeens raced into the forest.

"Wait! Who are you? Where did you come from?" She was trying to get one of them to stop and at first none did. Then Zila came by.

"These are the lost and forgotten. After you destroyed the golden grigeen and vanished, the oracles were able to release them from all across the world. That wizard had been trying to protect my people but misplaced most of them instead." He looked around. "Those who stayed with your human friend will now go to build a new safe place for our people in our homeland. I didn't go with them and joined these, since I failed to protect my kind." He gave a stiff nod and raced off.

"So, all of these grigeens are going to be living in those woods behind your palace?" Sean asked. He looked battered and beaten, and his left arm hung oddly across his waist. But at least he'd survived.

Nevaine knew they had the grigeens to thank for that.

"That's a good question." Nevaine didn't even try to count the grigeens that were still coming through the portal. And still more were coming. There were thousands.

"They do appear to be going toward my home woods. I should go and explain to my pack." Clait started to follow.

"Would it help if we came?" Her parents would be somehow notified when she returned, but Nevaine hadn't seen anyone from the palace coming to bring her back yet, and this could be important.

"Thank you for the offer. I know you want to go home." Clait grinned. "But I think this will have to be dealt with among my people before we bring news to the palace. Be well, both of you." She trotted off.

"There have to be tens of thousands of them," Sean said as he dropped to sit against a boulder.

Nevaine came over. "You're still hurt, and you didn't tell me." The grigeens had done a healing of the arrow wound, but they wouldn't have had time to check for other injuries.

"It's not bad. I took a hit when I blocked those people from following us down the cliff trail on the mountain—bandaged it, and didn't think about it." He'd been holding his right side with his injured left arm, making it look like he was only keeping his arm out of the way.

Nevaine moved his arm. "Sean, the injury on your side is soaking through. You can't keep lying. No more lying." She started moving the clothing and bandages. It was a deep cut and looked raw and dark. "I don't have enough magic left to heal you. Not now. Destroying the statue took the last from me. Why didn't you tell me?"

"Because it might have stopped you from doing what you had to do—the grigeens needed to be freed." A bit of blood came from the corner of his mouth. "And apparently I might have some internal injuries."

Nevaine tried to reach for anything: magic, sorcery, a combination of the two. She had nothing left. Sean's color was fading. He was dying in front of her. "No. You don't get to do this. You can't leave me. I love you!" She was almost as surprised at her words as he was.

"You implied that you couldn't trust me. That my duplicitous past made a relationship untenable." His grin was weak.

"I lied!" Nevaine fought her tears but they kept coming. There were only a few grigeens coming through now, and they had already passed them. "Help us! Please, get help!"

The grigeens looked like they were going to keep running, then spun back. "We will get help." A large gray striped one nodded to the others. Half of the group ran down the path, but faster now. Then the gray one and the rest came and put their paws on Sean. Grigeens *were* magic, more so than using it. But Nevaine felt magic flowing from them. "We need him to sleep. We can't heal him, there are no healers with us, but we can slow down time for him."

Sean looked doubtful, but Nevaine grabbed him. "Rest. You need to rest. Let them do what they need to do."

"Not sure about waking up...but sleep is good. By the way, I love you too. Even if you lie." He gave a weak smile, then his eyes closed and his head rolled back.

Nevaine put her hand on his chest. He was breathing, but extremely slowly. The grigeens kept doing what they were doing, and Nevaine just sat next to Sean, holding his hand and sobbing.

It felt like days, but she finally heard the sound of people running through the woods. Her immediate reaction was to draw a knife before she realized where she was.

Piallen, Finnian, and a slew of guards and healers were running toward them. Piallen dropped to the ground next to Nevaine, patting her for injuries.

"Not me. It's Sean. The grigeens are slowing it down, but he's dying. I have no magic. Can't heal." Her words came out in hiccups as she kept crying.

"Let the healers take care of this." Piallen made Nevaine look at her. "You don't look good, but I am so glad you're back!" She hugged her tightly.

Nevaine took a deep breath and forced herself to stop crying. "I wouldn't have been without him. And the grigeens." She looked over to where two of the senior palace healers were checking Sean and muttering spells. "I thought those two never left the palace?"

Piallen smiled. "Your grigeen friends might have implied that it was you who was near death. Our parents are right behind us, and Lizeth is trying to levitate herself the entire way here." She looked at the small group of grigeens, all now standing back and watching. "Those aren't from here, are they? Nor those?"

She looked past Nevaine, where the mass of grigeens was reappearing. Clait tore through them all to race to Nevaine.

"No, they aren't." Nevaine hugged Clait. "We almost lost him," she said brokenly into her white fur.

The healers had stabilized Sean and put him on a magically floating bed. "We need to get him back immediately." The question in his eyes was pointed. They'd come out for her, and if she needed them, they had to help her first.

"I am fine." A small lie, but she was beginning to get used to them. "My family will help me back. Please, do whatever needs to be done to save him."

Piallen made a shooing motion when both healers paused. "Go along now. Everything's fine here. Parents are on their way."

Finnian had been silent, but now turned to the healers. "My wife is now here. If there are any issues, I believe that she and Piallen can help their sister."

Lizeth was still in her wheeled chair, but she had it floating a foot above the ground and was singing a soft melody.

The two healers, Sean in his floating bed, and half the guards took off at a jog.

Lizeth watched them go. "That wasn't Nevaine."

"No, it was Sean." Nevaine got to her feet and ran to hug her older sister. "Thank you for coming to rescue me, though."

Lizeth nodded. "Anytime. But you *are* injured. Mother and Father are not far behind me."

Nevaine looked at her torn and bloody clothing. She looked worse than she felt—aside from the lack of magic—but that was a soul ache more so than a physical one. Lizeth sang another soft spell. Nevaine's clothes were neater, the blood was gone, and her aches and pains felt soothed.

Just in time, as another entourage came through.

"We saw that friend of yours, he doesn't look good, but I thought it was you who was injured and near death?" Her mother ran forward and grabbed Nevaine tightly, then looked at the grigeens. "Where did all of those come from?"

Clait grinned. "I know we can't talk of what happened in a Challenge to those who haven't gone through one, but I think these will need to be addressed. After everyone is healed, anyway." She said some soft words to the grigeens near her, and they all left. Clait marched forward. "I'll be going back with you for now. It seems neither you nor Sean can function without me." She shook her head and started trotting down the trail.

After a few more rounds of hugs from both her parents, Nevaine let Piallen help her back to the palace.

The palace was a wonderful thing to see, and Nevaine knew she still had to go officially in front of her parents and present herself. She was grateful that Lizeth had cheated a bit to clean her up. Dirt and mud were one thing, but blood-splattered clothing would have caused issues.

"Give us a few minutes to get into position, then come in." Her mother smiled at Clait. "Both of you." Then her parents entered the palace.

Finnian had been silent but now nodded. "Are these Challenges all this rough?" He winced and turned to Piallen. "Sorry, I forgot. Maybe things will settle down in two years."

Lizeth had a worried look on her face. "I think something is changing things. But that can wait for later." Her perky smile was back. "So, you brought home some grigeens? You know that will annoy the theorists who insisted they were all dead."

Clait grinned. "Idiots, one and all. My people weren't sure what happened to them, but we never believed they were dead."

A guard stepped out of the palace and waved to them.

"That's your cue, little sister," Lizeth said as Finnian wheeled her toward the palace doors.

Piallen followed them, and Nevaine and Clait went in through a smaller side door.

The ballroom was full, which wasn't surprising, but there was a group of people to the far side, all in black, who didn't look like they were from here. In fact, they had a sharp resemblance to Sean. None of them looked happy.

Nevaine took a deep breath as she and Clait strode forward.

"Princess Nevaine Laurel Gosslia, approach the throne." The crier's voice was loud enough that the grigeens out in the deep woods probably heard him.

Her parents smiled, and her father cleared his throat. "Daughter, we see you survived your Challenge. We welcome you back."

"Thank you. I did, and I was helped. The oracles sent Clait of the grigeens and Sean the blacksmith along with me. They both saved my life many times." She glanced toward the people who looked like

Sean. They were all watching her, but she couldn't tell if their expressions had softened or not. They might have gotten worse.

"We understand that the blacksmith is in the healing ward. Our best healers are attending him, and he is expected to make a full recovery," her father said. There was a collective gasp from the group in black, and the relief on their faces was obvious. "We are grateful for all he was able to do to assist our daughter. He will always have a place of honor in our kingdom."

Nevaine felt her chest relax at the news.

"Will Clait of the grigeens please step forward?" Her mother smiled and reached for a small chain as Clait went forward. "For saving so many, and helping bring grigeens back into the world, we name you royal counselor to the growing grigeen kingdom." She put the chain around Clait's neck. Clait nodded, but for once seemed at a loss for words.

The muttering around them meant people had caught the queen's words and were hoping for clarification. That wouldn't be happening just yet. It would be interesting to see what happened with the grigeens once they got used to being back in the world. And they dispersed from the forest behind the palace.

Her mother nodded to her, then looked around the room. "Princess Nevaine Laurel Gosslia, we officially recognize you as having successfully completed the Challenge. You will be named second heir at the ball tonight."

Her father flashed her a smile, then turned to the rest of the room. "You are all dismissed until this evening's ball." The king and queen left the dais.

Piallen and Lizeth came over to Nevaine. "Now we need to get you cleaned up and ready."

Nevaine watched everyone leave. "I want to see Sean."

"I won't lie. He's seriously injured. I'm not sure if seeing him will—"

"Let her see him." Piallen cut Lizeth off. "If that were Finnian, you'd be blasting your way over there."

"Fine. I was just trying to be protective." Lizeth started wheeling her way down the corridor.

Piallen took Nevaine's hand. "He will be okay; our parents wouldn't lie."

"I know, but..." She dropped her words as the group of people who looked like Sean's family crossed the hallway in front of them. A very old man, a middle-aged couple, and four young men. Nevaine steeled herself.

"You are the one who took our son on that journey? The *Princess* Nevaine?" If *princess* were a swearword, it wouldn't sound as bad as the way the woman, most likely Sean's mother, made it sound.

Nevaine pulled herself up, but she was still shorter than all of them. "I am. Your son joined me of his own will, and against my wishes, and saved many people, including myself. I am indebted to him."

"Pah. Royals can't be trusted. Let me tell you, once he's recovered, he's coming back with us." His mother was furious, but the rest of the family seemed to be waiting.

"I am sorry for what happened to you and your family in the land you left." She would have to be careful about what she said, but she had an idea where this anger was coming from. This woman had taken her husband and infant on a potentially deadly sea voyage to get away from royals.

"How do you know..." She turned to the rest of her family.

"I do. And I am so very sorry for the terror you went through." Nevaine was not a hugger at all. Plus, she was still dirty. But she stepped forward and held out her arms. "I would never let anything happen to your son."

His mother paused, then stepped forward and hugged her. Then started sobbing. "We...and then he...can't see him..."

Nevaine stepped back. "He might have been in surgery before, but regardless, they *will* let you see him now." She looked to the group of men. "All of you. Right, Lizeth?" As heir, Lizeth held almost as much power as their parents.

"They will most definitely let you all see him." She beamed her lovely smile. "I am Princess Lizeth, heir to the throne. This is our younger sister, Princess Piallen. We all admire and are indebted to your son, Sean." She exuded dignity and charm.

Then Lizeth turned to continue down the hall, with the rest following.

Sean's family stayed behind the princesses, but they seemed less hostile than before.

There were two guards in front of the royal healing wing doors when they approached.

"We can't allow strangers in, Princess Lizeth."

"Ah, but they are not strangers. I call them friends. You wouldn't deny me bringing people I call friends in." Lizeth sounded sweet, but there was steel in her voice.

The guards held their stance for a few moments, then both held open the doors and stepped aside. "Yes, Princess Lizeth."

"Excellent. Now carry on." Lizeth's chair moved forward.

"Why does Finnian push your chair if you can move it yourself?" Nevaine asked as they went down the pristine white corridor.

"Because he loves me." Lizeth grinned. "And I like to have him there. But he had other things to take care of this afternoon."

Piallen went ahead and held open the door for everyone else. Sean's family paused but her friendly smile got them to come inside.

The room was huge and immaculate, as expected. But Nevaine wasn't expecting Sean to be sitting up and joking with one of the healers.

Neither was his family. His mother raced forward and was hugging and kissing him so much it was a good thing he appeared to have responded well to the healing. The rest of his family came up a bit slower, but there was no doubt they loved him as well.

"Why are you here and why are you all in black?" Sean said once he recovered.

"We heard you had been kidnapped, then lost through some royal magic portal, then killed. We had no idea what was going on, so your mother brought us here." His father's voice was similar to Sean's, and he had the same eyes. His hair was lighter, though. "We have been waiting for days at an inn at the middle of town."

"We will move you here immediately." Nevaine bit her lip. "If you will accept it, we would be honored to have you stay here in the palace." She glanced toward Lizeth.

"Yes, we have guest quarters that would keep you close to your son." Lizeth paused. "Actually, Sean's cottage was destroyed, so he'll need a place for a bit as well. Not a worry; we have room."

His mother and father looked at each other, their faces neutral.

"These royals aren't like the ones you fled from," Sean said softly as he held his mother's hands.

"Yes, we would be honored. Thank you." His father smiled. "I am Padrick. My wife is Morian. My younger sons are Lucas, Ilian, Davith, and Jessup. We are very pleased to meet you all."

"We will give you some time with Sean." Nevaine smiled. At least his family didn't hate her on principle, so that was good.

"Actually, could I just have a few words with Nevaine first?" Sean asked. "Just a few...I know she has an event to get ready for."

"A full ball," Piallen said without much happiness as she walked toward the door. Dancing, mincing about, and dressing up were not her thing.

"Ah, should be fun." Sean's eyes twinkled.

His mother looked between him and Nevaine, then grabbed her husband's hand. "We will let you have some time alone. Then we'll come back and hear about your adventures." She gave Nevaine a small smile as she led them all out of the room.

"Very glad that you're doing so much better," Lizeth said as she and Piallen left.

Nevaine came forward to sit on the side of his bed. "Good of you not to die." Then she gave him a soft punch in his good arm.

"What was that for?"

"For not telling me how badly injured you were. You scared me." Terrified was a better word, but there was a hard lump in her throat.

"If it was me, or saving the grigeens...?" He shrugged.

"Fine, I might have done the same. We have to stop lying, though. Both of us," she added as he started to respond.

He took her hand. "Did you really mean it when you said you loved me?"

"Yes. Did you?" Nevaine hadn't been willing to admit it until she thought she'd lost him.

"I did. I'd say that's a start. I'll see about setting up a smithy of my own in town. Get a new house too."

She leaned forward and softly kissed him. "I'm going to ask to be allowed to go to university as my Challenge wish."

"Oh." His face fell.

"You could go, too."

"A bit awkward, courting the royal princess while she'd be in school housing."

"It wouldn't be if we were married." She looked into his eyes as she said it. She'd retract her words immediately if there was the slightest doubt there. There was none.

"Princess Nevaine, are you asking me to marry you?" His blue eyes were bright, but he was keeping his smile low.

"I wasn't sure how long it would take you to get to it." She put her finger over his lips before he could respond. "Think about it. I intend to only be married once."

Sean nodded. "The healers said I should be able to attend the ball, as long as I take things easy."

Nevaine got to her feet. "Then I shall see you at the ball. I'll send your family back in." She hadn't been nervous about her sideways asking him to marry her when she did it, but she found that her stomach was churning now. *What if he had said no?*

His family was just down the hall.

"He's waiting for you." She smiled, especially to his mother. A family of men, but there was no doubt who was in charge. "I look forward to seeing all of you at tonight's ball."

His mother smiled as they all went back into Sean's room.

Piallen and Lizeth were waiting just outside the healer chamber's main doors.

"So, is my little sister smitten?" Lizeth said as they went toward the stairs leading to the upper floors.

"She looks so to me. He is extremely handsome." Piallen's grin said they'd been talking about Sean while she was gone.

"He's also smart, charming, funny, a battlemage, and a sorcerer." Nevaine stopped when she realized she sounded like a love-struck teenager.

"What? He's a battlemage? I must talk to him." Piallen stopped herself. "Later."

Lizeth detoured away from the stairs. "Come around back here. There's a lift to get me upstairs—much easier than spell singing up."

The new contraption was a wood-paneled box that had sliding doors. Once the doors shut, the box slowly lifted.

"I was gone a week and you had this made?" Nevaine looked around the box. "I was only gone a week, right?" Lizeth's Challenge had been four weeks long, but she'd thought it was only one.

"Yup, seven days exactly," Piallen said. "Whatever weirdness that messed up Lizeth's didn't do that for yours. I can't wait until I finish mine so that I can hear about both of your adventures!" There was a level of wistfulness that made her look younger than eighteen. Out of the three of them, Piallen was the one who loved the idea of the Challenge the most.

"You'll get there soon enough," Lizeth said. "I have a feeling Nevaine will be spending her time for the next few months reading all of the past Challenges. There are some interesting stories."

The box halted on the second floor, and they went down to Nevaine's suite of rooms. She looked around, but while she didn't see anyone, that didn't mean there wasn't anyone. Her idea would wait until they got to her room.

"Oh, she has a secret!" Piallen laughed and held open the door. "Is it about a certain dark-haired, blue-eyed battlemage?"

Nevaine shrugged and went to flop on her sofa. "Actually, it has to do with my Challenge wish."

Piallen sat on a chair, and Lizeth wheeled closer.

"Oh? Nothing as dramatic as mine, I presume?" Lizeth leaned forward.

"Not really. I'm going to ask to be allowed to complete higher level studies at the University of Luzangberg."

"What? That's great!" Lizeth looked a bit envious; she'd wanted to go and Nevaine knew she'd fought to get her sisters to be able to go.

"But what about Sean?" Piallen asked. "I thought you two..."

"I know. I did too, then I didn't, then I did...sort of." Nevaine bit her lip. "But I know I want to go to the university." She didn't want to tell them what she'd asked Sean. Not yet.

"I don't think I've ever heard you babble." Lizeth narrowed her eyes. "There's something you aren't telling us, me thinks." She waved her hand. "Keep your secrets. I had my unused confirmation gown altered for you if you wanted to wear it tonight."

Nevaine was grateful for the distraction. "That would be lovely. Is it in my bedroom?" She couldn't try it on until after she had a nice long bath, but she hadn't given a thought to what to wear to the ball.

Lizeth had wanted to make a statement when she'd been confirmed heir, so she wore pristine white riding leathers. But she and her mother had designed a lovely gown.

That was hanging in Nevaine's closest.

It was just as lovely as she recalled, light colors of netting woven in the lush fabric. "I don't want to touch it as dirty as I still am, but it looks like it will fit." Considering that Lizeth was six inches taller than her, the fact the dress had been so expertly cut down to fit Nevaine was amazing.

"I'm glad you like it. Now, go bathe, then we'll bring our clothes and dress together like we used to." Lizeth smiled.

"What about Finnian?"

"Pah. He's no fun to dress. Too basic. He's off doing whatever now anyway." Lizeth waved her hand and turned her chair around.

Nevaine waited until they both left, then settled in for a long bath. She wasn't a contemplation-in-the-bath type of person, normally. Now was different. She'd planned to ask to be able to attend the university as her Challenge wish as soon as Lizeth got hers approved.

If Lizeth could get an entire law changed, Nevaine should be able to get this idea changed.

Which led her to her asking Sean to marry her. She hadn't planned that at all and was almost as surprised as he looked when her words came out. It wasn't that she as a woman had asked—both genders asked each other. It was that she, Nevaine, asked.

Part of her was almost hoping that he couldn't go to the ball so she could delay getting an answer. She took a deep breath and soaked some more.

Nevaine had just finished toweling her hair and getting her dressing robe on when there was a knock at her door. Nevaine swung the door open, expecting her sisters. "A bit early, but this works." Her words died in her mouth as three dark-clad people charged her.

Chapter Thirty

Nevaine yelled and tried to shut the door, but they were too fast. They were dressed like the descriptions of the people who'd taken Sean. One got his hand over her mouth so quickly that she barely got out a yelp. Up close, it was clear they were wearing Northalian army gear under their vaguely Laiandran-looking costumes.

Luckily, Nevaine had hidden weapons in her room along with her piles of books. She fell back against the couch and grabbed two knives hidden in the side cushions. She stabbed the closest attacker and got a decent swipe at the second.

Pounding on her door told her someone had heard her partial yelp and that these attackers had locked the door behind them.

She kicked the one she had stabbed away; he tumbled over, holding his stomach. She scrambled to the ledge behind her couch. "What are you doing? You won't get away with whatever it is."

The other two came forward slowly. "You shouldn't have come back. You were supposed to die." His voice was low and sounded like it was from the north, confirming Northalian involvement.

"Do you even know where I went?" Nevaine was stalling until whoever was pounding on the door could break it down. Her magic was still too drained to use right now.

"Doesn't matter. Our seers know you are an abomination." He lunged forward just as the door shattered, and Piallen and Sean rushed in. Lizeth was right behind them, already singing a spell to immobilize the attackers. It was a low-level spell, but she looked as shocked as Nevaine when it didn't stop them.

Piallen nodded and sent a spell at the attacker closest to her. He tumbled to the ground.

"Nice! That's a battlemage spell." Sean hit his opponent with the hilt of his sword. Clearly, like Nevaine, his magic was still drained.

Piallen beamed as Lizeth rolled forward and cast a second spell song, a much harsher one, on the injured attacker. He froze instantly.

Booted feet came running down the hall, and Lizeth and Piallen both turned to face them. Nevaine couldn't see who was coming, but when her sisters relaxed their stances, she knew it was palace guards.

Sean ran to Nevaine and helped her down from her perch. "Are you okay?"

"I am, thank you." She noticed her hands shook a bit as he took away her knives. "I think they were part of the group who kidnapped you."

"Is everyone okay?" The guards crowded around the door.

"My sister was attacked by people who managed to get inside. You need to check for more and lock down the palace." Lizeth sounded more and more like the queen she would become. "And notify our parents. Also, get my husband. He's with Gliandra."

"Yes, Princess." The guard yelled orders and dispersed most of the rest of the guards. Four stayed in the hall outside Nevaine's room.

Sean rubbed Nevaine's arms and looked her over. "You sure you're all right?"

"Yes. Sort of. After everything we went through this past week, I was hoping we were done with it for a while."

Lizeth looked at the shattered door. "Maybe it would be better if Nevaine changes and we all go to mine and Finnian's chambers. They're much larger and have locking, intact doors."

Sean peered into her eyes, as if she might be hiding secrets. "I'm going to make sure my family is secure. You are certain they didn't injure you?"

"I'm not the one with a history of lying about injuries." Nevaine kissed his cheek. "But, yes. Now go and get your family to Lizeth's rooms. The guards will show you the way."

Piallen escorted Nevaine to her bedroom and guarded the door while she quickly changed. "Are you sure you're okay?"

"I will be. My magic is still exhausted. I'm thinking we're not going to be having a ball tonight." She patted Lizeth's altered dress with a sigh.

"Not thinking so. You'll be lucky if our parents don't lock you up for a day or two until they sort it out."

"Thank you. Not the way I expected to spend tonight." They went to Lizeth and Finnian's chambers.

This suite of rooms was massive and its front room looked like a miniature version of one of the reception halls down below.

Their parents were chatting with Sean's grandfather, but the rest of his family was huddled in a corner. Lizeth and Nevaine went over and drew them into the rest of the room.

"I don't understand. Someone tried to kill the princess?" Sean's mother looked more comfortable in the large chair Lizeth had led her to, but there was still worry in her eyes.

"Just some Northalian troublemakers. Don't worry." Sean rubbed his mother's back.

"I don't understand how they got in, though." Nevaine looked to her mother.

"We found a compromised old entrance while you were changing. No portal this time. Gliandra set up protection spells radiating out to the borders while you were gone. It appears that the ones who attacked you were the only ones here, but it's still best we stay here for a few more hours. I am afraid your ball will need to be delayed a few days."

Piallen's eyes had lit up, then fell. A delayed ball was still a ball.

"That is most sad, as I had plans for tonight." Sean stepped to the center of the room, stopped before Nevaine, and dropped to one knee.

His mother almost swooned.

"Princess Nevaine, you are the most beautiful, intelligent, and ofttimes vexing woman I have ever met. Will you make me the happiest man in this, or any, world, and be my bride?" He held out an elegantly cut diamond ring.

Nevaine was startled. There was no way he'd had time to get that ring made since she asked him a few hours ago.

"I was planning on asking you before we had our little adventure." He held the ring higher. "Will you marry me?"

Nevaine put her hand in front of her mouth. "Yes. Yes, yes, I would be happy to marry you."

Sean's hands shook as he slipped the exquisite ring on her finger, then stood and kissed her as if they weren't standing in front of both families and assorted guards.

"Hear hear!" the king shouted, and clapped. Sean's family looked a bit stunned but soon they were clapping as well.

Nevaine just held onto Sean and the kiss.

Epilogue – a year later

Nevaine fussed with her wedding gown. It wasn't fancy like Lizeth's had been, which was good as she didn't want Lizeth to pay her back for pinning all those flowers in her veil three years ago. Nevaine's veil was short; her gown elegant, yet understated. And both Piallen and Lizeth had gasped when she'd come out of her room.

Now they were in the front of the exceedingly long, or at least it felt that way, main ballroom, waiting with everyone else for her to make her entrance.

Right after Clait walked the aisle. The situation with the grigeens coming back into the world was still a work in progress, and Clait was often in negotiations for land and repopulating the grigeens to their former locations. But she'd made it clear she was not missing this wedding.

She wore the collar Pantiar had given her. In the last year, she'd gained control over it and it glinted in the light of the candles, as she slowly strode down the aisle.

Nevaine came out behind her.

Sean's brothers all stood up with him and looked almost as happy as he did.

He, actually, looked delirious.

As she got closer, the music stopped. Piallen came forward to take her flowers and handed her the ring for Sean.

The words were simple vows; there was so much more to say, and they did say it, to each other. Sean's hand shook as he put the wedding band on her finger, and as much as she tried to stop it, her hands did too when she put the matching ring on him.

They were already kissing when the call came to do so.

After the kiss, Nevaine looked at Sean's chest. There had been an odd warmness over his right pocket.

He patted the pocket and shrugged. "I felt that Pantiar should be involved. I told him he's going with us down to university next month, too."

Nevaine laughed and turned herself and her new husband toward the now standing crowd.

And they lived happily ever after.

Dear Reader,

Thank you for joining me on a Nevaine's adventure! I hope that you enjoyed this second trip into this world and will also enjoy Piallen's Challenge! As always, I appreciate you for coming along on the newest escapade.

If you want to keep up on the further adventures of any of my characters, make sure to visit my website and sign up for my mailing list. http://marieandreas.com/index.html

You can also sign up on Amazon to follow me and they will keep you updated. Marie Andreas Amazon[1]

If you enjoyed this book, please spread the word! Positive reviews are like emotional gold to any writer. And mean more than you know.

Thank you again—and keep reading!

Marie

---

1. https://www.amazon.com/Marie-Andreas/e/B00SX81KIM/

About the Author

Marie is a multi-award-winning fantasy and science fiction author with a serious reading addiction. If she wasn't writing about all the people in her head, she'd be lurking about coffee shops annoying total strangers with her stories. So really, writing is a way of saving the masses. She lives in Southern California and is owned by two very faery-minded cats. She is also a member of SFWA (Science Fiction and Fantasy Writers of America).

When not saving the masses from coffee shop shenanigans, Marie likes to visit the UK and keeps hoping someone will give her a nice summer home in the Forest of Dean or Conwy, Wales.